AT THE *Hand* OF HER *Father*

BOOK TWO OF THE SYDNEY LEGAL SERIES

CHRIS TAYLOR

LCT Productions Pty Ltd
18364 Kamilaroi Highway, Narrabri NSW 2390

ISBN. 978-1-925119-48-0 (Paperback)

At the Hand of Her Father is a work of fiction. Names, characters, places, brands, media and incidents either are the product of the author's imagination or are used fictitiously. Any resemblance to actual persons, living or dead, events, or locales, is entirely coincidental.

Published in the United States of America.

BOOKS BY CHRIS TAYLOR

THE MUNRO FAMILY SERIES
(In order)

The Profiler
The Investigator
The Predator
The Betrayal
The Deception
The Negotiator
The Christmas Vigil
The Ransom
The Defendant
The Shooting
The Maker
(Available in Audio)

THE SYDNEY HARBOUR HOSPITAL SERIES
(in order)

The Perfect Husband
The Body Thief
The Baby Snatchers
The Final Bullet
The Debt Collector
The Lab Test
The Stolen Identity
The Cliff-top Killer
The Likeable Fraudster

THE SYDNEY LEGAL SERIES
(in order)

An Accidental Murderer
At the Hand of Her Father
A Woman Scorned
Lies and Deception
Ordinary Evil
The Ties That Bind
The Perfect Crime
Malicious Love
Toxic Inheritance

THE BARRINGTON FAMILY SERIES
(in order)

Broken Lives
Broken Promises
Broken Bonds
Broken Spirits
Broken Vows
Broken Minds
Broken Dreams
Broken Hearts
Broken Homes

THE CRAIGDON FAMILY SERIES
(in order)

Callum
Joel
Isabella
Nicholas
Sophia
Flynn
Noah
Logan
Elizabeth

Get a FREE book when you sign up for Chris Taylor's newsletter at: www.christaylorauthor.com.au

Love Audiobooks? Check out Chris Taylor Books on audio on Audible.com, Amazon.com and the iBooks store.

Join Chris Taylor's Facebook reader group/fan page and be among the first to receive news of book releases, read and review books prior to release and other amazing offers. Join Now at: www.facebook.com/groups/1758023621144744/

Find out more about all of Chris Taylor's books, by visiting her website at: www.christaylorauthor.com.au/about/books

DEDICATION

This book is dedicated to the people I love, especially my husband, Linden, my children, Angus, Imogen, Rory, Millie and Madeleine and my dear friends, Sue, Ally and Pru.

The world could do with a little more kindness and love. My life is better and brighter for knowing all of you.

Acknowledgments

As usual, no book comes into being without a lot of help and support by my friends and family. A world of thanks must go to my wonderful editor, Pat Thomas. Thank you for everything that you do to make my stories even more amazing than I could ever dare to dream. To former Detective Superintendent Michael Kilfoyle, thank you for lending my story credibility. Any mistakes are wholly my own.

To Damon Freeman, Alisha Moore and all of the staff at damonza.com, thank you for yet another fantastic cover. To my sister, Nicole Guihot and to my friend, Ally Thomson, thank you for your excellent editorial comments, proof reading skills and suggestions. I hope you like the final result.

To Amy Atwell and her dedicated staff at Author EMS who are so much more than book formatters. Amy, once again, thank you for your magic.

To the fantastic writer organizations such as Romance Writers of Australia, Romance Writers of

America and Romance Writers of New Zealand for all the help, support and encouragement they offer new and aspiring writers, including me.

To my readers, thank you for your support and love for my stories. Your encouragement and enjoyment make this journey all worthwhile.

And lastly, to my friends and family, especially my husband and children. Thank you for putting up with late dinners and even later conversations as I've emerged day after day from the sometimes scary but always enthralling world I've created on my computer.

PROLOGUE

The faintest sliver of pale moonlight leaked in through a gap in the curtains and gilded the soft, sweet curve of Lacey Johnson's cheek. Ian Johnson stared down at his young daughter and his heart clenched with pain. She was so small, so perfect, so beautiful with a halo of golden hair. She slept the sleep of the innocent, unaware of the turmoil that lurked all around her. At three years of age, what did he expect? It wasn't as if the child had spent much time in the outside world. No, most of Lacey's short life had been spent closeted and protected by her loving parents. That was, until their love ran out.

He squeezed his eyes shut tightly against the surge of pain the sad memories brought forth and pushed a fist up to his mouth in an effort to keep the agony from spilling out and waking his children. Even still, small whimpers of torture escaped him. He gazed across the room to the double bed that held his twin sons and was relieved to discover that Bailey and Darby continued to sleep soundly beside their little sister, equally oblivious to their father's dark thoughts.

A kaleidoscope of memories rushed through his mind and he shook his head slowly back and forth. *How had it happened?* He couldn't even pinpoint the time. He'd vowed to love Natalie until death did they part and he'd meant every word. Little did he know their love would dwindle slowly but surely, like fine sand through an hourglass, until all of it had gone.

He'd once thought they'd last forever. They'd been in love for more than a decade. In the end, it had taken less than seven years. Seven years of marriage and they'd gone from being passionately in love to spitting out hate at the sight of each other. The speed of the demise of his relationship with the mother of his kids still made his head spin.

Lacey murmured in her sleep. Her forehead creased in a frown. One of her small hands curled into a fist. He stared down at her and wondered what she was dreaming about. *Did she have an inkling that her world had been turned upside down? Did she know what it meant for her and her brothers to come from a broken home?*

Broken. Yes, that's what they were. All of them. Into a million pieces. Him, Natalie, and the kids— and nobody could pick up the pieces and put them together again. Not now. Never again.

CHAPTER 1

Natalie Johnson spooned the last of her cereal into her mouth. She pushed away from the kitchen table and took her bowl to the sink. Rinsing out the residual milk, she left the bowl on the dish rack to dry. She glanced at the clock on the wall above the fridge and frowned. Ian should've been there by now. If he didn't hurry up, the boys would be late for school and she'd be late for work. It was just like her ex-husband not to care about things like that—things that were important to her.

With a grimace, she picked up a stray hairbrush and ran it through her shoulder-length hair. Finding a hair elastic on the counter beside a basket of fruit, she secured her hair into a loose ponytail and then continued down the hallway to the bathroom. While brushing and flossing her teeth she peered at her reflection in the mirror and sighed at the woman who stared back at her.

It had been a rough couple of years. She'd lost

more than twenty pounds since the divorce—weight she couldn't afford to lose. Stress had a way of making her appetite disappear. Eyes that looked too big in her gaunt face stared back at her. There were dark circles beneath her eyes, evidence of another night where she'd tossed and turned and watched every hour come and go on the clock. It was always that way when the kids were at their dad's. Thanks to the judge, it happened every other weekend. At least the judge had seen it her way the last time.

The Friday just gone had seen her and Ian and their legal representatives come before the family court, yet again. The battle over who should have custody of their children had been a bitter one. There was no way Natalie was going to let her babies live permanently with their father. *Uh, uh.* No way. That was never going to happen. It was the reason she'd kept pouring every cent she had into the coffers of her lawyer's firm. She needed all the help she could get.

And it had finally all been worthwhile. The judge had found in her favor. He'd agreed that she was the best person to have custody of the kids. She was their mother and they were only babies. The twins were five and Lacey, three—she really was still a baby. Okay, a toddler, but way too young to live with anyone other than her mommy.

It wasn't surprising that Ian hadn't taken the judge's decision well. He'd screamed abuse at the man from his seat at the bar table and had then turned it on his lawyer. Natalie thought the corrections officers would step in and escort her ex from the building, but at the last minute, Ian closed his mouth and chose to depart the courtroom unassisted. Natalie had breathed a sigh of relief.

It was over. After two long years, the court had made final orders. She was still coming to terms with the fact that she need never step foot inside a courthouse again. Of course, it didn't mean her ex-husband was finally out of her life—he'd been given fortnightly contact with their children, after all—but brief contact with him while he collected or dropped them back was something she could handle. To know her children were finally, legally able to live with her on a day-to-day basis brought nothing but relief.

Returning to the kitchen, she glanced at the clock again and muttered a curse. *Where was he?* Even if he arrived in the five minutes, she was going to be late. She went to the front room and peered through the window. The driveway was empty. She swallowed another curse.

Dammit! Anger surged through her veins. It was at times like these that she was reminded of how rude and arrogant and aggravating her ex-husband could be. He thought only of himself. He always had.

Heading back to the kitchen, she grabbed her handbag and riffled through it for her phone. It wasn't there. No. It had to be there. She felt around again and came up empty. With a groan of impatience, she upended the handbag onto the counter.

A couple tubes of lipstick, a packet of tissues, a

pile of bills she'd meant to pay the week before during a lunch break. A wallet, three pens, two packets of gum, a pacifier—in case Lacey lost her usual one. A spare disposable nappy and a packet of baby wipes, a Snickers that had been in there more days than she could count. It all ended up in a pile on the counter, but it was clear there was no phone.

"Shit!" she muttered and wondered where it could be.

She went back into her bedroom and checked the nightstand. It wasn't there. She walked into the bathroom, but it wasn't on the sink. Finally, she returned to the kitchen and spied it across the room, poking out from under one of the seat cushions of the couch.

The night came crashing back in on her and she remembered spending the previous evening curled up on the sofa with a glass of wine, watching old movies and trying not to think about her kids.

She'd called them earlier and had spoken to each of them, asking about their day. She'd blown them kisses over the phone and bid them a good night. She'd wished them sweet dreams and assured them all she'd see them in the morning. She'd fallen asleep holding a cushion pressed tightly against her chest, tears drying on her cheeks.

Shaking her head impatiently, she pushed the sad thoughts away and snatched up the phone. Dialing Ian's number, she waited for him to pick up, relieved when he did.

"Ian! Where the hell are you? It's way past the drop-off time. We're going to be late!"

"For fuck's sake, Natalie! Back off, will you! I'm just a few minutes past the appointed time. Big deal."

"Don't swear in front of my babies, Ian. I won't stand for it! And for your information, you're twenty minutes late. The boys are going to be late for school and I'm going to be late for work. You promised the last time it wouldn't happen again, Ian. You *promised*."

"Jesus Christ, Natalie! You're always going on about something, aren't you? You just can't help yourself! No wonder I can't stand to be around you! I can't believe I once thought you were hot. I mean—"

"Shut up, Ian! Shut *up!*"

Natalie started shaking. She didn't want to fight with her ex, but somehow, they always ended up in an argument. Mostly because Ian broke the rules. The court had set strict pick-up and drop-off times and Ian barely paid them any heed. It was the same every time it was his turn to have the kids. His lack of respect for the scheduling of their lives drove her crazy.

"I'm heading out the door, Natalie, so just quit with your whining. Leave me alone!"

She saw red. "Don't put this on me! You're the one who hasn't been able to get out of the house on time! You're supposed to have them back here by eight and you know how traffic can be on Monday mornings. There's nothing new about any of this, Ian. You're doing this on purpose. You're doing this out of spite."

"Bullshit! I slept in, all right. The alarm didn't go off. I—"

"I don't believe you. You're just—"

"Yeah, that's right; call me a liar. That's what I am. Good on you, Natalie," Ian snarled.

She opened her mouth to retaliate in kind and then closed it again. It sounded like Ian had the phone on speaker and her babies were probably nearby. They might not be old enough to understand what was being said, but they sure could sense the anger. It wasn't fair to them. They didn't ask to be caught up in the middle of this. Taking a deep breath, she forced herself to calm down and then opened her mouth to speak again. Ian beat her to it.

"Look, I'll drop them off, okay? That way you won't be too late for work. I'll take the boys to school and Lacey to daycare. That's where she's going, right?"

His voice was thick with sarcasm. It took a gargantuan effort to ignore it. Ian hated that his daughter was in daycare when she could have been with him. He refused to face the truth: Lacey *couldn't* be with him. He was a self-employed plumber. Sometimes he was called out on a job. He couldn't take a three-year-old with him, no matter how much he argued otherwise. It was another bugbear between them. Lacey was safer where she was. She'd go to daycare and that was that.

"What about their school bags?" Natalie asked, changing the subject. "The boys need morning tea and lunch. I've already packed sandwiches and fruit."

"I'll give them some money. They can buy food from the cafeteria," Ian replied.

"What about Lacey?"

"I'll stop by the store. Yogurt and museli bars are her thing right now, aren't they?"

"Make sure you get those Kellogg ones," Natalie responded. "She doesn't like the other brands. And strawberry yogurt. It's her favorite. And a couple of cheese sticks. And a banana. She loves bananas."

"I've got it, all right. I'm her father. I think I know what to feed my own child."

Natalie bit back a retort and with effort held on to her temper. As much as she didn't want to be grateful to Ian for anything, she appreciated his offer and grudgingly told him as much. With him doing the school run, she might even make it to work on time.

"Tell them I love them and that I'll see them this afternoon," she said.

"Tell them yourself. You're on speaker."

Natalie had guessed as much. She smiled into the phone and lightened her tone. "Hi, Bailey! Hi, Darby! Hi, sweet baby girl!"

"Hi, Mommy!" came a chorus of high-pitched voices.

They sounded so happy, she couldn't help but widen her smile. They were fine. They were with their dad. For all his faults and failings, he truly loved his kids. It was only as a husband that he'd turned lousy.

"I'll see you this afternoon, okay?" she said.

"Okay, Mommy," one of the boys replied. She couldn't tell which.

"Have a good day, babies. I love you!" she cried.

The call came to an end.

———————

Ian hit the end button and canceled the call. It had gone on for long enough. His ex-wife already had his kids for way more days than he did and now that the judge had made a final decision that was unlikely to change for a long time. It infuriated him that someone else got to decide where and when and for how long. They were his kids as much as Natalie's. *Why should his ex-wife have them for most of the time?* It wasn't fair. It fucking wasn't fair.

A familiar surge of rage flooded through him. He ripped open the door to his HiLux twin cab utility and after shouting to the kids to get in, he climbed behind the wheel.

"Dad, you need to help Lacey with her seatbelt," Bailey said and Ian cursed again. Climbing back out of the car, he reached across Bailey and fastened the belt around his daughter where she sat in the middle and slammed the door shut. Thankfully, both boys were already buckled in the car.

Returning to his seat, he thumped the steering wheel with his fist. Pain shot up his arm, but he ignored it, in fact, he welcomed it. After all his ex-wife and the family law court had put him through over the past couple of years, a sore arm was the least of his concerns.

At the thought of the past tumultuous years, he ground his teeth and growled low in his throat. Even after all this time, after the court had found in her favor, his bitch of an ex was busting his balls about being late. *Didn't she get it?* She'd won the fight! The judge had sided with her and her fancy lawyer. The prick who sat so high and mighty, lording it over them on the bench, had taken Natalie's side over his. The knowledge sent a fresh wave of fury surging through him.

And now he was on his way to drop his baby girl at daycare. He'd been given two measly days with his kids and they were going to be left in institutions to while away the day. It was bullshit. Lacey should be home with him. He could work around her; schedule call-outs on another day. It only got tricky when he had to attend an emergency—like the other day when old Mrs Flaherty's toilet pipe burst. What a fucking mess!

Still, it didn't mean Lacey should be in daycare. He could look after her. He was a great dad. It was bullshit the courts had seen things differently. They'd ordered that his little girl spend her days in care while her parents were at work. He was perfectly capable of looking after her. He argued as much in court, but the sanctimonious bastard seated on the bench had ignored him. The crack of the gavel had sealed Ian's fate. The whole thing was bullshit.

Another surge of anger washed over him, flooding him with heat. He seethed with it. It was like he was combusting from the inside out. His head pounded and he cursed savagely. One weekend a fortnight. That was it. Fifty-two days a year. Fifty-two fucking measly days out of three hundred and sixty-five. It was total bullshit. He ought to buy a gun and blow that judge's fucking brains out. That would show him. That would show him Ian Johnson wasn't a man to be fucked with.

The idea appealed immensely, but a few minutes later, he dismissed it. *Who was he kidding?* The gun laws in Australia prevented purchases like that. He couldn't just walk into a gun shop and buy a weapon. There was all sorts of paperwork and red tape to plow through before they'd hand him a gun. He needed a permit to own one and they took weeks to be approved and there was always a chance he'd be turned down, rejected once again. Rejected by his wife of seven years, rejected by the courts...

Nobody cared about Ian Johnson and it was really pissing him off. The noise in his head increased to a roar. The traffic around him receded. He glanced in his rearview mirror and saw his kids. The twins, identical in nearly every way, sat either side of their sister. They were unusually subdued, as if sensing their father's dark mood.

The memory of his ex-wife smiling broadly as the judge handed down his decision ate into his gut. When her lawyer had hugged her in triumph, she'd even teared up. The stupid bitch had been crying, as if the decision meant so much to her. *Would it have been so hard if the judge had found against her, given Ian custody of his kids?*

He was their father, he deserved more than a stingy fifty-two days a year. It wasn't fucking right that Natalie got them the rest of the time. He loved them as much as she did. He took care of them just as well.

He and the kids had had a great weekend together. They'd gone fishing on the pier. They'd eaten ice cream and donuts and soda. Lacey had fallen over and skinned her little knee, but he'd stuck a plaster over it and wiped away her tears. He'd stopped by a department store and bought them all some toys. His little girl had fallen asleep with her new teddy bear tucked under her arm. She still had the stupid thing with her now, stuffed beside her car seat.

They were traveling on Anzac Bridge, heading north toward Lilyfield, where his kids went to school. Lacey's daycare center was nearby. The morning sun glinted off the water, turning it golden. It looked like it was going to be another great spring day, but what did he care about such things when his life was in free fall? When some fucking stranger had believed the lies of his ex-wife and had passed him over as the primary caregiver for his kids.

He punched the steering wheel again and this time cursed aloud. "*Fuck!*"

"Is everything okay, Daddy?"

Ian glanced again in the rearview mirror and narrowed his eyes at Bailey. "No, son. Everything's gone to shit. The judge said I could only see you on the weekend every fortnight. You have to stay with your mother the rest of the time. It's bullshit, Bailey! That's what it is and I'm not going to stand for it!"

Bailey's expression became pinched and frightened. Darby had also paled. Oblivious to the harsh words that he'd spoken, Lacey chattered quietly to her bear. Ian glanced from one child to the other and an idea formed in his mind. He couldn't buy a gun and blow the judge's head off, but there were other ways to make his protests known. Best of all, it would be a chance to strike a blow against his ex-wife. The thought brought a smile to his lips.

His gaze fell on Lacey and his gut tightened in anticipation. *Yes, she'd do.* She was exactly the right size. His lip curled up in a sneer. He'd show them not to fuck with Ian Johnson. He'd show them once and for all and his hoity-toity ex-wife who'd always thought she was better than him, and the judge who'd stared down his nose at him and had stolen away his kids, could both go to hell.

With his mind made up, he switched on his indicator and abruptly changed lanes. A car horn blasted behind him, but that didn't give him pause. With his foot planted on the accelerator, he steered the vehicle through the heavy morning traffic. For his plan to work, he needed to be in the lane furthest to the left.

Flicking on his indicator once again, he moved into the far lane and braked hard, bringing his truck to a halt. Another horn blasted behind him. Out of force of habit, he flipped on his hazard lights. Flinging off his seat belt, he climbed out and then opened the rear passenger side door. Bailey stared up at him in alarm.

"What are you doing, Daddy?" Bailey asked.

"Why are we pulled up?" Darby chimed in.

Ignoring their questions, Ian reached across Bailey and unstrapped Lacey from her seat.

"Wait, Daddy! My bear!" she squealed, but he hardly heard her over the noise in his head.

Pulling her across her brother's lap, he tugged her harder until she was clear of the car. Holding her on his hip, he used his free hand to pull them both up onto the bed of the pickup. From there, it was only a short stride and a step up onto the roof.

"Daddy! What are we doing?" Lacey cried out, her eyes wide with surprise. She clung to him with her small hands, her face turned up to his. Sweet and trusting, it tugged at his heart, but then the anger took over once again.

Ignoring her question, he eyed the steel and wire barricade that stood between him and the water far below. The fence was higher than he'd anticipated and it curved inward, which made it even harder. He'd need every bit of leverage to make this work.

The roar in his head grew louder. It thundered through his ears. Lacey's eyes widened in confusion and then they filled with sudden fear. He held her tight in front of him with both hands and braced himself. He would have to throw her high and hard if she were to clear the barricade. Taking a deep breath, he tensed in anticipation and then threw his daughter with all his might. She screamed in terror.

She went a long way up, longer than he thought possible. And then she was on the other side of the barricade and was free falling, all the way to the bottom. Her screams were abruptly cut short.

There, it was done. That would show them. The judge and his ex. Good riddance. Now he could get on with his day. Calmer, he climbed down from the roof and got back behind the wheel. Flicking on his indicator, he once again headed out into the traffic.

"Daddy! Daddy! What about Lacey? We have to go back!" Bailey cried, his eyes huge and dark in his pale face.

Ian glared at his sons through the rearview mirror. Tears poured down both of their cheeks.

"Daddy! We have to go back!" Darby repeated his brother's words. "Please, Daddy! Please! Lacey can't swim!"

"Lacey's fine," Ian snarled, his anger still raw and fresh. "Don't worry. The water's not deep."

"It looks deep," Bailey whispered brokenly, staring out the window.

"How will Mommy find her?" Darby asked, his voice cracking on a fresh sob.

"She doesn't finish work until late," Bailey added, fear stark on his pale face.

"Lacey's fine. I told you," Ian snapped, his patience wearing thin. "Now, shut the fuck up about it. I don't want to hear another word out of either of you until I drop you off at school."

The harsh reprimand did its job. Both boys fell deathly silent. Tears continued to roll down their cheeks, but Ian resolutely ignored them. He'd done what he had to do. It wasn't his fault. He'd been pushed into taking drastic action. It was too bad Lacey had borne the brunt.

But that was the way it was.

CHAPTER 2

Natalie frowned at the computer screen in front of her and once again tried to find the error in the figures that covered the page. She'd been entering the pile of invoices into the excel spreadsheet open on her screen, but something wasn't right. She made a sound of exasperation. Computers were all very good when the data entered into their programs was accurate, but they didn't take into account human error.

The truth was, she'd entered the wrong data somewhere, but she couldn't work out where the error was. She blamed her unusual ineptitude on the sleeplessness she'd endured over the weekend. Coupled with the stress of the morning that had come to a head with yet another argument with her ex, the week had begun just dandy.

She grimaced and rubbed her forehead. It was barely half-past nine and a headache was already beginning to form behind her eyes. The day stretched out in front of her, long and unrelenting. The only good thing about it was that the end of it would bring a reunion with her children. It seemed like a lifetime had passed since she'd seen them.

She sighed sadly. Now that the family law orders had been finalized, she faced more than a decade of missing every other weekend with her kids. She'd wanted to protest any time they spent with their father, but her lawyer had explained gently that such a thing was unrealistic and she knew it was true. Ian was their daddy. Nothing was going to change that. He was entitled to spend time with them, even a couple of days a fortnight. She shouldn't begrudge him. He was a good father and the kids loved him.

On a more positive note, now they'd finally finished with the courts, she could look to a more certain future and start getting on with her life. She felt like everything had been on hold since the day she and Ian had decided they were over. She wasn't kidding herself that her children hadn't suffered as a result. Of course they had. Kids were always the ones who suffered during a divorce. It wasn't their fault their parents had fallen out of love. They deserved the best mother she could be and now that life was back on course, she was determined to do all she could to see to their needs and live up to their expectations.

The phone at her elbow peeled and she absently reached over and picked it up, her gaze still focused on the computer monitor.

"Baker and Carr Construction. This is Natalie. May I help you?"

"Oh, Natalie. It's Kylie Bourke from Caring Kids Daycare Center. I noticed Lacey hasn't come in today. Is she sick?"

Natalie started in surprise and frowned in confusion. "What do you mean, she hasn't come in? Ian said he would drop her off. He had the kids for the weekend. She should have been there an hour ago."

"Well, I'm not sure if he stopped in. I didn't see him, and Lacey isn't here."

A swift burst of anger surged through Natalie. *The bastard! He'd taken Lacey to work!* She should have known she couldn't trust him. He hated having their daughter in daycare. She'd lost count of the number of times they'd argued about it.

Barely holding on to her temper, she thanked Kylie for her call and hung up. She immediately picked up the receiver again and dialed her ex-husband's number, fury pouring through her veins.

"Ian!" she shouted when he answered. "Where's Lacey? Why didn't you drop her off at daycare, like you promised? That's the last time I'm going to fall for that! What about the boys? Did they make it to school, or have you given all of them the day off?"

"*Tut, tut*, Natalie. You're always so angry. Of course the boys are at school. What do you think I am?"

His condescending tone grated on her nerves. She gritted her teeth and did her best to get a hold on her temper.

"What about Lacey? The daycare center just called me. You didn't drop her off. Where is she?"

"Oh, I dropped her off, all right. She's gone."

"What the hell do you mean, she's gone?"

"Like I said. She's gone."

Something in the icy calmness of his words sent a chill down her spine. Dread formed a pool in her stomach.

"Ian, stop playing games. I mean it. Where's Lacey?" She hated that her voice trembled with fear, but there was nothing she could do about it.

"Are you *stupid?*" he yelled. "I already told you! She's fucking gone!"

Natalie tried and failed to stem her panic. "Gone *where?*" she cried.

"I threw her off the fucking bridge."

A tightness started low in Natalie's belly and worked its way across her chest. She couldn't breathe. This couldn't be happening... Not to her baby... Not to Lacey... Natalie opened her mouth and screamed.

Work colleagues stared at her in shock. She barely registered their reaction. Out of control, she screamed and screamed again.

"My baby! He's thrown my baby off the bridge! Please! Somebody help me! Somebody call the police!" Sobbing with shock and horror, she dropped the phone, pushed away from her desk and promptly collapsed onto the floor. A haze of people gathered around her. Someone reached for her and tried to help her to her feet, but her legs wouldn't support her and she collapsed back to the floor.

"Somebody call an ambulance! This woman needs help!"

"No! No! The police," Natalie cried. Her voice seemed to come from a long way away. "Please, he's thrown my baby off the bridge. I need the police." Once again, her sobs overwhelmed her and she bent over, gasping.

"Natalie, look at me."

The stern voice of her boss broke through the terror that had overtaken her mind. She stared up at Jason Georgetown and did her best to control the panic that held her in a vice-like grip.

"J-Jason. He has my baby! He has Lacey!"

Jason knew all about the long, bitter, drawn-out battle she'd had with her ex over the kids. "Ian, right?" he asked.

"Yes! He just called me! He told me he'd thrown Lacey over the side of the bridge! He must be talking about Anzac Bridge. That's the usual route he takes. He was supposed to take her to daycare. Please, we need to call the police!"

Jason held out his hand and helped her to her feet. This time, with his support, she managed to stay upright.

"The police have been called," Jason assured her. "An ambulance is also on its way." He looked at her pointedly.

"No! I don't need an ambulance! I'm fine! I need to find my baby!"

"The police will be here shortly. You can tell them all about it. What exactly did Ian say?"

"He-he told me Lacey was gone. That he'd thrown her off the bridge."

Jason frowned. "He couldn't have possibly meant that literally. He's just playing games with you, Natalie. Like he's done so many times."

"But the woman from the daycare center said Lacey wasn't there! He must have her somewhere!"

"Yes. We need to find her. Oh, good. Here are the police."

Jason led her over to an empty desk and helped her into a chair. He greeted the officers that stood in the doorway of the large open office space and brought them over to where she sat.

"Natalie." Jason's voice was gentle, soothing. "These officers are here to help you. Tell them what you know."

In a voice that trembled with fear and confusion, Natalie relayed the conversation she'd had with her ex. The police looked disconcertingly concerned, particularly when they were made aware that she and Ian had been in the middle of a messy custody battle that had been finalized in her favor only the week before.

"What do you think your ex-husband meant when he said he'd thrown Lacey off the bridge?" the older of the two officers asked, his expression somber.

Natalie shook her head in bewilderment. Now that she'd had time to calm down, she realized that what Jason had said was true. Ian couldn't possibly have meant his words literally. No one in their right mind tossed their child over the side of a bridge. No, he must have meant something else...

Once again, desperate tears spilled down her cheeks. She bit back another sob. She didn't *know* what he meant. All she knew was that she wanted her baby back. *Now.* She needed to pull her little girl into her arms and know that she was safe. She needed to hold her close and never let her go. She needed to tell her she loved her.

She looked up at the police officer. "P-please," she sobbed. "You need to find her. You need to find my baby!"

"We'll do everything we can, ma'am. We need to get some more information. Can you give us your ex-husband's full name and address?"

Natalie gave him the information.

"Where does he work?"

"He works from home!" she cried, her patience exhausted. "Please, officer. I understand you need information, but my baby's out there! She needs me! You have to find her."

The officer regarded her with a sympathetic look and Natalie tried hard to get herself under control. He was only doing his job. He couldn't find Lacey without her help. She took a fortifying breath and tried again.

"I'm sorry. I... I'm a little overwrought. The phone call from Ian... It sent chills down my spine. I actually believed him when he told me he'd thrown Lacey off the bridge. It sounds ridiculous, now. I mean, who would do such a thing? He's her father! He loves her! He must have said it to upset me."

The officer studied her and waited for her to continue. She dragged in another deep breath. "We... We had an argument this morning. Ian and I. He was late returning the kids. They spent the weekend with him, but he was supposed to bring them home by eight. He told me he'd overslept and that he would drop the boys at school and take Lacey to daycare. Even though I was mad at him, I was grateful for his offer. It meant I wouldn't be late for work."

"How did he sound over the phone?" the second officer asked.

"He was annoyed that I was mad that he hadn't brought the kids home at the allotted time, but not anything over the top. He sounded quite reasonable when he offered to do the school run. But when I found out Lacey hadn't arrived at daycare and I called him a second time, he sounded quite different. He ended up screaming at me and swearing, saying over and over that Lacey was gone. When I demanded an explanation, he told me he'd thrown her off the bridge."

The second officer scribbled in a notebook. The older officer looked grim. "What kind of car was your ex-husband driving?" he asked.

"An early model Toyota HiLux utility. A twin cab. It's white."

"Do you know the plate number?"

"Yes. He has personalized plates. IJ 1987."

"1987. Does that mean he's thirty?" the first officer asked.

"Yes. We're the same age."

The second officer made a few more notes and then looked at his superior. "I'll call the station. Have them put out a BOLO on the car."

Natalie frowned. The officer noticed her confusion. "It means be on the lookout," he explained.

"I'll have a patrol car attend your ex-husband's

address. See if we can find him at home. With a bit of luck, he'll have your daughter with him," the older officer said.

"Th-thank you," Natalie managed and then another thought struck her. "I need to call the school. I need to make sure my boys are there."

"We can do that for you, Ms Johnson," the same officer offered.

"No, it will be quicker coming from me. Besides, I don't want to alarm anyone unnecessarily. As you say, hopefully Lacey's safe and sound at home with her dad." Natalie heard the tremor in her voice, but forced herself to keep her thoughts positive.

With something else to focus on, she felt stronger and quickly made the call to her boys' school. Her voice almost sounded normal when she asked the office lady if Darby and Bailey were there.

"Yes, I believe your ex-husband dropped them off earlier. I saw them running into the school a little while after the bell. He really should sign them in at the office if he's going to be late. That's the correct procedure."

"Yes, yes, of course. I'll speak to him." Natalie couldn't hide her relief. After asking the woman to keep an eye on her boys, she assured her once again she'd pass the request on to Ian and ended the call. She looked up at the officers standing nearby and gave them the news.

"So, the boys are where they should be," the senior officer replied. "That's a good sign. Let's hope he's only playing games with you about your daughter. We'd best get going."

The officers made their farewells and Natalie accompanied them to the door that led from the office out to the elevators. She grabbed the sleeve of the older officer. "You'll call me, won't you? As soon as you know anything?" she asked.

"Yes, of course. We'll keep you informed," he replied.

"Don't worry, Ms Johnson," the younger officer added. "We'll find her."

Natalie watched them disappear behind the sliding doors of the elevator and hoped he was right. As she returned to the office, Jason came up beside her.

"How about you take the rest of the day off, Natalie?"

She looked at him gratefully and nodded. "Thanks, Jason. I don't think I'm good for anything at the moment. Not until I know Lacey's safe..."

"I understand. Take as much time as you need. I'll let the police know where you are. Let's hope they find her soon."

In the end, it took the police two days to find Lacey's little body. She'd been swept along with the currents and the tide and was discovered by a fisherman washed up near a rocky outcrop several miles away. Natalie could still see the officer's face, pale and drawn, as he brought her the tragic news. She'd see his face and hear his words until the day she died.

"I'm sorry, Ms Johnson. We've found your daughter. I'm so very sorry. There was nothing we could do."

CHAPTER 3

Blake Harton Junior ran a hand through his short blond hair and thought about the weekend ahead. It was hump day and that was the perfect day to start planning some Friday and Saturday night revelry. It was one of the reasons he'd steered away from long-term girlfriends. They always ended up expecting something from him. He liked the freedom of choosing what he did with his time, including his weekends. Of course, that wasn't the only reason he was still footloose and fancy free at the ripe old age of thirty-one. His brother was most of it.

With a grimace, he forced the thought from his mind. Perhaps he'd take his boat out this weekend. The weather was supposed to be fine and sunny. There was nothing like the feeling of pushing his speed boat full throttle across Sydney Harbour, with the sound of the waves crashing across the bow and the wind lifting his hair. It had been months since he'd been on the water. This weekend might be the time. He'd call his work colleague and buddy, Ben Fitzgerald and Ben's new wife, Abby. They'd been married a month now. Long enough to want to come up for some air and touch base with the real world.

Reaching across his desk, he picked up the phone, intent on making the call. Now that Ben was a junior partner like him, they both worked on the same floor, but it was easier to buzz his workmate's office than to walk the gamut of female secretaries and young associates who would vie for his attention as he passed. It happened every time and was beyond annoying.

Before he could get Ben on the phone, there was a knock on his door and his secretary, Esther Otieno, appeared in the opening.

"Blake, I have a man by the name of Ian Johnson on the phone," she announced.

He frowned. "Ian Johnson? Why's that name familiar?"

"That's why I came in here instead of using the intercom. You have a client waiting out there. I didn't want her to overhear me."

Blake's frown deepened. "Why would that matter?"

Esther huffed an impatient sigh. Her fat cheeks wobbled with the effort. Blake had seen all the TV shows where the lawyers worked in glitzy offices with hot young secretaries hanging on their every word. Esther was almost as round as she was tall and was black and shiny like freshly washed coal. She'd emigrated from Kenya with her family and had been at Sydney Legal for more than ten years.

When Blake had made junior partner a few years earlier, he'd inherited Esther, along with a much nicer office. While he couldn't complain about the view out his window, Esther had been another story, but it hadn't taken him long to realize that there was nothing going on—both inside the office and out—that Esther didn't know about or could get access to. She was worth her weight in gold.

"Don't you ever watch television?" she asked, placing her hands on her generous hips. "It's been all over the news. Ian Johnson's the one who dropped his baby over the side of Anzac Bridge."

Blake stared at her in shock. Fragments of sound bites and film clips came back to him in a rush. He'd heard something about the awful tragedy. Most everyone in Sydney had. He couldn't believe the man who was supposed to have done it was calling him.

"Tell him I'm unavailable and I'll be that way for the rest of the year."

Esther raised her eyebrows. "You don't want to do it?"

Blake shook his head, impatient and bewildered. "Why would I want to represent a man who tossed his child over the side of Anzac Bridge?"

"Allegedly, Counselor. Don't forget whose side you're on."

Blake cursed under his breath. "I'm not on anyone's side and I sure as hell am not going to represent a man who could be capable of something like that. Tell him I'm not interested."

To his consternation, Esther stood her ground. "I agree, it's a nasty one, but I think you should take his call."

Blake narrowed his gaze at her. "Why?"

"The thing is, this man was in the middle of a bitter custody battle. He was at his wits' end. He told me he didn't mean for it to happen. It just...did."

Blake stared blindly at the papers on his desk, his mind in turmoil. Esther was one of the few people who knew the truth about his brother, David. After a long moment of silence, Blake raised his head.

"Where is he?"

"At home. He was released on bail earlier today. He said he can be here within the hour."

Blake sighed in resignation. No doubt he'd regret his decision, but right now, he didn't have a choice and Esther knew it. "Tell him to make an appointment."

His secretary nodded soberly. Blake's capitulation didn't appear to bring her any joy. "There's one other thing," she said.

Blake groaned and threw her a death stare. "What is it?"

"Johnson can't afford to pay a lawyer. He's spent all his money in the family court."

Blake seized upon the excuse he'd been hoping for. "Oh, well, that's too bad. Give him the number for Legal Aid."

Esther just stood there and continued to eyeball him in silence. Blake cursed again.

"Dammit, Esther! What do you want me to do?"

She shrugged. "It isn't like you don't do pro bono cases every now and then. Why would this one be any different?"

Blake glared at her. "You know why. Do I have to spell it out?"

Her expression gentled and her eyes filled with compassion. "No, you don't have to spell it out, but I think we both know you need to do this. This man has been through hell and it isn't over, yet. He needs you."

Blake clenched his jaw and ground his back teeth. He counted silently to ten, but the tension that had him coiled tight didn't ease. Esther had him over a barrel and she knew it. She knew he was going to say yes. His head screamed out all the reasons why he shouldn't do it...

"All right, you win," he heard himself say. "I'll take the case on for free. But you'd better tell him to get his butt over here as quickly as he can, before I change my mind."

Esther's face broke into a smile. Her teeth shone white against her dark skin. "Thank you, Blake. You won't regret it."

She shut the door behind her and Blake sat back in his chair with a sigh. It wasn't often his secretary was wrong, but this time at least, he believed she was. She'd barely cleared the doorway and already he was regretting his decision.

It was almost two hours later that Blake escorted Ian Johnson into his office. The man looked nothing like he'd expected. Of medium height and average build, Ian Johnson was quiet and soft-spoken. His nondescript, light-brown hair was a little long for the current fashion and he was in need of a shave, but he answered Blake's questions respectfully and with what Blake believed to be the truth.

"You've been charged with the murder of your daughter," Blake stated once they had the preliminaries out of the way.

Johnson stared at the carpet. "Yes."

Blake kept his gaze fixed on his client. He'd already read the police facts. Now he wanted to hear it from the man who'd allegedly tossed his daughter over the side of a bridge. "Tell me what happened."

With his head downcast and his elbows resting on his knees, Blake's client began to relay the events that had culminated in the terrible tragedy. He talked about the divorce and bitter custody battle and how he'd lost the right to see his kids.

"Two days every fortnight, that's all the judge gave me. Two days! How are they supposed to get to know me, to love me when I don't see them for most of every month? It's bullshit!" Ian's voice cracked on a huge sob that seemed to start from the bottom of his chest. He gasped and held his head in his hands. Blake sat in silence and let the man cry.

"They're *my* kids as much as hers!" he cried. "That judge didn't know anything! He took my kids away from me! My kids! My fucking kids!"

Blake understood the man's pain. While he

wasn't a father, he'd done his fair share of family law work. It was never easy dividing up the assets. When it came to the children and the orders to be made, tough didn't begin to describe it. There were never any winners in a family law dispute. It was one of the main reasons he'd turned his back on practicing that kind of law. He preferred to concentrate on criminal matters. Less heartache involved, most of the time.

"What happened on the day Lacey died, Ian?" he asked quietly.

The man took a moment to gather himself. When he started talking again, his voice was low and quiet.

"The day started out badly, right from the start. I overslept and was running late. I was supposed to have the kids back at my ex-wife's house at eight and it was already nearly that when I woke. She rang me, busting my balls over the fact I hadn't returned them on time. We argued. I eventually offered to do the school run myself."

"You had all three children with you?"

"Yes."

Blake absorbed the information and his gut filled with dread. *Had his client tossed the young child over the side of the bridge with his other children witness to it?* He forced himself to ask the question.

"Yes, all three kids were sitting on the back seat."

"What happened after you ended the phone call to your ex-wife? I take it she agreed to let you drop the kids off at school and at the daycare center?"

"Yes. She was happy. It meant she wouldn't be late for work. It was always about Natalie. Then, and now." His lip curled up in a sneer.

Ben didn't react. He'd seen it all before. In his experience, people who'd fought long and bitter custody battles didn't usually have good things to say about the other person. He let the comment slide.

"What happened after you ended the call to… Natalie, is it?"

"Yes. Natalie. I was still so mad about her giving me grief about being late and I couldn't stop thinking about the court decision. It was a final decision. It had been handed down the Friday before. The judge found in favor of my ex."

He spat the word and Blake caught the glint of anger in his eyes. Once again, he didn't judge the man for his reaction. It was, unfortunately, a normal attitude most divorced couples had toward each other.

"Let's go back to the weekend before," Blake suggested. "It was your weekend with your children, right?"

"Right. I picked them up at six on the Friday night from Natalie's. She doesn't get home from work until then."

"Where are the boys in between time?" Blake asked, curious.

"After school care," Ian snarled.

Once again, Blake didn't react. "So, you took them back to your place and you had a nice weekend."

Ian smiled softly. "Yes, we did. We played

football in the park across from my apartment and I pushed Lacey on the swings. We watched TV, went to the shops, and on Sunday we went fishing off the pier. We did the usual things—ice cream and stuff. We had fun."

"Did anything else happen?"

Ian stared at the floor and his hands clenched into fists. "Their mother called a few times to speak with them throughout the course of the weekend, including right before they went to bed. She reminded me to have them back on time, so they wouldn't be late for school. That's why she was so pissed when I overslept. Anyway, after I hung up the phone, I kept thinking about her and how the judge had given her my kids. I guess it got to me, knowing that it was finally over and she'd won."

He dragged in a ragged breath and continued. "I felt like going around to Natalie's and punching her in the face, but I knew that wouldn't be good for anyone, least of all my kids."

Blake stilled. "Was there violence in your marriage?"

Ian looked affronted. "Hell, no!"

Blake held up his hands. "I'm sorry. I had to ask."

"It's all right. I understand," Ian muttered.

"Good. Let's keep going," Blake said.

"Right. I woke up in the morning with a pounding headache and the kids screaming for me to get them breakfast. I realized I'd overslept and I knew Natalie would be mad. I was mad at myself for giving her the opportunity. Then she phoned and called me out about it and everything went downhill from there." He shrugged. "You already know what happened after that."

Blake pursed his lips and watched his client closely. So far, the man appeared to be telling the truth. "Yes, you pulled over halfway across Anzac Bridge. You removed your three-year-old daughter from her car seat, climbed onto the roof of your pickup and tossed her over the side, all while your young sons watched from the back seat. Did I miss anything?"

Ian's face turned red with embarrassment. He looked at Blake and anger flashed in his eyes. "I guess that's about it." His tone was belligerent.

Blake held on to his temper and stared at his client, trying to get his head around the enormity of what had happened. "Why did you do it, Ian? What made you throw your little girl over the side of the bridge, to her death?"

The man's hands clenched and unclenched and his breath came hard and fast. He stared at the carpet and Blake wondered if his client would answer. Ian had already told him he'd refused to participate in a record of interview with the police. *Would he be prepared to talk to his lawyer?* Blake was about to find out.

"I was off my head with anger," Ian started, his voice low and rough. "I was furious about the court decision. I was mad at Natalie for chewing my ass. I wasn't thinking straight. I wasn't thinking at all."

He fell silent. Blake continued to watch him steadily. "Why Lacey?" he asked finally. "The boys were in the car, too. Why not one of them?"

Ian compressed his lips and continued to stare down at the floor. "She was small enough to lift and throw over the fence. It's probably the best part of ten-feet high. The boys would have been too heavy to toss."

The words were uttered quietly and without inflection. To Blake, seated across from him, their effect was devastating. Shock reverberated in his head and chills were sent running up and down his spine. His gut twisted. He thought he might be sick. Fighting back the nausea, he distracted himself by scrawling down some notes on the blank legal pad in front of him. When he felt more in control of himself, he looked up at his client.

"I'm going to arrange for you to see a forensic psychiatrist. I'll organize an appointment for you as soon as possible. I'm hoping the medical diagnoses will support a defense that when you acted the way you did, you were in a dissociative state. There's no denying you tossed your child over the side of Anzac Bridge. Claiming dissociation is our only hope."

"What the hell is a dissociative state?" Ian muttered.

"There are a few different types of dissociation," Blake explained, "but generally it's defined as disruptions in aspects of consciousness, identity, memory, physical actions and/or the environment. The most common causes typically include some form of prolonged trauma such as sexual or physical abuse. The stress of war can also cause dissociation. I'm willing to argue that the prolonged stress of your divorce and bitter custody battle triggered the condition."

Ian nodded uncertainly. Blake continued.

"One of the signs of dissociation is a sense of detachment from oneself; seeing one's life as if it's a movie. From what you've described, I think that's what you were experiencing out on the bridge, but in order to successfully argue it as a defense to the murder charge, I need to back my hypothesis with medical proof."

"Hence the visit to the shrink," Ian said dryly.

"Exactly. And that's why we're going to plead not guilty," Blake added.

Ian's face flooded with relief. "You believe me? You believe me when I tell you I didn't mean to do it?"

An image of David as he'd been not long before his death appeared before Blake and he hurriedly forced it away. This wasn't about his brother. It was about a client who desperately needed his help.

"I believe you were in a dissociative state and you didn't know what you were doing. I'm prepared to take that argument to court and fight my very hardest to get a jury to believe it."

Moisture appeared in Ian's eyes and Blake could tell the man was trying to hold back tears. It moved him to know how important it was to Ian that Blake believe he hadn't meant to murder his daughter—and Blake suddenly realized it was important to him, too. Once again, his brother's image swam before him. This time, David was smiling. Esther had been right, after all. Blake was glad he'd taken on the case.

CHAPTER 4

From her position on the couch, Natalie stared vacantly at the clutter of casserole dishes, homemade cookies and cakes, vases of flowers, cards and other gifts that were piled up on every available surface of her open concept kitchen and living room. Lacey's pink-and-white baby blanket was clutched in her hands. It still smelled of her little girl. Natalie hadn't been able to put it down. She slept with it on her pillow and on the few occasions she'd been forced to leave the house, she'd stuffed it into her handbag, desperate to keep a little part of her baby close.

It was just over a week since her baby girl had been so cruelly taken and yesterday, she'd endured the pain of saying her final good-byes. The funeral had been well attended. At least, she thought so. She barely registered the crowd of friends and family and work colleagues who'd filled the church to overflowing. Her entire being had been focused on the tiny white coffin embossed with cherubs that took center stage at the front of the church. She couldn't take her eyes off it.

The arrangement of baby pink roses was beautiful and had brought a fresh wave of tears to her eyes. Pink had been Lacey's favorite color, like the teddy bear Natalie had taken from her daughter's bed and placed in the casket alongside the letters that had been written to Lacey by her brothers in their unformed, childish script.

At the thought of Bailey and Darby, Natalie's eyes closed on another rush of tears. Her sons had walked stoically by her side, all the way to the front of the church. They'd stared at the coffin with eyes that were wide and fearful and unbelievably sad. Tears had rolled down their cheeks. They'd turned to her, and as one, buried their faces in her jacket, sobbing quietly. It was all she could do not to turn tail and run out of there, taking them with her.

She wanted to find some dim, dark place to hide, and stay in there forever. She was numb from the inside out. She couldn't imagine ever feeling anything but cold desolation again. She had a hole in her heart that would never heal.

How was a mother expected to come back from burying her child? The circumstances of Lacey's death made the situation even more horrific. Natalie couldn't turn to the father of her child for comfort, like normal parents did, united in grief. No, her baby's father was the reason Lacey's tiny broken body now lay still and silent and cold against the white satin of her casket. She was just glad he hadn't dared to show his face.

A harsh sob tore through her and she pushed a fist against her mouth in an effort to hold it in. *It wasn't right!* No one should ever be expected to suffer through such agony, such unfathomable pain.

But she didn't have the liberty of falling apart. She had two little boys who were so sad and lost and forlorn. Their world had been turned upside down, too. It would never be the same again. They clung to her, looking for guidance, for some clue about how to act. They needed her now more than ever, and there was no changing that.

But what could she say to them? She had no answers. *How did anyone begin to comprehend how a father could murder his child?* It was inconceivable. And yet, that was now a reality in her life and the lives of her boys.

Her boys. They'd been through so much, experienced horrors they should never have been subjected to. There was no need for her to tell them their father was responsible for Lacey's death. Though they hadn't actually seen him toss her over the side of the bridge, they weren't stupid. Lacey had been with them in the car. Their father had removed her. They saw him climb on top of the roof of the truck with her. When he got back in again, Lacey wasn't with him.

Darby had tearfully confided in her that both boys had screamed for him to go back. They were scared their daddy had done something to her; scared that he'd thrown her over the side. They were home when the police came by to break the news. They were five years old and they knew too much...

The sound of the phone ringing in the other room registered in the back of her mind, but she paid it no heed. It had been ringing off the hook since the story had broken. There were so many people with questions. She didn't know what to say. She had to pull herself together, be strong for her boys. It was the least she could do for them. She hadn't been able to save her little girl, but she would do everything in her power to help and support and protect her sons.

With that thought in mind, she sat up a little straighter on the couch she'd barely moved from since she arrived home after the funeral. She pushed at a hank of hair on her forehead. Yesterday, her hair had been pulled back into a neat bun at the nape of her neck. Now it hung in loose, straggly waves, unwashed and unkempt.

She needed to take a shower and change her clothes. The black skirt and jacket she'd worn to Lacey's farewell were now wrinkled. The soft pink blouse was creased. The deodorant she'd applied yesterday morning had worn off and every now and then when she moved, she caught a whiff of body odor. No doubt she looked as bad as she felt.

That wasn't good enough. She had to be strong. She had to show her boys how much she loved them and how she would be there for them, protecting them, keeping them safe. One way to do that was to show them the mom of old; the mom they were familiar with; the mom they knew and loved.

Determined to set it in motion, she wriggled

forward until she was perched on the edge of the couch and then stood. Her best friend, Monica Radford came into the room.

"Natalie, I'm sorry," Monica said, coming toward her. "That was the police. They called to tell you that Ian has a lawyer. He's engaged the services of Blake Harton Junior from Sydney Legal."

Natalie's stomach clenched at the mention of her ex-husband's name, but she forced herself to respond. "Sydney Legal? I've never heard of them."

"They used to be known as Harton and Wentworth. They changed their name in recent months," Monica explained.

Natalie nodded. "Okay, that's a name I do recognize. Harton and Wentworth have been around forever. They're in one of those tall, glitzy buildings in Martin Place, right? I've never been inside their offices, but from the outside they look imposing enough. How can Ian afford a lawyer like that?"

Monica shrugged. "Who knows? Perhaps his family members have rallied around. I didn't see any of them at the funeral. It's obvious they're taking Ian's side."

Natalie made a sound of disgust. "They've always been on his side. They never liked me. Not even in the beginning. They always thought I believed I was too good for them. They used to talk about me behind my back—about the clothes I wore, the way I spoke, the fact I had a college education and worked in the city. There was always something for them to criticize. I ignored it most of the time, but that didn't mean it wasn't hurtful."

Monica shook her head in sad dismay. "What did Ian say?"

Natalie looked at her friend and was filled with sadness. "Never once did he defend me against them. That should have been the first sign that things weren't going to work out. At the time, I thought it was because it was easier for him to stay out of the arguments; to walk away. Little did I know he felt the same. He just managed to disguise it better—and for longer. I discovered during the divorce that he'd kept a list containing all the things that dissatisfied him during the course of our marriage. He threw many of them at me when the trouble between us began."

"I always thought you *were* too good for him," Monica stated.

Natalie opened her mouth to protest and Monica held up a hand to stop her and then added, "But in a good way, not in the way Ian thought you were."

Natalie shook her head sadly and sighed. "He was so insecure. So what if he didn't go to college? That never mattered to me. He just didn't believe that's how I really was... That truth was the beginning of the end."

Silence fell between them as they both got caught up in memories of the past. Monica had known Natalie since she'd started working at Baker & Carr Construction. Monica had been the first person Natalie had met there. They struck up a conversation in the staff tearoom. That was five years ago and they'd been friends ever since. Monica even had the honor of being Lacey's godmother. Natalie didn't know what she would have done without Mon during the long and bitter divorce and custody battle—and more recently, during the awful hours and days following Lacey's death.

"I probably shouldn't say anything," Monica began, rousing Natalie from her thoughts.

She frowned at her friend. "Say anything about what?"

Monica blew out her breath on a sigh. "It's about Blake Harton Junior."

"What about him?"

"He... He's kind of a big-shot lawyer. He's in the papers all the time. Apparently, he has an enviable success rate in the courtroom. He just got Roberto Pinnelli off those domestic abuse charges and everyone around him knows Pinnelli beats his wife."

Monica paused and Natalie slowly absorbed what her friend had said. "You mean, you think he might win this for Ian? Get Ian off? Is that what you're saying?"

Monica shrugged and looked uncomfortable. "I don't know, Natalie. I just... I just thought you should know. You know, so you can...be prepared."

White-hot anger surged through Natalie so quickly she gasped from the impact of it. Heat burned her cheeks. She shook her head vehemently back and forth. "No way! You're wrong! There's no way Ian's getting off this! He murdered my baby! The police told me there are a number of eye witnesses. They saw him do it. They saw him throw my little girl over the side of the bridge. There's no question he's the one responsible! Not the slightest bit of doubt. I don't care how good this Blake Harton Junior is, there's no way he's going to change the facts. He's not going to win this one."

Natalie's breath came fast. In the silence of the room, it sounded harsh to her ears. She forced herself to calm down and made attempts to slow her breathing. When she felt slightly more in control, she spoke again.

"Ian *has* to plead guilty. There's no other option. People saw him with Lacey. They saw him on the bridge. And then there was the phone call. The one where he told me he'd thrown her over. I don't care how good this lawyer is, there's no arguing against the facts." She paused and then added more quietly, "At least it should be over quickly. A trial that starts with a guilty plea isn't a trial at all."

A pained expression crossed Monica's face. At the sight of it, Natalie frowned.

"What is it, Mon? What aren't you telling me?"

Monica bit her lip. "I'm sorry, Natalie, but the officer I spoke to just then said he understands Ian will be pleading not guilty. The matter *will* go to trial. It's not going to go away any time soon."

A fresh wave of shock and anger hurtled through Natalie's veins. She stared at her friend and could hardly form the words that would give voice to her feelings. *Ian was pleading not guilty?* It was unbelievable! He couldn't *do* that! He couldn't do that to her or their sons! *And what about Lacey? How was she meant to feel?* Okay, so she was gone, but Natalie was certain her baby was now an angel, looking down on them. How would her little girl feel, knowing the man she called Daddy, the man she loved unreservedly, the man she trusted to keep her safe was refusing to take responsibility for her death? It was beyond comprehension. Natalie groaned aloud in an agony of anger and pain.

"Natalie? Are you all right?" Monica was there in an instant, touching Natalie's arm, looking at her with such a concerned expression, Natalie did her best to reassure her.

"I… I'm fine. I just… It's come as a shock that Ian wants to plead not guilty. The bastard! My poor, poor baby! Can't she be left in peace? This will be all over the news! And what about my boys? They'll be forced to remember the awful details all over again. How am I going to protect them from it? What can I do? I can't believe it!"

Monica made a sound of sympathy in her throat. "You're right. It *is* unbelievable, but if it makes you feel any better, it might very well be Ian's lawyer who's responsible for the not guilty plea, rather than Ian claiming he's not guilty. Harton doesn't sound like a man who's used to losing."

A fresh wave of anger rushed through Natalie and she dragged her hands through her hair in distress. "You're right. This has to be his lawyer's doing. Even Ian couldn't stoop as low as this. It's Blake Harton Junior. He's behind this. I know it!"

In a flurry of motion, Natalie dashed around the room, looking for her phone. She tossed aside cushions, pushed aside vases, looked under a pile of sympathy cards. She glanced across at Monica. "Get me the number for Sydney Legal. I'm going to talk to this man."

Monica frowned. "Natalie, I don't think that's a good idea. He's your ex-husband's—"

"Do it!" Natalie shouted, feeling more and more desperate. "And while you're at it, help me find my damn phone."

CHAPTER 5

lake tossed a ball of paper at the trash can he'd placed halfway across his office and cheered when the paper ball went in. He really should be working on the Johnson case, but he'd been at it all morning and he was restless. *Perhaps he just needed to go outside and take in some fresh air?*

The day looked inviting outside his window. The sky was clear and cloudless. The water of Sydney Harbour sparkled in the distance. People lay sprawled on the bright green grass around Hyde Park, enjoying some down time. The weather had also been perfect last weekend. He and Ben and Abby had filled picnic baskets and headed out on the harbor. Blake's Malibu Wakesetter had skimmed along the water and Blake was reminded how long it had been since he'd enjoyed a weekend off.

Now it felt like forever since he'd enjoyed some R and R and it was only Wednesday. It was going to be a long week. He'd been at work since six and hadn't yet ventured out, not even for coffee. He supposed he could call Ben and persuade him to take a break. He looked at the spread of papers on his desk and swallowed a groan. A coffee break with his buddy suddenly held immense appeal.

Before Blake could put his plan into action, the intercom on his desk beeped and Esther came on the line.

"Blake, I have Natalie Johnson on line two. She says she's the ex-wife of your client, Ian Johnson. I told her it wasn't appropriate for her to be calling here, but she insisted I put her through. Do you want to speak with her?"

Blake started in surprise and then frowned. The last person he expected to hear from was his client's ex-wife. *Should he talk with her?* Esther was right. It was highly unlikely the ex-wife of his client and the mother of the dead child would have anything supportive to say or offer anything that might help his client. Technically speaking, she was a witness for the prosecution—or would be somewhere down the track. Still, it might help to get her view of things... Blake vacillated back and forth, undecided.

"Blake? Did you hear me?" Esther said, her tone a little sharper.

"Y-yes, I heard you," he stammered, recovering his aplomb.

"Well, do you want to speak with her? I can always tell her you're out."

"No. No, don't do that," Blake replied, his curiosity winning out. He picked up the phone.

"Blake Harton."

"It's Natalie Johnson. I'm Ian Johnson's ex-wife."

"Yes. My secretary told me. What can I do for you, Ms Johnson?"

There was a slight pause, as if she was trying to collect herself enough to speak. "Th-thank you for taking my call," she replied. "I wasn't sure if you would."

"I'm very sorry for your loss, Ms Johnson. What happened was...unspeakable, but I'm not sure what you want from me. I'm representing your ex-husband. I probably shouldn't be speaking with you."

"Why am I not surprised by your attitude?" came the quick and angry reply. "You're gutless, aren't you?" she added, not waiting for him to speak. "You're prepared to defend my sorry excuse of an ex, but you don't have the courage to talk to me. She was my *baby!* My little girl! He *killed* her! And now you want to make excuses for him. You're going to do your best to convince a jury to let him go!"

Her voice had risen with her hysteria. Blake held on to his temper and let her awful accusations wash over him. Natalie Johnson had gone through a devastating tragedy. She was entitled to let off steam. If blaming him made her feel better, then so be it.

"I'm Ian's lawyer, Ms Johnson," he explained calmly. "Everyone's entitled to legal representation when they come before the courts. Your ex-husband's been charged with a very serious offense. He—"

"Do you think I don't know that? He murdered

my baby girl! He told me so! I spoke to him not long after he'd done it! He told me he'd thrown her off the bridge!"

Blake blinked in surprise. Ian had failed to tell him he'd confessed to his ex-wife, albeit while he was no doubt still suffering the effects of his dissociative state. Blake made a mental note to ask his client about it when next they spoke.

"Look, Ms Johnson—"

"No! Stop right there! Don't pander to me with your lame excuses! Don't you dare! Have the courage to tell me to my face why you think my ex-husband has the right to plead not guilty."

Once again, Blake felt a stab of surprise. He could only guess the police had told her his client intended to enter a not guilty plea, although how they knew, Blake didn't have a clue. *Perhaps they'd made an educated guess?* After all, he wasn't known around the courts for giving up without a fight.

"I'm sorry, Ms Johnson. I can't—"

"Don't you go telling me you can't and if you apologize once again, I swear I'll scream. You don't know me! You don't know anything about me! Don't presume you know how I feel."

"I'm sor—" Blake began but then cut himself off.

"I want to meet with you," the woman continued in the same high-pitched, desperate tone. "I want you to look into the face of the mother whose child was tossed over the side of a bridge and into the water by your client as if she were some unwanted piece of trash. She couldn't even swim! My baby couldn't swim..."

Her voice faded and was replaced by sobs. Blake ignored the stab of guilt. He felt awful for her loss, but what did she want him to do? He couldn't meet with her. She was the ex-wife of his client. He represented the man who'd been accused of the crime that had torn her life to shreds. He was helpless to do or say anything that would make things right.

"I'm sorry," he said again and hoped she'd accept he meant the words sincerely. He heard her drag in a ragged breath and when she spoke again, her voice was raw with pain.

"Look me in the eye and tell me how sorry you are."

Her voice had dropped to a guttural growl and was filled with ice and steel. Blake could only guess at how hard it had been for her to make the call in the first place. A shaft of admiration filtered through him and with it, a feeling of resignation. Faced with no other choice, he replied, "Okay."

"Give me a couple of hours," she replied a moment before the line went dead.

He stared at the phone in surprise. While he hadn't been expecting a thank you, he'd anticipated some sign of gratitude. With another frown and with a hand that wasn't quite steady, he returned the phone to the cradle and threw himself back against his chair. He stared blindly out his window and shook his head in dismay.

What the hell had he just agreed to?

Natalie stepped out of the shower and towel dried her hair. She had a little under two hours before her meeting with Blake Harton Junior and she wanted to look her best. He'd be expecting a woman whose life had fallen apart right before her eyes. She'd certainly given him that impression over the phone and that was fine because her life *had* fallen apart—but she didn't want to give him any more reason to think she was a crazy woman.

Monica met her in the hallway, a concerned expression still etched upon her face. "Natalie, I'm not sure this is a good idea. He's representing your ex-husband. What are you hoping to achieve?"

Natalie brushed past her and began searching for her handbag among the clutter on the kitchen counter. "I just want to talk to him, okay? I'm not going to do anything stupid. I just want him to see me, acknowledge me, look me in the eyes... Me, the woman whose child was murdered by his client. I want him to think about me when he stands before the court and enters a not guilty plea and then proceeds to make all manner of excuses for my ex-husband."

"Do you want me to wait?" Monica asked, still looking uncertain.

"No, but thank you. You've been wonderful. I don't know what I would have done without you. Go home. Get some rest. I don't think you've slept since you got here. I'll be fine. We're going to be fine." She wasn't sure if she was trying to convince herself or her friend, but either way, it worked. She felt better than she had since the police arrived on her doorstep with the sad news.

"What about the boys?" Monica asked.

"I'll be back in plenty of time to collect them from school."

Monica still looked undecided. Natalie gave her a nudge. "You're exhausted, Mon. You've been going day and night. Running around after the boys, heating food, answering phone calls... I really appreciate it, but you need a break. Please, go home. I'll be fine."

"All right. I'll call you later and you can tell me all about your meeting with Blake Harton. I must admit, I'm curious about whether he looks as good in person as he does on TV."

Natalie rolled her eyes and shook her head, but said farewell to her friend with a heartfelt hug and a smile that almost felt real. She'd been telling the truth when she'd told Monica how she wouldn't have coped without her. Monica's arrival had been a godsend.

After reminding her friend to lock the door on her way out, Natalie closed the front door behind her and climbed into her car. She thought of her sons and was glad she'd insisted they go to school. There had been enough disruption in their lives. They needed to return to their everyday routines and some sense of normality as soon as possible. It was what everyone around her urged her to do, and they were right, at least insofar as the twins were concerned.

The sun shone bright and warm in the sky. The gray clouds and rain showers that had dogged them yesterday during the funeral were nowhere to be seen as she set out. The early afternoon traffic was more congested the closer she got to the city, but she still arrived at the offices of Sydney Legal in plenty of time. Leaving her car in an underground parking station, she took the elevator up to the lobby.

The pale-gray and white terrazzo-tiled floor that spread across the expanse of the vast lobby was polished to a shine and gleamed with the reflected light from a myriad of downlights set into the ceiling high above. Natalie's heels clacked on the hard surface, momentarily distracting her from her mission. Conscious of not drawing attention to herself, she slowed her walk and made her way over to the information desk.

"I have an appointment with Blake Harton Junior from Sydney Legal," she told the nattily dressed twenty-something male who sat behind the counter.

"May I have your name?" the young man asked.

"Natalie Johnson."

The man gave no sign of recognition as he picked up the phone near his elbow and Natalie swallowed a sigh of relief. Her name and photograph had been splashed repeatedly over the news and all the major morning television shows as the people of Sydney discussed and argued and wondered about the man who'd tossed his baby over the side of Anzac Bridge and the family that now had to live with the consequences of his inexplicable actions.

Moving slightly away, Natalie gave the man privacy to speak with who he needed to speak with to confirm her right to be in the building and a moment later, he waved her over.

"Mr Harton's office is on the twenty-third floor. Take one of the elevators to your left. They will take you straight there."

Natalie forced a smile of thanks and headed off in the direction he'd indicated. She'd decided, on the drive over, that she wanted more from Blake Harton Junior than for him just to acknowledge her existence: She wanted him to drop the case. She wasn't sure how receptive he'd be to that idea and the thought of putting her proposal to him made her nervous.

A case as sensational as this one would draw a big crowd. People would be talking about it everywhere and for a long time. The media attention would be enormous. She understood the appeal such a high profile case might have to a criminal lawyer on the way up, but she hoped to appeal to his better nature, have him see how it just wasn't right for him to represent a man who could cold bloodedly murder his baby out of anger and spite.

She twisted her lips at the thought. As much as she wanted to deny it, she wasn't under any illusions. She was certain Ian had been motivated by rage and his desire to get back at her for the court deciding in her favor, and that desire for vengeance had caused her baby's death. The knowledge sent a fresh wave of sadness and regret rushing through her. She fixed on the image of her little baby, as she'd been before that last weekend with Ian—giggling, running with excitement, her little blond pigtails bouncing—and was almost overcome with desolation. With an effort, she forced the image and feelings aside.

The elevator moved smoothly and silently up the progression of floors. Way too soon it opened for Natalie to disembark on the twenty-third floor. She stepped onto plush carpet that was the color of a stormy summer sky. The walls were painted a muted gray in a slightly lighter shade. Expensive artwork, illuminated by special lighting, hung on the wall. The overall effect was one of wealth and opulence. The offices of Sydney Legal screamed success. Instead of making her feel better, dread formed an icy lump in her belly.

She walked into a reception area that was equally well designed and furnished with fashionable, expensive pieces. A large black woman, who appeared to be in her mid-fifties, sat behind a Tasmanian oak desk. An incongruous, bright pink headband perched in a nest of thick afro hair.

"May I help you?" she asked. Her voice was soft and mellifluous. It was at odds with her solemn expression.

"Yes. I'm Natalie Johnson."

"Oh, Ms Johnson. Take a seat. I'll let Mr Harton know you're here."

Natalie could feel the woman's curious gaze upon her as she turned and walked over to the plush leather couch and perched on the edge of it. She clasped and unclasped her hands and tried to calm her nerves. Now that the moment was upon her, she wasn't quite sure what she'd say.

A door to her right opened and a tall, blond man with broad shoulders, narrow hips, and possessing a pair of the bluest eyes she'd ever seen, walked toward her. He held out his hand.

"Ms Johnson. I'm Blake Harton."

Distractedly, she shook his proffered hand and noted somewhere in the back of her mind that his handshake was firm and warm. He was younger than she'd expected. Close to her age. Thirty, maybe a little older.

"Please don't call me that. Natalie's fine," she replied belatedly.

The lawyer merely acknowledged her request with an inclination of his head and then showed her to his office. Natalie preceded him into a spacious room with a bookshelf that took up almost the entire length of one wall. A second wall was made up entirely of glass. He paused in the open doorway and turned to address the woman who sat behind the reception desk.

"Esther, do you mind bringing us some coffee?"

Closing the door behind them, he gave Natalie a moment to get her bearings. She looked around the office and noted the expensive furniture, the desk that was covered in papers, the magnificent view. Blake Harton was obviously a successful lawyer and a prized employee. Nobody came into possession of an office like this one without bringing in some serious money. She wondered idly how many hours he billed each week. Probably eighty, at least. Then again, his father was a senior partner. *Maybe the nice office had more to do with that?* Her lips twisted on a grimace.

"Let me start by saying how sorry I am," Blake started before taking refuge behind his desk.

She frowned. *What did he think she was going to do? Fly at him in a desperate rage?*

"If you were really sorry, you wouldn't be doing this," she bit out, lifting her head and staring at him challengingly.

His gaze remained steady on hers. "I don't know what you expect of me, Ms—Natalie. Your ex-husband came to me needing a lawyer. Like I told you on the phone, everyone deserves the right to legal representation."

"Not a man who murdered his baby daughter in cold blood," Natalie snapped, unable to help herself.

Blake Harton remained infuriatingly calm. "I don't think it was cold blood, Natalie, but if it was, even cold-blooded murderers deserve a lawyer."

"But, why you?" she cried, suddenly at her wits' end. "I've heard about your reputation. You have a success rate surpassed by none, and you love to dig in and fight. That's why he chose you! Don't you *get* it? Ian thinks you can beat this thing!"

The man continued to regard her steadily. "I can't change the evidence, Natalie. All I can do is present it to the jury. It's up to them to decide."

She made a sound of disgust. "Don't give me that nonsense! We all know how it works! You'll say things, twist the truth, make it sound different than how it was. And the jury will eat it up! They'll take one look at your pretty face and your charming ways. They'll listen to your silver tongue and they'll think you know what you're talking about. My ex-husband will walk free—free to get on with his life—while my life will be left in so many pieces I'll never be able to put them back together again."

To her horror, hot tears welled up in her eyes and her chest tightened on a sob. Try as she might, she couldn't hold it in. Within seconds, she was going from being a reasonably calm and rational woman to a blithering, blubbering mess—and there didn't seem to be a damn thing she could do about it.

Blake stared at the tears that poured down Natalie's cheeks and was immediately beset with panic. Crying women had always been his weakness. He didn't know what to do with them, but something inside him always felt the need to offer them comfort, to do anything he could to make things right again. Only, this time he couldn't heed that urge.

What she was asking of him was impossible. He'd already agreed to take on the case. He *wanted* to take on the case. She had no business knowing his reasons, but the simple fact was, he wasn't going to remove himself, and that was that, no matter how her tears tore him up inside.

A knock at the door snagged his attention and he almost sighed in relief when Esther appeared, carrying a large silver tray laden with coffee things. She set them down on the low table that stood in front of his three-seater couch and then headed back the way she'd come. He wished briefly that he could ask her to stay, but discounted the idea as ridiculous. Surely he could handle a woman in distress, no matter how fragile and beautiful.

Yes, she was beautiful. He hadn't expected that. In truth, he didn't know what he'd expected, but it wasn't the tall, athletic-looking woman with softly curling, shoulder-length red hair and skin so pale it was almost translucent even with the scattering of freckles. She looked so natural and normal, like tragedy had never touched her life and yet every day for the rest of her life she would live with the knowledge that her ex-husband had caused the death of her child.

Guilt rushed through him and he angrily pushed it aside. *What did she expect?* He was only doing his job. If it weren't him, it would be some other lawyer who'd step in and offer their services and if they wouldn't do it without charge, like he was, the court would appoint a lawyer from Legal Aid.

The woman was kidding herself if she thought the whole thing would go away if he agreed to step down. Any lawyer worth his salt would advise his client to plead not guilty and take his chances with the jury. *After all, what was there to lose?*

Blake recalled the look of devastation and horror on Ian Johnson's face when he'd recounted the moment he pulled over, climbed up on the roof of his car and tossed his child to her death. No doubt his ex-wife wouldn't want to hear it, but it was the truth. There were no winners here, no matter what she thought.

Moving over to the coffee tray, Blake poured a cup. He went to add cream and then paused. A woman that slim and fit-looking probably watched her weight. Cream and sugar were no doubt off the list. He handed her the cup of black coffee and she took it with a murmur of thanks.

Blake poured himself a cup and added cream and sugar before settling back on the couch. He sipped from his coffee in silence. Finally, Natalie moved closer and perched on the armchair opposite. He set his cup on the coffee table and cleared his throat.

"What happened was a tragedy no matter which way you look at it or whose side you're on. I'm not going to dispute that. But Ian is just as devastated about what happened. I spoke to him personally last week. This has really cut him up."

Within seconds, her green eyes lit up with fury. She launched herself to her feet. Coffee sloshed from her cup all over the carpet, but she paid it no heed.

"Don't you talk to me about Ian's devastation!" she cried out in outrage.

Blake regarded her calmly and leaned over and took another sip from his cup in an effort to diffuse some of her anger. He drew in a breath and eased it out before continuing.

"I understand how you feel, Natalie. I'd feel exactly the same way. But the truth is, your ex-husband didn't know what he was doing. His actions were out of his control. It was like he was in a dream. None of it seemed real. He can't believe what happened, that little Lacey is dead. He loved her like you did. He wishes desperately that he could start the day over, bring her back. But he can't."

Once again, Blake paused. From the closed look on Natalie's face and the anger that still flashed in her eyes, his words weren't having their desired effect. He tried again.

"Your ex-husband came to me for help. He's a desperate man and he's desperately sorry for what he's done. He needs good representation." Once again, he paused and this time she met his gaze. "And I'm going to provide it."

His words sent a fresh wave of anger flooding across her face. Twin spots of bright color infused her cheeks. She set her cup on the coffee table and stood with her hands on her hips. She opened her mouth...and let him have it.

"Don't you *dare* presume to know how I feel! You don't understand anything!" She pointed at him, accusingly. "You sit there and tell me how much my ex-husband regrets his actions, how sorry he is, how much he wants his daughter back. Well, guess what? She's not coming back because he *murdered* her! No matter how you dress it up with fancy words and phrases, that's exactly what happened and *no one* can argue with that."

She began to pace his office, her arms now crossed defensively over her chest. "It's all right for him to feel sorry now, but nothing's going to bring my baby back! If it weren't for him and his selfish, cruel actions, she'd still be here!" She spun on her three-inch heels and eyeballed him, her breath coming fast. "Tell me *that's* not the truth!"

Blake stood slowly and moved toward her. His

heart was filled with compassion. No matter that he wasn't going to drop the case, this woman, this mother was hurting desperately and it was awful to see. He wished he could take her pain away, but nobody could do that.

"I don't know what you want me to say, Natalie, but one thing's for sure. I *do* know how you feel."

She stared at him in disbelief and shook her head slowly back and forth. "How the hell would you know how I feel? Have *you* lost a child?" she scoffed.

Blake paused and thought about what he was about to say. Coming to a decision, he spoke again.

"No, but my brother, David, was caught up in a bitter custody dispute. Two young kids he loved to death. I mean that literally. The day the courts handed down their final decision, awarding his ex-wife sole custody, was the day he tied a belt around his neck and hung himself."

CHAPTER 6

Barely aware that she had Blake Harton Junior's business card scrunched up in her hand, Natalie stumbled across the gleaming floor of the foyer she'd admired less than thirty minutes earlier and headed through the automatic doors into the sunshine. She hurried through the crowds that lined the sidewalk, desperate to put as much distance as possible between her and the offices of Sydney Legal. The noise of the traffic, the hum of the pedestrians, horns, shouts of greeting, cries of alarm—all of it disappeared into a void of nothingness. The only thing she could think about was what Blake Harton Junior had just told her.

Six months earlier, his brother had committed suicide over a custody battle. The announcement had blown her away. She'd stared at him in shock, unable to believe what she'd just heard. The shock was followed closely by an overwhelming need to vomit. His brother had killed himself after losing a court battle over custody of his kids.

Though part of Natalie sympathized with Blake for his loss, for the most part, the news terrified her.

It had become immediately and terribly obvious that for Blake Harton Junior, Ian's case was personal and the lawyer's pain was still fresh. He was never going to give up this case. Nothing would stand in his way to do whatever it took to win. A win would be like a tribute to his brother and everyone knew how much Blake Harton Junior liked to win—and how good he was at doing just that.

A fresh wave of nausea rushed through her and she stumbled down the steps of Wynyard train station in search of a public restroom. Tumultuous thoughts filled her head, going round and round in circles, making her dizzy.

Oh, God! What if Blake Harton did his thing and Ian got off? He'd walk right out of that jail cell and wouldn't look back. Lacey's murder would go unavenged, soon to be forgotten amidst other, more sensational news—and Natalie would be left to live with the consequences. The thought horrified her.

Lurching from side to side, she finally found the restrooms and stumbled into a stall. Her stomach clenched. Barely managing to close the door behind her, she found the toilet bowl, and just in time. Hot, acrid vomit spewed from her mouth and her nose. She retched until there was nothing left. She couldn't remember the last time she'd eaten, but her stomach didn't seem to care about that.

All she could think about was how her ex-husband might very well go free. She couldn't let that happen. She had to try harder to convince his lawyer to drop the case. It was even more imperative now that she knew about Blake Harton Junior's motive and what the driving force behind him would really be.

Of course, she was sad about his brother, but this was *her* life they were messing with and the lives of her boys! She had to make him see! This wasn't just about his job and a client who needed him. This was life and death.

She didn't know what she'd do if Ian weren't punished. He should be sent to jail! He should be kept in there the rest of his life! She wished Australia still allowed for capital punishment. She'd be the first to flick the switch! She didn't care how sorry he was or how much he wished he could turn back time and she didn't put much stock in his remorse. The fact was, her little baby girl was dead. She was never coming back.

He'd murdered Lacey out of spite. She *knew* it. She just knew it, no matter how much his lawyer tried to pretty it up. It should be an eye for an eye. Ian's life for Lacey's. Even the Bible backed her on that.

Never would her baby see another birthday, go to school, grow up and kiss a boy. Lacey's life had been stolen and that was the pure unadulterated truth. A fresh wave of fury surged through her. She wanted Ian dead! *Dead! Dead! Dead!* As dead as her baby girl.

A sob tore from her throat and she gasped and cried out. With her hands still clasped around the toilet bowl, she slowly slid to the floor. Tears poured from her eyes and ran down her cheeks. No doubt the makeup she'd applied so carefully in anticipation of her meeting with Blake was now a smudged black-and-green mess. But what did that matter compared to the loss of her child? She doubled over on another heart-wrenching sob.

A knock sounded on the door. "Are you all right in there?"

Natalie heard the woman's voice, as if from a far distance, but was too weak to reply. With her head resting on the cold porcelain, she continued to cry.

"Somebody call an ambulance! There's a lady in here who needs help!"

Once again, Natalie heard the words, but they bounced off the walls and fell flat. The next thing she knew, the door to the stall was forced open and people milled around. She saw legs covered in pantyhose, a nice pair of sparkly silver high-heels. Then there were other legs covered in navy-blue pants and much more sensible shoes.

"Paramedics. Please stand clear. Excuse me, miss. We need to get through."

The crowd of onlookers dissipated and all of a sudden, Natalie was left staring into the kindly, calm face of a middle-aged woman dressed in a uniform.

"Hi, I'm Mary-Jane," the woman said, crouching down beside Natalie and offering her a quick smile. "What seems to be the matter?"

Natalie shook her head, helpless to answer. The vomiting had stopped, but the tears still flowed and her breath was fast and choppy. An oxygen mask appeared and was fixed over her mouth and nose.

"Okay, honey. It's okay," Mary-Jane murmured comfortingly. "Easy now. Big slow breaths. In and out... There. That's better."

Natalie tried to concentrate on the paramedic's words, but it was a struggle. Her head was spinning with images of Ian and her little baby girl.

"We're going to transport you to the hospital, if you're okay with that." Mary-Jane said.

Natalie nodded, beyond words.

"Here's the stretcher now," the paramedic added and then stood. "Stand back, people. Give us some room."

Another paramedic appeared in Natalie's line of sight. In no time at all, she was helped up onto the stretcher and wheeled out to a waiting ambulance. The last thing she remembered was the sound of the doors closing behind her.

Blake strode toward the automatic double glass doors that led into the emergency department of the Sydney Harbour Hospital and headed straight for the desk. He'd received a call from one of the nurses to say that a young woman, about thirty years of age had been brought in by ambulance. When he'd questioned the nurse about why she was calling *him*, she informed him that the patient was unable to tell them her name and had arrived at the emergency department without any ID. His business card had been found in her hand. Hence the call. They were hoping he'd be able to tell them who she was.

Before the call had even ended, Blake's heart kicked into overdrive. He'd left the office immediately.

"Hi," he now said to the nurse seated behind the triage counter. "I'm Blake Harton. Someone called me about a patient who carried my business card. From the description I was given, I believe it's Natalie Johnson. I'd like to see her, please."

The woman glanced at him and nodded and then turned her attention to the computer on her desk. She typed on the keyboard for a minute and then looked back at him.

"She's being seen by the doctor. No doubt he'll be out in a moment. Take a seat."

"Is she... Is she all right?"

The woman's expression didn't change. "Like I said, the doctor will be out in a moment."

Blake did his best to stem his impatience and took a seat in the crowded waiting area. The room was filled with the usual assortment of people with cuts and scrapes. Mothers with young children and an elderly man hunched over in the corner coughing and rasping like he only had half a lung.

Blake sat as far away from the coughing as possible. He felt like pulling out his handkerchief and using it as a mask. He never had been good about dealing with germs. He wasn't exactly obsessive compulsive, but he sure liked things clean. The smell of disinfectant in such a place was like perfume to his nose.

A set of automatic doors between the waiting room and the area that Blake presumed led into the emergency ward, slid open and a middle-aged man with salt-and-pepper hair and wearing a white doctor's coat appeared. A stethoscope was draped around his neck. He looked around the collection of patients gathered nearby and his gaze settled on Blake. The man moved closer.

"Are you Blake Harton Junior?" the man asked.

"Yes."

The man stuck out his hand. "I'm Doctor Arthur Schofield. I've been treating the woman we believed was your client. She's since recovered enough to tell us her name."

Blake nodded and shook the proffered hand and then quickly asked, "How is she?"

"Are you a relative?"

"No. I'm...her lawyer. And a friend."

The doctor studied him. "I wouldn't normally share a patient's information with just a friend, but seeing as you're also her lawyer..."

The doctor watched him expectantly and Blake fought to keep the guilt from his face. "Yes, of course, I understand," he managed. "And thank you. Is she all right?"

"Yes, she's going to be fine. She had what we call a panic attack. It left her dazed and confused for a little while, but she's fully conscious now. The attack was probably brought on by some unexpected shock. It happens. She told us she's been stressed out lately...?"

The doctor's gaze became more pointed, but Blake purposely kept his expression blank. It was obvious Natalie hadn't elaborated about the reasons for her stress. If she wanted to keep her private life private, that was her business. It wasn't Blake's place to explain.

Ignoring the doctor's unspoken query, Blake changed the subject. "Can I see her?" he asked.

The doctor took a step back and nodded. "Sure. Follow me. In fact, she's now free to go."

Blake followed the doctor through the automatic doors the man had entered through and down a long corridor lined with wheelchairs, IV poles and other medical equipment. Finally, he opened another door and strode into a large open ward where the beds were partitioned with curtains.

"She's right over there," the doctor said and pointed across the room.

Blake muttered his thanks and headed for the bed the man had indicated. Because the bed was surrounded by taupe curtains, Blake didn't catch sight of Natalie until he tugged one of them slightly open. She was pale and still against the sheets. Her hair was spread out across the pillow. Her eyes were closed, as if in sleep. She looked much younger and frailer than she had in his office. He didn't want to think their conversation might have had something to do with the onset of her panic attack. The last thing he needed was guilt over someone else's mental health.

As if sensing his presence, her eyelids fluttered open. At the sight of him, her eyes widened in surprise.

"Mr Harton. W-what are you doing here?"

"They found my business card in your hand and they called me. Don't you remember?"

Tiny frown lines marred the smooth skin of her forehead. "No, I don't."

"Yes. I got a call from a nurse to say that someone with my card had been brought in here by ambulance. They said you were dazed and confused. Initially, you couldn't tell them your name. You had no ID on you." He shrugged. "So, they called me."

She turned away and faced the opposite direction, but not before he caught the flush of embarrassment on her cheeks. Her hands clutched the sheets.

"I'm sorry," he said. "I'm probably the last person you want to see. Is there someone else I can call? A brother or a sister? Your mother? A friend?"

"No, there's no one," came the soft reply.

"There must be someone."

"No, there really isn't," she said. "I'm an only child. My parents died a few years ago. My best friend, Monica, would come, but she's not long gone home after spending the last week looking after me and my kids in Lilyfield. She lives in Parramatta. I couldn't ask her to come into the city. She's probably asleep."

Blake fell silent. There was nothing he could say to that. "Can I take you somewhere then? I could drive you home."

She shook her head so vehemently he was a little taken aback. "No! I don't want anything from you! They shouldn't have called you."

Blake tried not to take her words personally. She was upset and probably still feeling the residual effects of her panic attack.

"I understand," he said soothingly, "but you can't stay here. The doctor said you're free to go. Either you can come with me, or you can make your own way home. You choose."

She frowned again, deepening the lines on her face. She looked torn, as if the last thing she wanted to do was go anywhere with him. When she looked back up at him, there was a mutinous expression on her beautiful, pale face.

"I could call a cab," she stated.

"Apparently, you don't have your handbag. The hospital couldn't find any ID, remember?"

She bit her lip. Tears glinted in her eyes. Even upset, she was beautiful. Blake's gut clenched involuntarily. It was a shame they'd met in such awful circumstances... And then he immediately dismissed that thought.

He wasn't into commitment, not now, not ever. And that was that. But as much as he wished he could, he couldn't ignore her distress. Fishing in his pocket for a clean handkerchief, he handed it to her in silence. It was made from the finest cotton and monogrammed with his initials. It had been a birthday gift from his grandmother.

With the briefest look of gratitude, Natalie took the handkerchief from his hand. She wiped her eyes and blew her nose gently, elegantly. He hid a smile. Even her nose-blowing technique was delicate.

She carefully refolded it and handed it back to him and then flushed with embarrassment. She pulled her hand back and then paused, as if she wasn't quite sure what to do with it. In the end, she tucked it inside her blouse. Blake tried hard not to notice how the movement caused the fabric to pull tight across her breasts.

For Pete's sake, Harton. Get your head out of the gutter. This is so not the time or the place, he silently admonished himself. As a peace offering, he extended his hand.

"Here. Let me help you."

Carefully, she eased herself upright and with his help, slid her legs sideways and put her feet on the ground.

"Where are your sandals?" he asked, noticing her bare feet.

"I think they put them in that cupboard," she replied, pointing to a nightstand beside the bed.

He opened the door and located them. Crouching low, he took one of her feet in his hand to slip the sandal on. She pulled her foot away.

"I can do it," she muttered.

He stood, embarrassed. *Hell, he was only trying to help. Couldn't she see that?*

Turning away, he gave her a few moments to put on her shoes and straighten her clothing and then, once again, he offered his arm. Once again, she shunned his chivalry.

"I'm fine," she said and took a few wobbly steps forward.

"Are you sure? I can rustle up a wheelchair," he replied.

"No, I don't need a wheelchair. I'll be fine. It's just that...I haven't stood upright for a while."

With a determination he couldn't help but admire, she left the emergency department unaided and slowly walked with him to his car. The silver Aston Martin V8 Vantage Roadster convertible was his pride and joy. He'd saved up every penny to buy it and even then, his bank still owned a hefty portion of it. Still, it was low and sleek and stylish and was the same car driven by James Bond.

What more could he say?

He moved around to the passenger side and opened the door for Natalie. If she was impressed by his wheels, she didn't say so. He didn't hold her lack of enthusiasm about his car against her. She had a lot going on.

Climbing behind the wheel, he started the ignition and then turned to her.

"Where to?"

Chapter 7

Keeping up with the speed of the traffic, Blake headed east and followed Natalie's directions to a nice street at the northern end of Lilyfield. They pulled up outside a dark brick, freestanding federation home that looked like it harkened back to the 1920s. A picket fence painted the same shade of cream as the trim around the windows closed the front yard off from the street. The lawn was freshly mowed and a neat row of colorful petunias lined the pathway on either side. It was a nice house, a pretty house. It was a house that beckoned you in from the street.

Natalie opened her door before he could get to it and she practically leaped out of the car to avoid his help. He joined her beside the garden gate that fronted a path leading to the front door. She'd been quiet throughout the ride over and he hadn't wanted to intrude on her thoughts, though he couldn't help but wonder if she should be left alone.

"Is there anyone at home?" he asked.

She shook her head.

"Are you sure there's no one I can call?"

"No."

The afternoon sun still shone bright and warm, but she rubbed her arms, as if warding off the cold.

"What about your boys? Are they at school? Who's picking them up?"

A look of sheer panic crossed her face. Her gaze clashed with his. "Oh, my goodness! I've left my car in the city. I didn't think. *Damn!* The boys are going to be out of school in ten minutes. How could I have been so stupid?"

"Hey, don't worry about it. I'm happy to swing by and collect them."

"No! They're still traumatized by what happened. I don't want them having to deal with a stranger—"

"I didn't mean I'd go alone," he interrupted. "You can come with me."

She bit her lip and looked away and he could tell she didn't want to be any more beholden to him than she already was. But it was nearly three o'clock. She didn't have any choice. As if coming to the same conclusion, her shoulders slumped on a quiet sigh.

"All right, I'll come. But we need to hurry. The school's about six minutes' drive away. We'll be lucky to get there in time."

Without further ado, Blake opened the passenger side door and waited for Natalie to get back in. Closing the door after her, he hurried back around to the driver's side and climbed behind the wheel. The V8 engine made short work of the journey and they arrived just as the bell rang. Young children of various ages raced out from everywhere. Smiling, laughing, skipping, bouncing with energy; accosting parents with hugs and cheery greetings. Watching them, Blake felt a pang. For the first time, he wondered what it would be like to be a dad. For the first time in a long time, he thought about his niece and nephew.

How were they doing, without their dad? It shamed him to realize David had been gone six months. *Six months.* That's how long it had been since he'd seen his brother's kids... His thoughts turned to his own father and he felt another pang.

Blake Harton Senior had been a good provider. Blake and his brother had never wanted for anything...except their father's presence. He was always at work. He'd leave early in the morning and return late at night. Even the weekends saw him leave straight after breakfast and often it would be well into the afternoon before he returned.

Blake's mother, Annette Harton, would tell them it was because their father wanted to make junior partner. He had to work hard, bill a lot of hours, win more cases than anyone else. When his dad made junior partner, Blake had been overjoyed. Naïvely, he'd thought, at last he'd see more of him, but it didn't work out that way.

Next there was senior partner to aspire to and that meant even longer hours and more time away from home. There had been no time for his father to attend soccer matches or football practice. Their father hadn't even made it in time to see David star in the school play.

Blake had been astonished when his dad made it to his high school graduation. He hadn't been surprised when Blake Harton Senior had left the ceremony early and returned to the office: He was in the middle of a complicated criminal trial; he had witness depositions to attend; there were a million things he needed to prepare for before Monday arrived. That always seemed to be the case.

The truth of it was, Blake Harton Senior was a brilliant lawyer who'd done extremely well in life, but who hardly knew his children. Now there was only one left. Blake had wondered if things would change with David's sudden tragic death, but if anything, his father got worse, absenting himself from his family for even longer periods of time. Blake guessed it was his father's way of coping, but he didn't know for sure and he couldn't help but wonder how his mom felt about it all. She must be very lonely. *What was the point of being married when her spouse spent more time away than at home?*

It was ironic that Blake had also become a lawyer, but as much as he loved his job, he tried hard to strike a balance. Besides, he had no wife and family, wondering when he'd come home. Most of the time, it was easier that way.

"There they are!"

Natalie's shout interrupted his musings and pushed his dark thoughts aside. Climbing out of the car, she headed toward two young boys who were walking slowly, dejectedly toward her. They greeted her with brief smiles, their behavior in stark contrast to that of the rowdy children around them. He watched her go down on one knee and gather her sons close. The three red heads were crowded together.

Slowly, she came to her feet and, taking one hand in each of her own, she guided them back to Blake's car. As they got closer, he saw how much the boys looked alike. In fact, he couldn't tell them apart...

"Bailey. Darby. I want you to meet...a friend of mine. Boys, this is Mr Harton. He's been kind enough to offer us a ride home."

"Where's *your* car, Mom?" asked one of the boys. Blake couldn't tell which one.

"I... I left it in the city."

"How come?" the same boy asked. The other twin just eyed Blake's car in silence.

"What kind of car is this, mister?" he asked.

"It's an Aston Martin V8 Vantage Roadster," Blake replied, not bothering to disguise the pride in his voice.

"It's real nice," the same boy said, his gaze running along the car.

"Thanks," Blake replied. "Would you like to take a ride in it?"

The boy looked doubtfully across at his mother. "Can we, Mom?"

"Of course, Darby," Natalie replied. "I already told you. Mr Harton gave me a lift from the city. He's going to drive us home."

"Cool!" Darby replied, his eyes lighting up.

He stepped closer to the car.

The other boy—Bailey—held his ground and frowned. "You always told us not to talk to strangers, Mom, and definitely not to get into their cars."

Natalie smiled softly and hugged him close. "You're right, Bailey and you're such a good boy to remember that. But Mr Harton isn't a stranger. Not to me, at least, and I'd never do anything to hurt you." Her expression sobered and she stared closely at her son. "You believe me, don't you?"

He offered a reluctant nod, his gaze fixed at his feet. "Yes, but I didn't think Daddy would hurt us, either and he did. He hurt Lacey. He hurt her really bad." The child lifted his head toward his mother and Blake saw the gleam of unshed tears.

"I *told* him not to, Mom! I *told* him to go back. But he wouldn't listen. He wouldn't listen to me."

Blake's heart broke at the desolation on Bailey's face. The child's tears that had threatened now rolled silently down his cheeks. Blake's gaze shifted to Darby. The boy wore a closed expression on his face and his fists were clenched by his side. His excitement over Blake's car seemed a distant memory.

Blake glanced at Natalie and his gut clenched at the pain that was clear on her face. It had seemed like such a good idea to come and collect her children from school. Now it was all blowing up in his face. After all their mother had been through that day, a meltdown from her sons in the schoolyard was the last thing she needed. He thought fast.

"Hey, boys! Who wants to go to McDonalds for ice cream?"

Natalie stared at Blake, surprised and relieved. She mouthed a *thank you* and went warm all over when he winked at her and followed it with a cheeky grin. Blushing furiously, she ducked her head and busied herself getting the boys into the car. Opening the passenger side door, she pulled up short. There were no car seats. She bit her lip and looked across at Blake.

"Oh, I'm so sorry. I didn't think. The boys are only five. They need car seats."

Blake grimaced and followed it with a shrug. "There's not a lot of room back there," he said, indicating the rear seats with a movement of his head. "They should fit pretty snugly. We don't have far to drive. I'm willing to risk it if you are."

Natalie was flooded with indecision. *Would it be all right to drive a few miles without car seats?* Blake was right. They were literally only a half dozen minutes from home. His offer to go for ice cream had gone down well with her sons, but she'd simply explain to them that they weren't going to be able to make any detours. They'd need to go straight home. What choice did she have? She was still without her handbag. She had no money for a cab or ice cream. They could probably walk home, but it would take the best part of an hour with the boys tagging along.

Blake was also right about the snug fit. A glance behind her revealed two black leather seats that looked luxurious and outrageously expensive, but were each barely big enough to hold a child, and a small one at that.

Decision made, she helped the boys into the back and both she and Blake made sure her sons had their seatbelts on. She caught Blake's eye as he leaned across Darby and buckled him in and a fresh wave of warmth washed over her. The feeling was weird and confusing and put her on edge. He was her ex-husband's lawyer. He was determined to help set a murderer free. And not just any murderer, but the man who'd killed her baby...

Blake Harton Junior wasn't her friend. He was her enemy.

The thought sobered her. All of a sudden, she wanted to put as much distance between them as she could, but it was impossible in the close confines of his car. She opened the door and climbed in, seating herself so that she sat on the very edge of the seat and clung to the door handle.

The Aston's engine rumbled to life and Blake pulled out into the traffic. She glanced at his profile and tried not to notice how handsome he was. He was her adversary...and yet, ever since he'd arrived at the emergency department, he'd shown her nothing but kindness. If he wasn't her ex-husband's lawyer, she might even like him...

But she was well aware they were on opposite sides of what was a very nasty case and now all she wanted to do was to get away from him as quickly as she could. Their arrival back home couldn't come soon enough.

As calmly as she could, she turned toward the boys and explained that they couldn't stop for ice cream. Amidst their cries of protest, Blake shot her a questioning look, but didn't argue.

"The car seats," she said to him by way of explanation. "I don't want you to risk getting a ticket."

He nodded in understanding and turned his attention back to the traffic. Minutes later, they pulled up outside her house. She swallowed a sigh of relief and released her grip on the door handle. She climbed out before Blake could make it around to her side. Then she helped Bailey from the car. Darby climbed out on Blake's side and stood there, once again admiring the sleek car.

"Come on, boys. We need to go. Say thank you to Mr Harton."

"Thank you, Mr Harton," they chorused.

Shooing the twins inside, she turned to him, intent on adding her own reluctant thanks. She found him staring at her, a curious expression on his face, as if he was trying to work something out. A flutter of nerves filled her belly. With his blond hair ruffled and his designer tie loosened and slightly askew, he looked like a menswear model fresh from a photo shoot for the cover of some glossy magazine.

Her heartbeat picked up its pace. Despite the fact he was representing Ian, Blake Harton Junior was a good-looking, kind-hearted man. She was truly grateful for all he'd done for her that day. If only...

There was no point considering the *if only*s. That was surely an exercise in futility. He—

"What about your car? It's still in the city, isn't it?"

His question brought her thoughts to a halt. She frowned and then slowly nodded. "Yes. But don't worry about it. You've done enough already. I'll work something out."

"But what about the boys?" he insisted. "Won't they have to get to school in the morning? You don't even have your wallet. Here." He peeled off a small bundle of hundred-dollar bills. "Take this. It should see you through until you can locate your bag or, if it doesn't turn up, until you can get to the bank."

Natalie stared at the money, reluctant to take it. He'd already been so generous with his time. She didn't want to be beholden to him any further.

"Thank you, but no. I'm fine. I'll call the train station. I'm sure I left my purse in the bathroom. It's probably been handed in."

He shot her a look of disbelief and she grudgingly offered him a grin. "Okay, I'm being totally optimistic, but who knows? I'm sure there are still some honest people in the world. Maybe one of them found my handbag?"

"I think you should call the station right away and then start cancelling your cards. I hate to break it to you, but chances are, the bag's been stolen. You might never get it back."

Her shoulders slumped on a sigh of defeat. "You're right," she said, unable to keep the dejection from her voice. It was just another blow during what had been an awful day and that wasn't even counting Lacey...

Still, at least she and her sons were home, safe and sound—and she had Blake Harton to thank for that. The rest she'd deal with later. She offered him a handshake.

"Thank you again, Mr Harton."

"Call me Blake, please."

"Thank you...Blake. I... I appreciate everything you've done for us today."

"Are you sure I can't arrange—?"

"No, it's fine," she said, cutting him short, once again feeling the urge to put some distance between them. Blake Harton Junior was dangerous and in ways she never imagined when she made the decision to drive into town and confront him in his office.

He shot her a look of surprise and she forced herself to modify her tone. "I'm sorry, I shouldn't have snapped at you. It's been a difficult day. Thank you for your offer. You're very kind, but I'll do what needs to be done. Now, I need to go inside and check on the boys. They need to get ready for bed."

His eyebrows flew upwards and she cursed silently under her breath. What a stupid thing to say. It wasn't even half-past three. Still, she needed to get away from him before she said or did something really stupid—like inviting him inside.

The thought was enough to motivate her.

Ducking her head and giving him a brief wave of farewell, she turned on her heel and headed toward her house to join her boys.

———————

Blake stared at Natalie as she disappeared up the paved pathway, past a display of healthy-looking tropical plants and flowers and up the front stairs. He tried not to notice how good she looked from behind. Her figure was tall and slender, enhanced by the close-fitting clothes. Her red hair had come loose during her stay at the hospital and hung in waves around her shoulders. In fact, she looked almost as good from the back as she did from the front.

His body stirred involuntarily and he swore quietly and forced himself to turn away. She was the ex-wife of his client, a man he was defending against a murder charge. She was a witness for the prosecution and no doubt he'd be forced to cross-examine her in due course. The thought didn't sit well with him. Still, that was the reality of the situation and as much as he might wish things were different, they were what they were.

And then he shook his head. *Really? Did he really wish things were different?* He was Mister No Commitment. Had been that way for thirty-one years and he had good reason for being that way. A beautiful woman with a drop-dead-gorgeous figure, filled with sadness and vulnerability, was not going to change the way he was. Not now, not ever. He only had to think of his brother, and the painful divorce and bitter custody battle that had ended with his death, to remember that marriage and long-term commitment weren't for him.

With that memory firmly re-established in the forefront of his mind, Blake unlocked his car and opened the door. He climbed behind the wheel, started the engine and drove away. He didn't look back.

Chapter 8

Natalie stood in line behind two other people who waited outside Wynyard Station's lost property counter. She still couldn't believe her handbag had been handed in by someone who'd found it on the floor of the public restroom. The knowledge restored her faith in humankind and allowed her forget for just an instant her ex-husband's monstrous act of barbarity.

"May I help you?"

With a start, Natalie realized the attendant behind the counter had addressed her. She hurriedly stepped forward. After offering her name and a description of her handbag, in short order it was returned. She thanked the woman behind the counter and checked inside it. Everything seemed to be there, including her purse which still contained eighty-five dollars in cash. That was a good thing.

Everything she'd owned with Ian had been halved in the divorce. Money was often scarce now. Title to their matrimonial home had been transferred to her and she'd re-financed the loan. She'd spend most of the rest of her life paying for it, but at least her kids could remain in the only house they'd known and could continue to attend their school. Keeping those things consistent was important to her and even more so after what had happened to Lacey.

Natalie had also organized for the boys to attend counseling, but there was no getting around the fact that they'd all been through a series of traumatic events in a relatively short space of time. First the breakdown of the family unit and the subsequent divorce. Then the battle over who would have the right to have them live with them. That had gone on for two years. And lastly, the tragedy of Lacey's death... A tragedy played out in full view of her boys.

Would any amount of counseling help them through it? Would they ever be happy again?

Her therapist kept telling her that children were resilient; that they'd come to accept what had happened and adjust to not having their father, and now Lacey, in their lives. Children adjusted a lot better than adults did, the therapist assured her. Natalie hated that her boys had to adjust at all.

They still woke up with nightmares every night. She knew because they slept in her bed. Ever since Lacey's death, they were terrified of the dark and often woke crying out against an unknown, horrifying monster. She understood how they felt. She woke from nightmares, too. Sometimes Ian's features materialized, sometimes it was her daughter's. Those were the hardest to deal with. Lacey, screaming in terror, her sweet face contorted with fear.

"Mommy! Mommy! Mommy! Help me!"

Natalie scrunched up her face and fought off a rush of tears. She was still standing in the underground train station with people all around. She didn't want to suffer another debilitating panic attack and be taken to the hospital all over again.

Forcing deep breaths into her lungs, she clutched her handbag to her chest and pushed through the crowd hurrying to and from the train platforms and the shops that lined the walkways. After getting out of bed earlier than usual so she could walk the boys to school, she'd called her office and explained that she'd be late for her first day back at work.

If her secretary was curious about the details, she didn't say anything. Natalie was relieved. Though everyone who worked at Baker & Carr Construction knew about Lacey, it was only natural for people who hadn't been through it to assume that, since the funeral had come and gone, she was over the worst of it. She didn't blame them. They didn't know any better.

The truth was, she'd never get over the loss of her child. She knew that as well as she knew what she looked like. Her work colleagues were wrong on both counts: The worst was yet to come.

She didn't kid herself that facing Ian across a courtroom, knowing he was contesting his culpability surrounding their daughter's death—when there was no way she'd ever believe he hadn't done it as a twisted act of revenge against her and the system—would be the hardest thing she'd ever done and would take all the courage she possessed. She just hoped she was strong enough to endure it.

Her thoughts went to Blake and her stomach knotted with a mix of nerves and dread. In another lifetime, she might have been taken in by his suave good looks and old-fashioned manners, but he was Ian's lawyer; he was the man who would stand before a court of law and argue her ex-husband's innocence—or at the very least, make excuses for the fact he'd murdered his little girl.

It didn't matter that Blake was probably a decent man doing his job to the best of his ability. The fact was, he was most definitely the enemy and was as dangerous to her family as her ex.

———

Ignoring the horde of cameramen and reporters that crowded around the steps of the courthouse, Blake pushed his way past their shouted questions and requests for interviews and entered the building. Passing through security, he glanced at his watch. He had thirty minutes before court would commence. He'd asked his client to meet him inside. He only hoped the man had taken his advice and used a side entrance well ahead of the appointed time to avoid the barrage of questions from the media.

Blake hadn't spoken to Ian Johnson face to face since their initial interview in his office more than a month earlier. He wished he hadn't met Natalie. Knowing her and her sons, and the stress they were under, complicated an already difficult case. Usually he could focus completely on his client and what needed to be done, but every time he thought of Johnson, he saw the man's beautiful, haunted wife. Ex-wife. Whatever. The fact was, Blake's heart went out to her. He felt her pain and that wasn't a good thing.

No. He needed to forget about Natalie Johnson, put her completely out of his head. He had to clear his mind of everything he knew about her and focus on the job at hand.

"Mr Harton?"

Blake turned at the sound of his name and spied his client coming toward him. The man was neatly dressed in an off-the-rack, dark-colored suit and a cheap, plain blue tie. His face was drawn and lined, but he was clean shaven and his hair was wet, like he was fresh from the shower. Blake put out his hand in greeting and Johnson shook it.

"How are you doing?" Blake asked.

His client merely shrugged. Blake didn't press him. "Let's go somewhere we can talk in private," Blake suggested and led the way into a vacant interview room on the far side of the floor. Several similar-sized rooms lined the wall, available for members of the legal fraternity and their clients.

Johnson pulled up a chair and took a seat at

the cheap, government-issued table. Blake sat across from him. Opening his briefcase, he brought out a fresh legal pad and pen.

"Let's go over a few things. Have you ever been to a criminal court before?" he asked.

His client wiped his palms on his pants. "No."

"All right, well, let me explain how this works. The judge will deal with some preliminary issues, including any questions that have been raised on points of law, venue, media presence and the like. Then we'll select a jury. Twelve in all. That will take some time, depending upon who we draw. It's important to get the right mix of jurors; people favorable to our case."

"How do we do that?" Ian asked.

"Both the crown prosecutor and I get a number of strikes—that's what we call it when we decide a juror isn't a good fit. Of course, the strikes are limited, so in the end, we get a few jurors we want, they get a few they want and we hope we can live with the rest. Once the jury's been selected, the trial starts.

"The prosecutor will lead the talking. He'll make an opening statement which is basically a summary of his case and then I'll have my turn. I'll make a similar statement explaining things from our point of view. Of course, the opening statements will be in direct conflict with each other. That's the way it works. By the end of the trial, the jury will be asked to choose."

Johnson looked troubled and Blake understood why. After becoming aware that Johnson had told his ex-wife shortly afterwards that he'd thrown their daughter off the bridge, Blake had phoned his client and had put the question to him. After some prevarication, the man finally admitted that the conversation with Natalie had taken place. It was now imperative that the psychological evidence show that Johnson was out of his mind—dissociating—at the time of the offense even if he was rational when he made the call. If the jury didn't buy it, they were going down. Blake hoped there weren't any other surprises in store for him.

He swallowed a sigh at the thought of what lay ahead. There was no point showing his client how stressed his lawyer was. Besides, Blake had run difficult trials in the past. In fact, he did some of his best work while under pressure. It was weird, but true. He hoped the Johnson trial wouldn't be the trial that broke that mold.

"When do the witnesses get called?" Ian asked, interrupting Blake's introspection.

"The prosecution will call their witnesses first. The detectives who investigated the case are usually called at the beginning. Their evidence will pretty much follow their statements. Then there will be testimony from any eye witnesses to the incident."

"Will they call Natalie?" Ian asked, his expression grim.

Blake nodded. "She's on their list. I assume they'll call her."

"She'll tell them about the phone conversation we had right after... Right after, won't she?"

Blake refused to give his client false hope. "Yes, she will."

"Shit," Johnson cursed. "I should never have told her. If only I'd kept my fucking mouth shut. I—"

"There's no point in talking about *if onlys*, Ian" he interrupted. "We need to deal with the reality. That's the only thing worth talking about."

Johnson fell silent and stared morosely at his feet. "Will I have to testify?" he asked, his tone somber.

"No, and the judge will instruct the jury that they aren't to read anything into the fact you choose not to—but... I think you should speak, just the same. It's risky because it means the prosecution will be entitled to cross-examine you, and no defense lawyer is ever keen to expose his client to such a risk, but I think the jury needs to hear from you."

Blake stared hard at his client, hoping to get Ian to see. "We're talking about the death of a child. You can bet your ass the prosecutor will do his hardest to paint you out to be the meanest son of a bitch he can think of; a man who cared nothing for the life of his little girl. The jury will want to hear from you that you loved her and that you didn't mean for her to die."

Johnson squirmed in his seat. An uncomfortable expression crossed his face. "I don't know if I can do it."

"Do what?"

"Face them. Face *her*."

"Who?" Blake asked, already suspecting the answer.

"My ex. Who do you think? She's never going to believe I didn't mean to do it."

Dread formed a hard knot in Blake's gut. If his client didn't think he could convince his ex-wife he didn't mean to do it, what hope did they have with a jury? Presumably Natalie Johnson knew her ex-husband better than most. To the jury, he was a total stranger. This was troubling, to say the least.

His only option was not to call his client to the stand and that wouldn't go down well with the jury, either. They'd be left to wonder how Ian really felt about his little girl and what his state of mind had actually been at the moment when he decided to throw her to her death. And a jury left wondering was an unpredictable jury—the kind of jury Blake dreaded the most. Still, there was time yet, before a decision about Ian testifying had to be made. Right now, Blake had a trial that was about to commence.

He glanced at his watch and noticed their time was up. They had exactly two minutes to get inside the courtroom, take their seats and wait for the judge. He told his client as much and Johnson reluctantly got to his feet.

"Are you all right?" Blake asked quietly.

"Just dandy," came the sarcastic reply.

Blake had nothing to say. He understood Ian's attitude, even as it grated on him. In grim silence, he left the room with Johnson trailing behind him.

The first person Blake saw when he entered through the doorway that led into Judge

Chamberlain's courtroom was Natalie. It had been more than a month since he'd seen her, but she was as beautiful as ever. She wore a loose-fitting navy-blue skirt and jacket. A peach-colored blouse with a frothy neckline and a simple strand of pearls completed the look.

She was dressed well for the jury. Her red hair was pulled back from her face and was captured in a neat bun at the nape of her neck. She was pale and drawn. There were dark circles beneath her eyes. She looked every bit the grieving mother.

Blake guessed she was having trouble sleeping and the thought brought out his protective instincts...which he immediately quashed. It was none of his business that she was struggling to sleep. He was representing her ex-husband. From this day until the trial was over, they were adversaries. He best remember that. No doubt that was foremost on *her* mind.

As if she sensed his scrutiny, Natalie shifted slightly in her seat and looked in his direction. Her expression froze and he was almost certain her cheeks lost more color. He glanced behind him and saw Ian following in his footsteps and wasn't sure whether the look of horror that now filled Natalie's expression was for him or her ex.

Blake felt a stab of something that felt very much like disappointment in his gut. He wanted to acknowledge her, give her some sign of comfort and encouragement, a friendly hello, but he couldn't. They were at opposite ends of the bar table, literally and figuratively. Though the table in question was less than ten feet long, they might as well have been seated on opposite sides of the Grand Canyon.

———————

The walls were closing in. The thought went through Natalie's mind as her gaze bounced off the padded, soundproof walls, the modern seats, the gathering of legal personnel, media, court reporters and spectators. The quiet hum of muted conversation filled the courtroom as people came in, looked around, made their way to their seats.

And then Blake Harton Junior appeared. He was followed closely by her ex-husband. A wave of nausea rolled through her and she clamped her hand across her mouth. Her already-tense belly knotted painfully and nerves banded tightly around her chest. She forced herself to breathe through the feeling of suffocation, knowing that if she didn't, the horrible sensations could quickly escalate into a full-on panic attack. That was the last thing she needed.

The one and only time she'd experienced one had been in the train station, but all of a sudden, another attack seemed likely. Already, she could feel the pounding of her heart as her stress levels skyrocketed. It was the sight of Ian that had done it. She hadn't seen him since that Friday afternoon when he'd stopped by to collect the kids. It seemed so long ago, and yet, it also felt like yesterday. Lacey had still been alive, laughing, skipping down the front path—excited to see her daddy.

He'd picked her up and twirled her around and she'd squealed in delight. The boys had stood by watching, grins stretching their mouths wide. For all Ian's faults and failings as a husband, he'd always been a good dad. There had been arguments and occasional cross words, but he'd never been violent toward them—until he'd decided to toss their baby daughter over the side of Anzac Bridge.

Her stomach clenched in pain again and it was all she could do to hold back a sob. Even now, so many weeks after the awful events of that day, the thought still brought her to her knees. Knowing she was going to have to sit through testimony from eye witnesses as to just how the tragic situation had come about was almost more then she could bear.

How would she be able to sit there and listen to strangers talk about the last moments of her baby's life? It would be torture. She didn't know if she was strong enough to withstand it, but she had to stay, to force herself through it. She owed that to Lacey.

Blake looked every bit the powerful, successful lawyer, dressed as he was in his black barrister robes and ivory-colored wig. He strode toward her and came to a stop at the opposite end of the bar table. Ian stood beside him wearing a suit and tie she'd never seen before. He looked like he'd lost more than twenty pounds. She was filled with an involuntary surge of sympathy and then remembered what he'd done.

Blake turned to his client. After a murmured

exchange, Ian frowned and then turned and took his place in the dock set a little distance from Blake's chair. As far as Natalie was concerned, it still wasn't far enough away.

A pretty, young female with short brown hair, dressed in a smart charcoal-gray suit and pale blue blouse walked up to the bar table carrying an armful of files. She set them down beside Blake. He glanced up at her arrival and pushed away from his chair, but she was seated before he could gain his feet. Once again, Natalie was reminded of his good manners.

Natalie guessed the woman was his instructing solicitor who would assist him throughout the trial. The crown prosecutor was also instructed by a solicitor. Natalie had met Colby Shearer weeks earlier, when the matter had first been set down for trial. He was young and smart and enthusiastic and was good looking enough to turn heads. He'd gone over her evidence with her and had also given her a rundown on what to expect. She was grateful for the tutelage, but it felt like everything she'd learned before the trial had disappeared out the window with the arrival of Ian and Blake.

Of its own volition, her gaze went back to Blake. He looked so cool and calm and confident. She glared at him. In that moment, she disliked him and all that he represented. He was there to offer excuses, to plead clemency for her ex-husband. Ian had shown no such clemency when it came to her baby girl.

Anger surged through her and Natalie turned away in disgust, fixing her gaze on the high bench in front of her. Unlike in the movies, this courtroom was modern, with shades of taupe and cream and light-colored wood. There wasn't a dark and dreary surface to be found. It was slightly off-putting and reminded her of the modern interior of the family court where she and Ian had battled so fiercely over their kids. Now they fronted another courtroom, brought there by the worst of circumstances. It would have been somewhat fitting to have her surroundings echo the knots of darkness and gloom in her heart.

A man, similarly bewigged and gowned like Blake, came toward her and held out his hand. Natalie spied Colby Shearer behind him.

"Ms Johnson, I'm Greg Villa, the crown prosecutor. I'm in charge of the case for the prosecution."

Natalie shook his hand that felt warm against her icy palm. She pulled back her hand as quickly as she could.

"Please, let me tell you how sorry I am," he added. "Rest assured, we're going to pull out every stop to win this thing. Between me and Colby, we have more than thirty-five years' experience in the courtroom. Don't worry, you're in good hands."

Natalie nodded in acknowledgement. His words of reassurance helped her feel a little better, as well as the knowledge that he'd done this many times before. But there was no denying Villa's pockmarked face, thick gray hair and short portly figure were no match for the good-looking, tall, broad-shouldered man who sat at the opposite end of the bar table. Natalie only hoped the jury wouldn't be swayed by such inconsequential things.

Colby moved closer and frowned at her in concern. "Are you all right, Natalie?"

She drew in a deep breath and did her best to offer him a smile but was sure she failed miserably. He kneeled down beside her chair.

"It's going to be, okay," he murmured. "I'm not going to lie and pretend this isn't going to be one of the hardest things you've ever done, but you're so strong! You can do this! You can do this for Lacey. Okay?"

Natalie nodded, barely listening. She'd met him a couple of times before and had spoken to him recently over the phone when he'd called to confirm the trial date and to go over her evidence. She'd been grateful for his attention, but most of the conversation had been a blur. All she knew was that she was going to have to sit through hours of testimony, including being told exactly what her ex did to Lacey and then listening to others make excuses for him and try and convince the jury he didn't mean to kill their baby girl.

Hard didn't begin to cover it.

CHAPTER 9

Aloud knock coming from somewhere out of sight behind the bench caught everyone's attention. A door off to the side and behind the bench opened and a young woman entered carrying a staff. She was followed by a gray-haired man dressed in robes the color of fresh blood. On his head was an impressively long wig. Natalie assumed he was the judge.

"All rise," directed the woman with the staff.

The crowd got to its feet. With Australia being a member of the British Commonwealth, Natalie joined the people in the courtroom in the traditional show of respect for the Queens's representative. Judge Chamberlain came to a halt behind his chair. The members of the legal fraternity and a few of the spectators bowed toward the bench. Natalie would have thought it was another sign of respect for the judge if her family law lawyer hadn't explained that it was the presence of the Royal Coat of Arms that hung on the wall behind the bench that the lawyers and other people present bowed to. Once again, it was a ritual that showed respect for the Queen's justice. She only hoped Lacey would receive justice that day.

When the judge was settled, the people returned to their seats. In short order, he called upon Greg Villa and Blake Harton Junior.

"I refer to the matter of Regina versus Johnson," the judge said. "Are the parties ready to proceed?"

"Yes, Your Honor," Greg replied.

The judge turned his attention to Blake. "Mr Harton?"

"Yes, Your Honor. The defense is ready to proceed."

"Very well. Are there any preliminary matters that need to be dealt with before we get to the business of selecting a jury?" The judge addressed the question to the barristers. Both men murmured in the negative.

"All right, then. Let's get started." Judge Chamberlain turned to the woman who sat below him on the bench. "Miss Lindsay. Can you instruct the sheriff to have the prospective jurors brought up, please?"

The woman who'd entered in front of the judge picked up a phone at her elbow and spoke into it. Natalie saw her lips move, but couldn't make out the words. A few minutes later, there was another brief knock and a side door opened to reveal a man dressed in a sheriff's uniform. He directed a line of men and women to fill the vacant chairs beside him.

Natalie's gaze was drawn to them. They were a mix of men and women, old and young, of various ethnicities. A true cross section of her city and that was the way it was meant to be, at least in theory. She'd never had anything to do with a jury, but she'd watched enough TV shows to know that the lawyers had some right to choose or discount one person over another.

Her gaze traveled over them again. They looked so normal. A little scared and apprehensive, but who wouldn't be? Twelve of these people would ultimately decide her ex-husband's fate. Twelve of these people would listen to the evidence and the inevitable legal arguments and they would then return to their cloistered jury room and debate Ian's guilt or innocence.

Colby had explained to her how juries in Australia were required to come to a unanimous decision. Twelve out of twelve had to agree on an outcome, or else the judge would declare a mistrial. *Please, God, not that.* It would be hard enough to sit through the next few days, to listen to a blow by blow account of how her little girl had died. She'd never be able to do it a second time.

"Miss Lindsay, are you ready to call the ballot?" the judge asked.

"Yes, Your Honor," the woman replied. Tucking a stray strand of hair behind her ear, she picked up a box that sat on the bench in front of her. She reached in and drew out a small white card.

"The first prospective juror is Juror Number 6795," she said.

A white-haired grandmotherly type stood and

began to walk toward the jury box. Blake got to his feet.

"We'd like to use one of our peremptory challenges, Your Honor."

Natalie stared at him, but his gaze remained focused on the bench.

"Very well, Mr Harton. I'll make a note of your first peremptory challenge," the judge replied before turning his attention to the juror.

"Juror Number 6795, it appears we won't be needing your services in this trial. Thank you for coming. You're free to go."

The woman looked surprised, but then shrugged and returned to her seat. Natalie leaned over and whispered in Colby's ear.

"What was wrong with her?"

"She's a mother of three and a grandmother to seven children. All under the age of five. It's no wonder Harton challenged her."

"So he can do that? Object to whoever he wants?"

"Yes, but he only has three peremptory challenges. Twelve people make up the jury. Don't worry, he can't handpick them all."

Natalie pursed her lips and continued to stare in Blake's direction. He exuded calm and confidence, like he already had this trial won. The very thought made her stomach clench with nausea and nerves.

"How many challenges do we get?" she whispered.

"We get the same number as the defense."

"Oh." She tried to keep the disappointment from her voice.

"It's only fair," Colby said.

"Yes, I guess so," she replied.

"We can still challenge for cause," he added, a hopeful look on his face.

"What does that mean?"

"It means that if someone has a particular objection to the charges, or for example has previous history with child custody proceedings, we can challenge their right to be on this jury. The whole point of the jury selection process is to form a fair and unbiased group of people who will listen dutifully to the evidence and then come to a decision. If they arrive here with previous attitudes or misconceptions, it can skew the balance one way or the other."

Natalie nodded and tried to hide her unease. Colby hoped they'd get a fair and unbiased jury. She didn't know if that were possible, given the subject at hand. She couldn't imagine anyone— regardless of their age or gender—thinking it was acceptable for a child's father to toss that child over the side of the bridge. She was counting on that fact.

The jury selection began to move at a faster pace as one person after another was either sworn in or dismissed. Both Blake and Greg used all three of their peremptory challenges. Two other men were dismissed on the basis of their history—involvement in messy family law disputes.

When the twelfth juror was sworn in by the officer of the court, Natalie surveyed them carefully. Seven women, five men. A range of ages and ethnic backgrounds. She looked each of them in the eye, hoping to make some sort of impact on the twelve strangers who would decide her ex-husband's fate—and ultimately her own. There was no hiding the fact that any decision would affect her for the rest of her life.

It had taken the best part of two hours for the jury selection. The clock above the judge's head struck twelve as the last juror was sworn in and took their seat. The judge looked over his half-moon glasses to the lawyers seated below.

"Are the parties ready to proceed?"

"Yes, Your Honor," Blake replied.

The crown prosecutor murmured his assent.

"Very well. Mr Villa, we'll take a short adjournment and thereafter we'll start with your opening statement."

With that, the judge stood. His robes fluttered around him, like a river of blood flowing freely from a mortal wound. Natalie shivered and hoped the fleeting image wasn't a premonition of what was to come.

"All rise," the court officer called out.

The lawyers stood and along with them, the crowd. Natalie followed suit. After bowing toward the bench, Colby moved closer to her.

"I'm afraid you're going to have to wait outside now, Natalie. Remember what I told you in my office? You're a witness for the prosecution. Until you've testified, you can't hear what the other witnesses have to say, including the opening statements which will be made by the barristers. Don't worry, it will only be the two detectives in charge of the case and then you'll give your evidence."

Natalie nodded. Though she wanted to sit through every minute—she owed it to her baby— she understood the rules. The court didn't want her testimony to be influenced by the evidence given by any other witness. Once she'd testified, she could remain in the courtroom for the duration of the trial.

Bending to gather up her handbag, she headed toward the exit. The route took her past Blake. She caught a faint whiff of his expensive cologne, but kept her eyes averted. Ian sat in the dock, right behind his lawyer, a stoic expression on his face. His gaze was filled with desolation and remorse.

Tears burned behind her eyes and then spilled over. She blinked hard, determined to get out of there without breaking down. Ian had no right to be upset! He was the reason they were there! He was the one who'd murdered their baby! He was the reason little Lacey was never coming back!

How the hell was she going to endure days of this? The trial hadn't even begun. She couldn't do it... She couldn't do it—

She *had* to do it. For Lacey.

She had to sit there and listen and remind every single one of those twelve jurors that she was that little girl's mother and her baby would never be forgotten.

With a gargantuan effort, Natalie bit down hard on her lip and steeled herself against another round of tears. Raising her gaze and staring straight ahead, she walked quickly down the aisle and left the room.

———————

Ian stared after his wife—ex-wife—and slowly shook his head. He couldn't believe he was there, in court on murder charges. *How had it happened? How did he go from living a normal, mostly happy life, to this?*

He and Natalie *had* been happy. They'd been together for ten years and married for the best part of seven. Somehow, they'd let the day-to-day drudgery get to them. Worry about money, job security, a health scare with the twins... Gradually, they'd let their concerns and stresses drain all the love from their marriage until there was nothing left but the fighting.

Then Natalie had walked out one night after a particularly vicious argument. She'd been gone for hours. When she came back, she told him they were through and that she was going to file for a divorce.

He hadn't argued with her decision. All the fight had gone out of him. It was only when the kids came up for discussion that he'd become fired up again. Time and time again, he fronted up to the family law courts and time and time again, he was told he couldn't have custody of his kids: They were too young. They needed their mother.

In the beginning, Lacey was barely a year old, the twins only three. They needed a stable, secure, familiar home. At first the judge had ruled he could see them on weekends for a few hours at a time. There would be no sleepovers until they were older... Like that was ever going to be enough. Most recently the judge had said he could see his kids every second weekend. He'd stormed out of the final hearing that Friday afternoon only hours before he was due to collect them, intent of making the most of his time with them.

They were overjoyed to see him, especially Lacey. The way she hugged and kissed him and told him how much she missed him—it had made his heart smile. And to think what he'd done to her...his little baby girl... And all because he wanted to get back at Natalie and that judge, to make them pay.

His heart clenched in agony and he buried his face in his hands. He didn't realize he'd groaned aloud until his lawyer shot him a concerned look.

"Are you all right, Ian?"

He looked up and squinted at Blake Harton. Tall and confident, with broad shoulders and a strong neck that only emphasized his regal bearing, the man was the epitome of a successful lawyer. Ian was pathetically grateful Harton had agreed to take him on.

Ian had done his research. Blake was the best in the game. Ian would never have been able to afford his fees, but had asked him just the same. Without a shit-hot lawyer, he'd be facing definite jail time. There was nothing more certain. He wasn't sure what had clinched the deal, but he was thankful for whatever it was that had made up Harton's mind in his favor.

Blake's frown deepened and Ian realized he hadn't answered the man's question. "I'm fine," he muttered.

His lawyer continued to regard him for a moment longer before turning back to face the front. There was a loud knock and then the same clerk's voice ordered them all to rise. The judge came back in and made his way toward the bench. He looked like he was past retirement age and yet, he seemed sharp as a tack. His long white wig hung halfway down his back, and coupled with the red robes, it reminded Ian of Santa Claus. Only, instead of excitement, Ian's gut was filled with an icy dread—and no matter the outcome, there would be no laughter or joy in this room.

Ian looked around him. Natalie hadn't reappeared. He wondered where she'd gone and then recalled Blake telling him she was a witness for the prosecution. He knew enough about the legal system to know that she wouldn't be allowed to remain in the courtroom until after she'd given her testimony.

He was glad. It was going to be hard enough to sit there and listen to the tragic details of that awful day. It would be even worse with his ex-wife sitting only a few yards away... He forced the thoughts aside and focused on the judge. The man settled himself behind the bench and everyone took a seat, including Ian.

"Is the prosecution ready to proceed?" the judge asked.

The crown prosecutor got to his feet. "Yes, Your Honor."

The prosecutor was an older guy, probably not much younger than the judge. His hair had turned gray and he was short and stout, but he still had a certain presence. His voice was deep and resonant. Ian was sure the jury would respond to a voice like that. He only hoped his lawyer was up to the challenge. Ian's liberty depended upon it.

CHAPTER 10

Natalie paced the floor opposite the courtroom where the trial of her ex-husband had just commenced. She could only imagine the words being spoken by the crown prosecutor and the defense. They were talking about her and Ian and their family; they were talking about her children and the last moments of her little girl's life. They were talking about things so awful, Natalie felt sorry for the people who were forced to listen. Though she was determined to be there for her daughter, she was selfishly glad she'd been asked to wait outside until after she took the stand and gave her testimony.

At the thought of what was being said behind the closed wooden doors, her heart rate picked up its pace and her palms turned sweaty. She hid her hands in the pockets of her jacket and continued to pace. No doubt the prosecutor was delivering his opening statement to the jury and then it would be Blake's turn. The trial had begun.

Greg Villa cleared his throat and got to his feet. Blake ignored the flurry of nerves that rushed through his belly like they usually did right before the start of a trial. He busied himself with the notes he'd made for his opening statement while Villa turned to face the jury.

"Ladies and gentlemen of the jury, you've heard Judge Chamberlain read out the charge: murder in the first degree. You're here to decide if Ian Gregory Johnson intended to kill his daughter when he made the decision to toss her over the side of Anzac Bridge."

Blake stared at the jury. Already, some of them were looking grim and had tightened their lips. He understood their reaction. This wasn't going to be easy...for any of them.

"Lacey Maree Johnson was a beautiful, happy three-year-old when her father made the decision to take her life," the prosecutor continued. "You'll hear evidence from eye witnesses who saw him enter Anzac Bridge in his vehicle, pull over into the far lane, climb onto the roof of his truck with his daughter and throw her off the bridge."

The courtroom was still and silent. It was as though everyone present was holding their breath, including Blake. Ian Johnson was his client, but he could barely breathe past the band of tension in his chest when he considered what his client had actually done.

Villa cleared his throat and continued. "You'll also hear evidence from the defendant's ex-wife, who was involved with the defendant in a messy custody battle over their children. In fact, only three days before Lacey's murder, the family court handed down its final decision with regard to the Johnson children: They were to live permanently with their mother and although the defendant was given reasonable access, apparently it wasn't enough.

"You see, the defendant stewed over the court decision during the course of the weekend. By Monday morning, October ninth, he was livid with the courts, and most especially with his ex-wife. He came to the decision to hurt her the way she'd hurt him and the best way to get to her was through her children."

Nausea swirled in Blake's stomach. Hearing the words aloud made it seem that much worse. He thought of his brother and was pathetically grateful David hadn't taken the lives of his kids. David's suicide was hard enough to bear. Burying his innocent children would have been too much. Blake sucked in a breath and willed the sad thoughts away. This wasn't about him or David. He needed to remember that.

"Now, the defense will try and tell you it was an accident; that the defendant didn't intend to kill his daughter," the prosecutor continued. "You'll hear their expert witness give evidence to the effect that the accused was in a state of dissociation, a state of mental impairment which excuses what he did."

Villa shook his head slowly back and forth, his expression grim. "Well, I don't buy it. I don't buy it for one second and the reason is the evidence you're going to hear from a forensic psychiatrist with experience second to none. He'll tell you about the many signs the defendant exhibited in his behavior, before and after, that demonstrated just how normal his state of mind was.

"No," Villa continued. "Make no mistake. There was nothing mad about what the defendant did; the only madness came from his determination to seek the most awful kind of revenge on his ex-wife. The fact that his little girl lost her life as a consequence was, in the defendant's mind, nothing more than collateral damage, sad but unavoidable. Nothing more; nothing less."

The prosecutor returned to his seat. Those gathered in the courtroom sat in stunned silence. Blake understood how they felt. He couldn't imagine anyone deliberately throwing their child to her death, and yet, that's what his client had done. If he didn't believe Ian had been in a state of dissociation, he'd have never been able to take on the case. He only hoped his expert witness was up to the job of convincing the jury as much. If not, they were doomed.

Blake had made no notes throughout the prosecutor's opening statement. It was no surprise that the prosecution was setting up his case to prove intent. Without it, they would fail to make out the most important element in support of the murder charge. The jury's belief that what Ian did was anything less than a deliberate move to end Lacey Johnson's life would result in a manslaughter conviction for his client. Manslaughter was better than murder, but Blake hadn't gained a reputation for being one of the best defense lawyers in Sydney by pleading to lesser charges. No, Blake went for acquittals. Nothing else would do.

Now it was his turn to address the jury with his opening statement. He had the text printed on the pages before him, but he'd memorized it days before. In fact, from his very first meeting with Ian Johnson, he'd known what angle to take. Meeting Natalie hadn't been part of his initial plan and he wished he could pretend that knowing her hadn't had an effect on him. He was glad she wasn't in the courtroom right now to listen to his opening statement.

Still, at the end of the day, he had a job to do and he couldn't let his sympathy for the mother of the dead child interfere with his work. He represented a man accused of murdering his own daughter. Blake was convinced the man hadn't meant to do it and he intended to do all he could to ensure his client wasn't convicted of that charge.

"Mr Harton, are you ready to proceed?" the judge asked.

Blake nodded and got to his feet. "Thank you, Your Honor." He picked up the sheaf of papers in front of him, glanced down at them and then eyeballed the jury.

"Mr Villa, would have you believe that my client, Ian Johnson, is a cold-hearted killer who thought nothing of murdering his child in order to get back at his ex-wife. To the prosecutor, Mr Johnson's actions were nothing more than a deliberate act of murder by an angry man bent on revenge. But nothing in life is that easy and when it comes to murder, things get even more complex.

"There is no dispute that my client threw his daughter over the side of Anzac Bridge and that, as a consequence, the child died. What is in dispute, and what you must decide, is whether Mr Johnson intended for his daughter to die. That can only be decided after a close examination of my client's state of mind prior to and at the time of the offense.

"You'll hear testimony from a renowned forensic psychiatrist who will convince you that at the time my client made the decision to climb onto the roof of his car and throw his child off the bridge, he was suffering mental impairment, a form of dissociation from his surroundings, from reality, during which time he could not be held responsible for his actions. After his testimony, you'll be shocked, appalled and ultimately filled with understanding and compassion because you'll accept that though Ian Johnson did the unthinkable, he didn't realize what he was doing. And then, ladies and gentlemen of the jury, you'll have no choice but to acquit him."

Blake returned to his seat, satisfied that he'd done enough, at least to this point in time. The jury had hung on his every word and toward the end, a few had been nodding. That was a good sign. He only hoped it was a portent for more good things to come.

———————

As Blake sat down, the prosecutor got to his feet and advised the court he was ready to call his first witness. He asked the court officer to call for Detective Constable Peter Jones-Smith. Blake listened as first one detective and then the other took the stand and delivered their testimony.

Their evidence followed closely the police statements Blake had been provided with in accordance with the rules. Any witness the prosecution intended to call had to make a formal statement to the police prior to the commencement of the trial, including the investigating officers, and these formed part of the brief of evidence, a copy of which had been provided to the defense.

"You received an emergency call at eight-forty-one on the morning of October ninth, is that correct?" the prosecutor asked the second detective who had identified himself as Detective Senior Constable Warren Holloway.

"Yes," Detective Holloway replied.

"What did the dispatcher tell you about the call?"

"I was told that there was a stationery vehicle heading in a northerly direction in the far eastern lane of Anzac Bridge and that a man had climbed onto the roof of his vehicle. He had a child in his arms. It was strange enough behavior that the passerby who called it in thought it warranted police attention."

"So, you and Detective Constable Jones-Smith attended the scene, right?" the prosecutor asked, making reference to the detective who had already given evidence to that effect.

"Right."

"Did you interview any witnesses?"

"Yes. A few people had pulled up after seeing a man throw something off the bridge. Some of them thought it looked like a child. Others thought it was a doll. Detective Constable Jones-Smith and I interviewed them. A few of them came down to the police station later and made formal statements."

"How did you identify the defendant as the driver of the vehicle?"

"We'd been given a physical description by some of the witnesses. We were also given the make and model of the car. One witness remembered the license plate. We ran it through our database. It came back to the accused. We then contacted his ex-wife. She confirmed it was Ian Johnson's car. By that time, someone from Ms Johnson's office had already been in contact with the police. They'd made a call to the emergency line to report the suspected murder of a child."

"Did the defendant's name come up in that report?"

"Yes."

The prosecutor paused before continuing. "Where did you locate Mr Johnson?"

"We found him outside a police station in Lilyfield."

"What state was he in?"

"He appeared almost catatonic. He didn't speak. He was pale and trembling and his demeanor indicated he was suffering extreme shock and distress."

"Did you think his reaction was genuine?"

Blake got to his feet. "Objection, Your Honor. This witness isn't qualified to give such an opinion."

Villa looked at the judge and responded. "Your Honor, I'm not suggesting Detective Holloway is an expert in psychiatry or even in body language, but he was one of the first law enforcement officers to come across the defendant after the offense. He also has formal training in making observations. It's my contention that those observations are relevant."

The judge appeared to consider the arguments. "I'll allow it," he eventually said.

The prosecutor returned his attention to the witness. "Detective, when you first observed the defendant's distress, did you think that distress was genuine?"

The detective eyed the prosecutor steadily. "Yes, I did. And given what we understood to have happened, it didn't come as a surprise. I would have thought it strange if he'd acted otherwise."

"Did the defendant participate in a formal interview at that time?"

"Yes, although he only responded to our preliminary questions and very early on requested to see a lawyer. After that, he refused to be interviewed."

"Did you do anything else while you had the defendant in custody, Detective?"

"Yes. We tested him for drugs and alcohol."

"And what were the results?"

"They were both negative."

"So the defendant had neither drugs nor alcohol in his system at that time, shortly after the offense?"

"That's correct."

The prosecutor nodded in acknowledgement. He looked down at his notes for a moment before resuming his questioning.

"Are there any security cameras on Anzac Bridge?"

"Yes."

"Were you able to obtain any CCTV footage of the defendant?"

"Yes. The cameras captured the moment he entered the bridge and when he departed it. Unfortunately, he brought his vehicle to a stop between two camera points and we were unable to obtain any vision of that time."

The prosecutor asked a few more questions and the replies were similar to the account given by the officer's colleague. Detective Holloway's testimony also included the fact he'd organized for police dive teams to search the water.

Blake made scant notes. The evidence given by the detectives provided little in the way of surprises. He eased a breath out from between taut lips and turned and gave his client a reassuring nod and then braced himself for the next witness. Next on the list was Natalie Johnson. As much as Blake loved his job, he looked forward to interrogating her over her evidence like he'd look forward to having a root canal.

———————

Natalie splashed water over her face in the restroom and patted it dry with a handkerchief. Her hands shook and her belly twisted with nerves. Colby had confirmed that she would be called as the next witness. He assured her he'd be right there, helping her through it. All she had to remember was what they'd talked about. Keep her answers short and simple. Don't offer anything more than was asked. Soon it would be over.

The thought of giving evidence terrified her, but staying silent when Lacey had no other voice but hers kept her there. She thought of Ian and the certainty she had that he'd murdered their baby out of spite. Anger boiled inside her. His deplorable actions were nothing more than a cruel and heartless act of revenge that had ended in the death of their child. It was his way of saying, 'If I can't have her, you won't either.'

The thought was beyond shocking and made her so furious, she could hardly contain the anger that burned at a fever pitch inside her. She clenched her hands into fists and then forced them to relax. She was determined to get through this without showing Ian how much his actions had destroyed her. She wouldn't give him that satisfaction. She just hoped she could stay strong. With a last look in the mirror, she thrust back her shoulders and lifted her head and strode outside. Colby waited for her.

"We're ready," was all he said. His expression was grave. Something in her face caught his attention. He shot her a look of sympathy. "Don't worry, it isn't easy for anyone to take the stand, even lawyers who are well practiced in the art of public speaking, but you'll do fine. Just answer the questions like we rehearsed and listen when Harton speaks. Hopefully he won't be too hard on you. After all, they're not denying his client carried out the act. They're hanging their defense on the fact that your ex-husband wasn't thinking straight when he did it."

Colby shook his head and a flicker of admiration showed in his eyes. "You have to hand it to the defense team. It's a smart move. With all the eyewitnesses and the fact your child was fished out of the harbor, there was no point denying it was him. Going for mental incapacity was the only choice. A lot of the members of the jury will struggle to accept the defendant was acting in sound mind when he did what he did. I know I would. We have our work cut out for us."

Natalie cringed at the mention of her daughter, but listened to his murmured conversation. Her stomach clenched with nerves. A fresh wave of despair washed over her at the memory of what had happened to her little girl. *Oh, Lacey! Her baby! This whole thing was so unfair!*

Her chest went tight. Pressure built behind her eyes. An image of her little girl appeared before her. Dressed in her favorite pink princess outfit, including a glittering tiara, Lacey smiled at Natalie and then laughed at a butterfly that landed near her feet. She bent to pick it up, but it flew away again. Then a familiar frown creased Lacey's brow.

Natalie bit her lip against a surge of emotion and quickly blinked away the tears that threatened. She owed it to Lacey to hold herself together. She needed to get through the next little while, projecting as much calm and confidence as she could. Her evidence was crucial to them establishing her ex-husband's state of mind before and immediately after the offense. Coupled with the testimony from the prosecution's expert witness who would give evidence of Ian's mental status, she hoped it would be enough. Nothing less than a guilty verdict for murder would suffice. Even then, it wouldn't bring back her baby, but it would go some way to avenging Lacey's tragic death. It was the least the justice system could do for her little girl.

"We have to go in, Natalie. It's time."

Colby's quiet words broke through her sad thoughts. She blinked to clear them away and offered him a shaky nod. "Okay."

Ignoring the flutter of nerves and nausea that swirled in her stomach, she followed him into the courtroom and took her seat in the first row of chairs directly behind the prosecution's end of the bar table. The judge was not yet on the bench and the jury seats remained bare. Greg Villa was seated at the bar table and twisted in his chair to face her.

"Are you all right, Ms Johnson?"

"Yes, thank you," she managed.

She was so far from fine it was laughable, but what choice did she have? Colby shot her an equally concerned look, but after a moment, returned his attention to the files piled on the bar table in front of him. A loud knock on the door indicated the arrival of the judge. From the corner of her eye, Natalie saw Blake take his seat.

"All rise."

CHAPTER 11

The crowd of spectators and lawyers came to their feet and everyone bowed toward the bench.

"Mr Villa, are you ready to call your next witness?" the judge asked after he was once again settled in his chair.

"Yes, Your Honor," the prosecutor replied, getting to his feet.

"Very well." Judge Chamberlain turned to the sheriff who stood adjacent to the jury seats. "Send in the jury, please."

The sheriff nodded in response and opened the door next to him and disappeared. A short time later, the door reopened and the jury appeared and were quickly seated. The judge nodded toward the prosecutor.

"Mr Villa."

Once again, Villa got to his feet. "The prosecution calls Natalie Johnson."

Hearing her name said aloud in the quiet courtroom sent a quiver of apprehension down

Natalie's spine. Now that the moment was upon her, she didn't know if she could go through with it. Butterflies multiplied and swarmed in her belly, along with a fresh wave of nausea. Blood rushed through her ears. The prosecutor shot her a look of concern and she forced herself to her feet.

She made her way to the witness box and prayed that she wouldn't trip over in her four-inch heels. She was dressed in her best navy-blue suit teamed with a soft peach blouse that picked up the color of her hair. She wore her grandmother's pearls. They were only brought out for special occasions. Lacey had always loved them. Natalie wore them to court for her little girl.

Once Natalie was seated, the court officer approached her with a Bible in her hand. "Are you prepared to take an oath or would you rather make an affirmation?" the woman asked.

"I'm happy to take an oath," Natalie replied.

The court officer handed her a Bible and a small white card with words printed on it. "Please read the oath aloud," the woman instructed.

Natalie looked down at the card and cleared her throat. "I swear by Almighty God that the evidence I shall give will be the truth, the whole truth and nothing but the truth."

Satisfied, the court officer collected the Bible and returned to her seat. The judge invited the crown prosecutor to begin his examination. Natalie dug her fingers into the sides of her seat and prayed for the time to pass quickly. Greg Villa got back up on his feet and went through the preliminaries. He established that she was thirty years old. She lived in Lilyfield and worked as an in-house accountant for Baker & Carr Construction in the city. Most importantly, she was the ex-wife of the defendant and the mother of Lacey Johnson.

The routine questions were meant to put her at ease and she appreciated the prosecutor's efforts, but she wouldn't breathe freely until her time in the witness box had come to an end. It was as simple as that.

"Ms Johnson, I'd like to take you to the afternoon of Friday, October sixth," the prosecutor continued and Natalie's stomach clenched.

"Did you see your ex-husband that day?"

Natalie drew in a breath and eased it out between taut lips. "Yes. We had our final hearing in the family court that day. Ian was there with his lawyer."

"Who else was with you?" Villa asked.

"I was also there with my lawyer, Damian Price. He'd represented me throughout the divorce and property settlement proceedings. He also acted on my behalf in relation to the children."

"You have three children, with the defendant, don't you, Ms Johnson?"

"Yes. We have five-year-old twins, Darcy and Bailey and...Lacey."

The prosecutor blanched, as if he'd only just remembered that one of her children was now dead. Natalie forced herself to keep breathing evenly. She was sure the oversight was an innocent one. She did her best to ignore it.

"Right. And you were involved in a pretty nasty dispute over who should have custody of the children, weren't you?"

Blake jumped to his feet. "Objection, Your Honor. He's leading the witness."

"Withdrawn," Villa muttered. "Let me rephrase. Ms Johnson, were you seeking sole custody of your children?"

"Yes. Lacey was only twelve months old when Ian and I separated. The twins were only three. I wanted them to live with me."

"Can you describe for the court how your ex-husband reacted to your request for sole custody of your children?"

Natalie was besieged with a wave of bad memories, of the awful fights and bitter arguments she and Ian had over their children. She compressed her lips. "He didn't react well. He thought the children should live with him, or at the very least, that we should have joint custody."

"How long did you fight your battle through the courts?"

She sighed sadly. "Two years."

"And that Friday I mentioned, the Friday three days before Lacey's death, was a significant day, wasn't it?"

"Yes. The judge handed down his final decision."

"And what did he find?"

"He found in my favor. He gave me sole custody of our children."

Natalie heard an angry sound come from the direction of her ex-husband. She kept her gaze directed on the prosecutor. She couldn't bear to witness Ian's anger. She'd been subjected to it for far too long as they'd battled their way through the family law court.

"Did you speak to the defendant that day?"

"No."

"What about afterwards? After the decision came down?"

"No. Ian was angry and upset. I saw him arguing with his lawyer. I... I just wanted to get out of there. I left as soon as I could."

"Did you see your ex-husband again that day?"

"Yes. It was Ian's turn to have the children for the weekend. He came by to collect them about six o'clock that evening."

"Did you speak to him then?"

"Yes."

"How was he?"

"He was still angry and upset over the judge's decision. He tried to argue about it with me, but I shut him down. The children were nearby, waiting to go with him. I'd tried very hard over the two years since the breakdown of our marriage to keep our disagreements between us and out of the kids' hearing. Ian knew I didn't like arguing in front of them."

"Did he respect your wishes this time?"

"Yes, eventually. I told him that the judge's decision was final and there was nothing more to discuss. I gave him the overnight bags I'd packed for the children and I kissed them good-bye. It was the last time I saw Lacey."

Natalie's voice hitched on a sob she tried hard

to prevent. Tears burned behind her eyes. She dug her fingers harder into the sides of her chair and sucked in a breath, determined not to break down in front of everyone, and most especially in front of Ian. She glimpsed Blake out of the corner of her eye and the look of sympathy on his face almost did her in. Resolutely, she stared at her lap.

"Over the course of the weekend, did you speak with Ian again?" the prosecutor asked quietly.

Natalie nodded. "Yes. I called a few times and spoke to the kids. I usually do that when they're staying with Ian."

"Any reason in particular? Were you concerned for their safety?"

"No, of course not. I would never have let them go with him if I didn't think they'd be safe. Ian was always a good father and only occasionally lost his temper with them. I called them because I wanted to talk to them, hear their voices, tell them goodnight, tell them I loved them. I missed them."

"And how did Ian react?"

"To my calls?"

"Yes."

"He was okay, I guess. By the end of the weekend, he was getting a little irritated and I remember he said something about me checking up on him all the time. I denied that, of course, and we argued. At the time, I was adamant my frequent calls had nothing to do with that, although now that I look back on it, I think subconsciously I probably *was* checking up on him. He'd been so angry at the courthouse and he'd collected the children not long afterwards..."

"You wanted to make sure they were all right?" the prosecutor finished.

Natalie saw Blake lean forward as if to stand and then appeared to think better of it. She answered the prosecutor's question.

"Yes, I guess I did. I also wanted to remind Ian to return them early on Monday morning. The boys had to go to school and Lacey... Lacey had to go to daycare."

The prosecutor acknowledged Natalie's response with a nod and then flipped through some papers on the bar table in front of him before resuming his questioning.

"I now want to take you to that morning— Monday, October ninth. Can you tell the court what you remember of that day?"

Once again, Natalie drew in a breath and steeled herself for what was to come. "That day started out like a normal Monday. Ian was often late returning the kids after a weekend visit. I was convinced he did it to annoy me and it irritated me that it worked. That Monday wasn't any different. Ian was late with the kids, as usual. I was running around trying to get ready for work. I called him, upset that he hadn't brought them home on time, like I'd asked."

"How did Ian respond to your phone call?"

"He was angry and short with me and accused me of flying off the handle for no reason. I explained as calmly as I could that I was going to be late for work if he didn't get there soon. That's when he offered to drop the boys off to school and Lacey off to daycare. I... I didn't think anything of it. If anything, I was relieved. It meant I would get to work on time."

"Had Ian ever dropped the children off to their respective schools before?"

"When we were still together, he often did the school run. As a self-employed plumber, his time was a little less regulated than mine. After we separated and during the divorce, it rarely happened. Maybe only once or twice before that Monday."

"Did the defendant give you any reason to suspect he was angry enough to do what he did?"

Natalie stared at him. "Are you asking whether I had any idea he was about to murder my child?"

"N-not exactly," the prosecutor stammered, blushing. "What I mean is, how was Ian's mood when you spoke to him over the phone?"

"Like I said, he was rude and sarcastic and angry over the fact I was giving him a hard time over being late, but relations between us were often like that. I actually thought he was trying to make it up to me by offering to do the school run. It never occurred to me he'd do what he did."

"Had he ever exhibited dangerous behavior in the past?"

"Nothing like that. Nothing that would have me questioning the decision to let him have access to my children. Toward the end of our marriage, there were more and more arguments, many of them heated, but I never felt my safety was threatened or the safety of my children."

She sighed quietly. "I was happy to give Ian visiting rights. That was never in dispute. He was their father. They loved him and he loved them. I wanted him to be a part of their lives. The only reason the court case went on for so long was because Ian wanted sole custody and I refused to give him that. They're my babies. I'm their momma! They need me and I need them! I... I wanted them to live with me!"

Without warning, she was overcome with a barrage of memories of that awful time. The tears, the heartache, the anger, the despair. The feeling that the struggle to keep her children would never come to an end; that she'd never be happy or at peace again.

A sudden surge of emotion tightened her chest and made it difficult to breathe. She put a hand up to her mouth in an effort to keep it all in, but a gasp escaped and tears burned in her eyes. Despite her best efforts, she was about to fall apart. She fumbled in her jacket pocket for a tissue and prayed silently for the questioning to come to an end. Her prayers went unanswered.

"Do you need a moment, Ms Johnson?"

Though the question from the judge was asked kindly, Natalie wasn't fooled. He wanted the matter to proceed and by taking time out, she was only going to delay the inevitable. She had to get through her evidence and then she'd be free to leave. Well, not leave. She owed it to Lacey to stay until the last witness had testified and the final sweeping comment had been made by the lawyers and possibly the judge.

"No, I'm... I'm fine," she managed and in an effort to prove it, dabbed at the moisture in her eyes and sat up straighter in her chair.

The judge surveyed her a moment longer and then turned back to the prosecutor. "All right, Mr Villa, you may continue."

"I'm sorry, Ms Johnson. I appreciate how difficult this must be for you," the prosecutor said, looking genuinely contrite. "I only have a few more questions."

She nodded and clenched her hands together in her lap.

"You called Ian that morning and he told you he would drop the children off at school, right?"

"Yes, that's right."

"What did you do next?"

"I continued to get ready for work. I left the house not much past my usual time and actually managed to get to work on time. I remember feeling grateful that Ian had done the school run." She grimaced at the memory.

"When did you first realize something was wrong?" the prosecutor asked quietly, his expression grim.

Natalie closed her eyes. She drew in a breath and held it and then released it slowly. The moment she dreaded was upon her. The moment she discovered her baby was seriously injured or even more likely, dead. She was determined not to let Ian see how much his actions had hurt her.

"Ms Johnson?" Villa prompted gently.

She opened her eyes. "I received a call from Lacey's daycare center. It was about half-past nine. Her teacher called to ask about Lacey. When I told her that Ian was supposed to have dropped her off, I discovered she wasn't there."

"Did you become alarmed?"

"I wouldn't say alarmed," Natalie replied. "My initial reaction was anger that Ian hadn't done as he'd promised. He said he'd take her to school and he hadn't. I assumed he'd taken her home with him, instead."

"What did you do then?"

"I called Ian."

"Did he answer?"

"Yes, he did."

"What did he say?"

"I asked him about Lacey and the boys. I asked him where they were."

"What did he say?"

"He told me he'd dropped the boys off at school. When I asked him where Lacey was, he said she was gone."

"What did you think he meant by that?"

"I didn't know. I asked him to explain."

"And what did he say?"

"He repeated that she was gone. He sounded so...weird. I got frightened. I asked him where she was gone."

"And what did he say?"

Natalie drew in a deep breath. "He told me he'd thrown her off the bridge."

There was an audible gasp from the direction of the jury. Natalie was glad they were as horrified as she was at her ex-husband's actions, but she didn't have it in her to raise her gaze from where her hands lay tightly clenched in her lap. The memory of that horrific phone call was still sharp in her mind, as was the nightmare that came afterwards. Despite her best efforts to remain stoic, fresh, hot tears burned in her eyes and she looked at the prosecutor in despair. Taking note of her distress, he gave her a brief, sympathetic look and continued more gently.

"Did Ian say anything else?"

"I'm not sure. I'd gone into shock. If he did, I didn't hear anything more."

"What happened next?" the prosecutor asked gently.

"I-I can't really remember everything. It was all a bit of a blur. I remember shouting for someone to call the police. I also remember calling the boys' school. I needed to make sure they were all right, and to see if Ian had been lying about that."

"Did you talk to someone at your sons' school?"

"Yes. I was advised both boys had been dropped off there by their father." Her voice had dropped to a whisper. She was almost at the end of her endurance. Noting her distress, the prosecutor nodded briefly in acknowledgement.

"Thank you, Ms Johnson." He gazed up at the judge. "I have no further questions."

CHAPTER 12

Blake stared at Natalie from where she sat in the witness box and steeled himself against what was to come. If she thought giving her evidence through the prosecutor was tough, wait until she faced off with Blake during cross examination. He had no intention of hurting her unnecessarily, but he had a job to do. It was obvious she was doing it tough and who wouldn't be under these circumstances?

She'd recounted the harrowing moments when her ex-husband had told her he'd tossed their child over the side of the bridge. Now it was Blake's turn to elicit whatever sympathy he could for the man responsible for it. With no choice, he drew in a deep breath, organized his notes and got to his feet.

"Ms Johnson, did you believe your ex-husband when he told you he'd tossed your daughter over the side of the bridge?"

Natalie regarded him steadily and Blake couldn't help but admire her resilience. In a soft voice tinged with weariness, she replied. "I... I didn't know what to believe."

"Right," Blake said. "Because if any of us here had taken such a call, we would have been unable to comprehend that such a thing could happen, that anyone could throw a child over the side of a bridge to what was almost certain death."

Natalie winced and her face lost color. Blake felt a twinge of guilt, but forged on. He turned to face the jury.

"The fact that Ian did just that is still incomprehensible to us. We know it happened and yet we are almost numb with disbelief. How could it happen? How could it be? The questions keep piling up and there don't appear to be any answers."

Blake turned back to Natalie. "All of us here, in fact anyone you might ask, would find such behavior incomprehensible. Just like you, right?"

Natalie nodded slowly. "Yes."

"This wasn't normal behavior, even for your ex-husband, was it, Ms Johnson? I mean, you just told us you'd never had any concerns for your safety or for the safety of your children while they were in the care and company of my client, correct?"

"Correct."

"He'd never given you any reason to distrust him, to think that you might be putting your children at risk, had he?"

"No."

"Even through the sometimes tense and angry moments that can arise during a messy divorce.

You were never once fearful of your ex-husband or thought that he posed a threat, right?"

"Right."

"Because, just before this tragic event, your children had stayed with their father over the weekend and you were happy for them to go, right?"

"Yes."

"You're a good mother, aren't you?"

A tiny frown line appeared between her eyebrows, as if she wasn't quite sure where he was headed. A moment later, she answered.

"I'm not perfect, but yes, I think I'm a good mother."

"You love your children?"

"Yes, of course. They mean everything to me."

"And therefore, as a good, loving mother, it's inconceivable—if you thought there might be the slightest chance that my client would harm your children—that you'd let them go with him. That's true, isn't it?"

"Yes."

"So when Ian told you Lacey was gone and that he'd thrown her over the side of the bridge, you thought he was joking, didn't you?"

The prosecutor got to his feet. "Objection! The question has been asked and answered. The witness said she didn't know what to believe."

"Sustained. Mr Harton, ask your next question."

Blake glanced down at the bar table to the papers scattered across the space in front of him and then glanced back at Natalie. She looked calm and composed, although her hands were clenched in front of her.

"You said Ian sounded weird when he spoke to you in the moments before he told you he'd thrown Lacey over the bridge. What did you mean by that?"

Natalie shrugged. "I'm not sure. He sounded cold and scary and…weird. It frightened me."

"And yet, at some point, you thought he was joking."

Once again, Villa got to his feet. "Objection! We've already been over this. The witness told the court she didn't know what to believe."

"Sustained," the judge replied. "Move on, Mr Harton."

Blake took another moment to look down at his notes before continuing. "When you ended the call to my client, you immediately told your work colleagues that your ex-husband had killed your daughter and you asked them to call the police. Is that correct?"

Natalie's gaze lowered to her hands. Her voice trembled as she answered. "Yes."

Blake waited a moment for her to collect herself. There was no point upsetting her unnecessarily. He wouldn't win any points from the jury by attacking the grieving mother.

"Ms Johnson," he said in a soft tone, "why did you tell your work colleagues that my client had killed your daughter?"

Blake saw Natalie's chest rise and fall on a deep indrawn breath before she raised her gaze to his. "There was something in Ian's voice, a madness. It terrified me. I didn't want to believe what he told me, but then I remembered how angry he'd been on the Friday afternoon, after the court case and then he hadn't returned the kids on time and we'd argued again..."

"But you weren't frightened for their safety on Friday afternoon, were you? Despite my client's display of anger after the judge's decision, you were happy for your children to spend the weekend with him, weren't you?"

"Yes."

"What my client did to Lacey... It wasn't planned, was it?"

Natalie looked uncomfortable. "I don't know."

Blake was insistent. "Yes, you do. If you thought there was even the slightest chance of Ian harming your children, you wouldn't have let them go, or you would have insisted he return them home to you. Instead, you were *grateful* when he offered to do the school run. You gave evidence to that fact. Are you saying you lied about that?"

A flush stained her cheeks. She stared at Blake with defiance and anger. "No, I wasn't lying about that. I'm not lying about any of it. I had no idea Ian was going to do what he did."

Blake paused. When he spoke again, his tone was almost conversational. "You were married to my client for seven years, correct?"

"Yes, give or take a couple of months."

"And you were together for three years before that, right?"

"Right."

"It would be fair to say you know him as well as anyone, don't you think?"

Natalie shrugged. "I guess."

"In all those years, the best part of a decade, he never once gave you cause to think he was capable of something like this, did he?"

"No, at least, not to the children. He treated them a lot better than he treated me."

"Why did you file for divorce, Ms Johnson?"

She compressed her lips and looked reluctant to give him an answer, but finally she did. "We fell out of love."

"It was something as simple as that?" Blake asked.

"Yes."

"He wasn't violent, was he?"

"We had some pretty heated arguments from time to time, especially toward the end."

"Those arguments never turned physical, did they?"

"No."

"In fact, you were shocked when the police told you what happened, weren't you?"

"Yes. I think any normal, sane person would be shocked."

"Of course. And you were shocked your ex-husband could do such a thing."

"Yes."

"You never saw it coming."

"No."

Once again, Blake paused, as if to gather his thoughts. In reality, he wanted to allow time for the jury to process all that had been said. When he spoke again, it was in a much gentler tone. He instinctively knew it would go better with the jury.

"How do *you* explain my client's actions, Ms Johnson?"

Natalie shook her head slowly back and forth. Blake could see her distress. Still, he needed to press on. They weren't finished yet.

"Could you please answer the question, Ms Johnson?" he said.

"I... I can't explain what happened."

"I understand," Blake replied sympathetically. "Ian's actions were totally out of character, weren't they?"

"Yes."

"Something you could never have imagined?"

"Yes."

"A brain snap?"

"Objection!" the prosecutor interjected. "This witness isn't qualified to answer these kinds of questions."

The judge peered down at Blake. "Sustained. Move on, Mr Harton."

"Yes, Your Honor." He turned back toward Natalie. "You loved your ex-husband very much, didn't you?"

She drew in a deep shuddering breath. "Yes. For a long time, things were good between us."

"He was a good father, wasn't he?"

"Yes."

"A good provider?"

"Yes."

"In fact, like most of us, Ian Johnson worked hard, provided for his family and looked out for his wife and kids. Is that fair to say?"

"Yes."

"And then, one day it all went horribly wrong and he lost his baby girl."

Natalie's eyes flashed with anger and she sat up straighter in her seat. "He didn't *lose* her, Mr Harton! He threw her over the side of Anzac Bridge and he did it to get at me." She practically snarled.

Blake ignored her anger and continued to regard her steadily. "He loved Lacey very much, didn't he, Ms Johnson?"

"I thought so," she replied, breathing hard.

"She was his little girl, wasn't she?"

The question broke through Natalie's composure. Anger forgotten, she cried out with a sob. "Yes. She was always his little girl."

Tears filled Natalie's eyes and spilled over. Blake felt hollow inside. It killed him to upset her, to dredge up the awful memories, but he had a job to do. He didn't have a choice.

"No further questions," he said and with a sympathetic nod in her direction, he returned to his chair.

In quiet tones, the judge thanked Natalie for her testimony and excused her from the witness box. She gratefully stepped down and made her way back to her seat. Tears continued to well up in her eyes and run silently down her cheeks. She swiped at them with the back of her hand and kept her gaze averted.

A loud sniffle caught her attention and she

looked up and saw that Ian was crying, too. She almost combusted with fury. She hated him for what he'd done. She wanted to rant and rave and scream. He'd stolen the life of her baby! Lacey would never laugh or cry or smile again. It was all Ian's fault! He had no right to feel sadness, or to feel sorry for what he'd done.

Then Natalie looked at him again and saw the abject defeat in the slump of his shoulders and the quivering of his mouth; in the tears that ran freely down his cheeks. He made no attempt to staunch them.

What had happened in those fateful minutes when their worlds were turned upside down? Would they ever know? One thing was for certain: There were no winners here.

Her gaze drifted to Blake. He stared grimly at the papers in front of him. There was a quiet somberness in the courtroom. It was like every single person was trying to get their head around the enormity of the tragedy that was playing out before them. She was glad she didn't have the burden of determining guilt or innocence.

How would she feel if it were someone else's child they were discussing? Someone else's family who'd been torn apart? Would she be able to view the matter so clinically, and determine so matter-of-factly the only possible outcome? That tore her up inside. A guilty verdict was all that she'd accept. Anything less was unthinkable. Despite his obvious remorse, Ian *had* murdered their baby. *Surely it was as simple as determining that?*

And yet, she knew in her heart of hearts that there was nothing simple about what had happened. As she'd admitted during Blake's cross examination, she couldn't explain Ian's actions and she knew him better than anyone. *How could she expect twelve strangers to understand and agree?*

The judge addressed the lawyers. He noted the time and suggested that the parties adjourn for the day. Natalie was glad. She was weary beyond mention and wanted nothing more than to escape the courtroom for a while. She had endured about as much as anyone could be expected to endure that day and looking around at the jury, it appeared they felt the same.

After excusing the jury and waiting for them to depart, the judge dealt with some administrative matters and finally brought the gavel down. He stood and the crowd stood with him. Another bow of respect toward the bench by those present, and amidst a swish of flowing crimson robes, the judge departed the room.

Natalie blew her breath out on a heavy sigh and gathered her handbag from beneath her seat where she'd stowed it earlier. The crown prosecutor came over to her and patted her on the shoulder.

"You did well up there," he said.

"Thank you," she murmured.

"I know how hard it was for you," Villa continued. "You did a great job."

"Thank you," she said again and then asked, "What time will we resume in the morning?"

"If you can be here by a quarter to ten that would be great. The trial will recommence at ten."

Natalie nodded. Slinging her handbag over her shoulder, she came to her feet and after murmuring good-byes to the prosecutor and to Colby, she headed toward the exit. It was nearly four. She needed to call Monica and make sure she'd collected the boys from school. Her friend had agreed to take them home with her until after the trial. They both agreed it would be easier on everyone if they slept over at Aunty Mon's place for the week.

With Natalie being a fixture at the supreme court for the next few days, it made sense for Monica to take over their primary care. She'd ferry them to and from school and everything in between. Natalie wasn't looking forward to walking into an empty house, but the least amount of disruption to the twins' routine was best for everyone—and most especially for them.

She reached the exit to the courtroom at the same time Blake did and her heart skipped a beat at his nearness. Lines of fatigue had etched themselves into the corners of his eyes and around the downturn of his well-formed mouth. Still, he looked suave and confident and in another lifetime, she might have found him attractive. But right here, right now departing a courtroom where he'd just peeled back her soul, layer by painful layer, she felt nothing but sad resignation.

He stepped back and let her precede him. She appreciated his courtesy. Inclining his head in her direction, he opened his mouth and she thought he was going to say something. But, as if thinking better of it, he closed it again and simply waited in silence for her to pass through the doorway and into the foyer.

Without pausing, she strode across the carpet and headed straight for the stairs. She was glad Blake hadn't tried to speak with her. After what had gone on between them in the courtroom, there was nothing left for either of them to say.

CHAPTER 13

Blake loosened the tie that had hung all day around his neck and undid his top button. He usually spent the evening, after a long and draining day in court, winding down at a bar near Circular Quay, or kicking back with a drink in his luxury bachelor pad that was within walking distance of his office.

So why was he standing outside the front fence that bordered the neat garden that led up to Natalie Johnson's front door? The hell if he knew. What he did know was that ever since he'd watched her walk out of the courtroom earlier that afternoon, he hadn't been able to get her off his mind.

It wasn't just the sad and haunted look that had deepened the shadows in her green eyes or the air of quiet despair that surrounded her. It wasn't just that he'd pushed hard to get the answers he wanted and had succeeded, to the point where he'd left her in tears.

Her distress had made him feel like a prick, but

still he had done what he had to do. His client expected it; Blake expected it. It was what made him such a good barrister. Still, he couldn't shake the feeling that he should apologize.

Yes, apologizing...

That was the reason he found himself outside her door. If he told himself that often enough, he might even believe it.

The truth was, he found her honesty and vulnerability compelling, and he wanted to get to know her better. It was foolhardy on so many levels and in some respects, downright wrong. He was her ex-husband's lawyer, for Pete's sake. Today, he'd grilled her on the stand. No doubt she didn't want to have anything to do with him and he wouldn't blame her for that. But he had to at least try and make contact, to explore the unexplainable need in him to talk with her, connect with her; to reassure her he wasn't the monster he'd appeared to be in the courtroom.

With a sudden surge of determination, he opened the gate and strode up the path, climbed the steps and knocked on the door before he lost his nerve. He was still second-guessing the wisdom of his actions when the door opened and Natalie stared at him with narrowed eyes from the other side.

"What are you doing here?"

He grimaced. *Good question. What was he supposed to say?*

Heat crept up his cheeks and he was thankful for the shadows of the night that hid his discomfort from her gaze. Still, he couldn't stand there on her porch without saying something. "Natalie, hi. I... I hope you don't mind. I... I came by to see if you were all right."

Her eyes narrowed even further. "I'm. Fine." She bit off each word.

His gaze drifted over her. The tight bun had come loose and her hair now hung in soft waves around her shoulders. Her eyes were red-rimmed, like she'd recently been crying and an air of sadness and despair still lingered. "No, you're not."

As if on cue, her eyes welled up. She ducked her head and hurriedly brushed them away. "I told you. I'm fine," she repeated but her voice trembled with the effort.

"May I come in?"

For a long moment, she stared at him in silence, as if debating the wisdom of acceding to his request. At last, and with obvious reluctance, she stepped back and opened the door wider before turning her back on him and disappearing down the hall.

Blake let himself in and closed the door behind him. The house was quiet. He guessed the kids were either in bed or were staying elsewhere. His footsteps echoed on the polished floorboards and the high ceilings lent the hallway a grand, majestic air. A soft, golden glow from intermittent light fixtures illuminated a muted mint-green color on the wall.

The hallway opened into a wide open-concept kitchen and living room that was furnished in harmony with the age of the house. A scarred wooden table that seated six. A beautiful bowl of pink roses in a silver dish. Modern appliances that sat comfortably side by side with antique kettles, copper saucepans and a set of fine bone china that was displayed in a glass cabinet on one wall.

The overall look was soft and charming and undeniably feminine. He didn't know what the room had looked like when she'd shared it with Ian, but there wasn't a scrap of masculinity in evidence now. Not that it bothered him. The space was all Natalie and he liked it. He liked it a lot.

He found her with her back to the counter. Her arms were crossed defensively over her chest. She eyed him steadily, distrust and suspicion still clouding her gaze.

"Should you be here?" she asked bluntly.

He compressed his lips and shook his head. "Probably not."

She continued to stare at him. He shifted his weight from one foot to the other and tried to ignore the guilt that filled his gut.

"I'm not breaking any rules, if that's what you're thinking and you've already given evidence," he added in an attempt to put her at ease.

She shrugged and looked away, but her lips tightened and he caught a fresh glimmer of tears, as if she was remembering the traumatic events of the day.

"Can I get you a coffee?" she asked quietly, still not meeting his gaze.

Blake eased out the breath he hadn't been aware of holding and nodded. "Thanks. That would be nice."

"How do you take it?" she asked, turning away and walking around the counter.

For the first time, Blake realized she was barefoot. Somehow, it made her look younger, more vulnerable. His heart ached at what she'd been through. Resolutely, he forced the feelings aside.

"Cream and one sugar, please," he replied trying not to notice how good she looked in her clothes. She was still dressed in the fitted skirt and peach-colored blouse she'd worn to court. Along with her high heels, the jacket had been discarded.

She reached up into a cupboard and took down two mint-colored mugs. Her blouse pulled tight across her back, revealing the outline of a lacy white bra. Once again, Blake averted his gaze.

To his relief, she suggested he take a seat at the kitchen table and he didn't need to be told twice. He was there to apologize and offer her his condolences for the difficult day. Nothing else.

In short order, the kettle boiled and she brought over two steaming cups. Blake noticed she took her coffee black—like he'd guessed the last time. He murmured his thanks and took a sip. She sipped from her cup, too. Then she set it down in front of her and stared at him, her gaze now clear and direct.

"Why are you here, Blake?"

He looked away and yet again, heat crept up his neck. *How could he explain the inexorable pull she had on him?* He'd felt it from the first time they'd met. But he couldn't tell her that. She'd run like hell and he wouldn't blame her. Keeping his gaze fixed to the black-and-white checkerboard pattern of the floor tiles, he cast around for a suitable reply.

"I... I wanted to apologize for the rough day you had and my part in it...and to check that you were all right."

"I already told you, I'm fine," she said quietly. "And seeing as you're the one who caused most of my distress, you being here wondering how I'm doing is a little hypocritical, don't you think?"

He blushed and lowered his gaze. He should go. He had no business being there. Only, he didn't want to leave.

"Tomorrow we'll hear from the eye witnesses," he blurted, grasping for something to say.

Her lips tightened and she paled. He cursed under his breath. *Dammit. Why did he have to go and remind her of what was yet to come?* He could only imagine how difficult it was going to be for her to sit in the courtroom and listen to strangers talk about the last moments of her little girl's life.

"After that, the psychiatrists will testify," he added in an attempt to shift her thoughts from what had happened on the bridge.

She stared at him dully. "Yours or mine?"

"Yours," he replied. "Mine will testify after."

She was silent for a moment and then sighed heavily. "I hope we get some answers." Her voice was pitched low.

He bit his lip and nodded. "Yes. And I'm truly sorry about today."

She offered him a shrug, but didn't reply. Her lips trembled. Tears glinted in her eyes. Her gaze was fixed on a point somewhere across the room. He wasn't fooled by her offhand manner.

"I was only doing my job," he added. "But I'm still sorry."

"It's very sad all round," she said in the same flat tone. Her voice hitched. "Nothing's going to bring my baby back. Nothing's going to change what happened. I wish this would all go away. That we could go back to the way we were. I keep expecting Lacey to come racing down the hall, shouting and squealing with laughter, asking me to lift her up, complaining that the boys are giving her a hard time. It's never going to happen! Never again will I hear her, see her, hold her. I can't stand it!" she cried, and this time a sob escaped. "I can't *stand* it!"

The single sob morphed into an avalanche of tears. Natalie buried her face in her hands. Blake stood and, without thinking, came around to her side. He urged her upwards and into his arms. He held her against his chest. She tensed and then as if the effort of resisting was too much, she went limp in his arms and cried like her heart was broken. He was sure that it was.

She cried for a long time. Gradually, the sobs quieted. Without even being aware that he was doing it, he tilted her chin up with his fingers. She stared at him with tears in her eyes, devastated and devastatingly beautiful. He lowered his head until his lips barely grazed hers. She gasped in surprise, but didn't pull away. He stared down at her, his heart pounding.

What the hell was he doing?

Natalie stared at Blake in surprise and did her best to get control of her racing heart. She tried not to think about how good it felt to be held by him. The turmoil and heartache of the day, coupled with arriving home to a dark and empty house, had set her spirits plummeting and she'd given in to a few tears of self-pity before resigning herself to putting in a silent and lonely night.

Having the boys stay over with Monica had seemed like a good idea at the time, but the reality of spending the next few days alone while enduring the hell that was the trial was suddenly overwhelming. After the harrowing day, she could have really done with one of Lacey's special hugs.

That thought had brought tears to her eyes and she'd kicked off her sandals and had collapsed on the couch. She'd just finished pulling the pins from her hair when Blake knocked on her door. To say that she'd been surprised was putting it too lightly. Once she'd gotten over the shock of seeing him, she'd debated the wisdom of letting him in. He was her ex-husband's lawyer, for heaven's sake. Only hours before, he'd interrogated her on the stand. And when he'd done that he'd forced her to remember all the details of the most horrific day of her life.

She understood that he was only doing his job, but that didn't make it any easier. Or right. She could barely bring herself to look at him on her way out of the courtroom. And now, here he was, in her kitchen, drinking coffee and then, holding her, murmuring words of comfort while she cried her eyes out.

And now they'd shared a kiss...

Sweet and tender, it had touched her deep inside. His arms were strong and firm around her, protecting her from the world outside. It had been so long since she'd been held by a man. She'd forgotten how good it could feel. No, scrap that. Ian's arms had never felt so good. It was Blake. Blake was the difference and that realization scared her.

As if sensing her unease, Blake loosened his hold and reached up. He ran the pad of his thumb down her cheek. The tenderness in his gaze stole her breath and fresh tears burned behind her eyes. She couldn't remember the last time she'd felt kindness from a man. She wasn't sure she could deal with that feeling now.

Once again, Blake seemed to read her mind. He stepped away and cleared his throat. His arms hung by his sides.

"I... I'd better get going," he said, his voice rough with emotion.

She nodded. "Yes."

He closed his eyes and when he opened them again he acknowledged her response with a nod and a sad smile of resignation. In silence, he turned on his heel and left the way he'd come.

With a sigh, Natalie picked up the coffee mugs and put them in sink. Not bothering to rinse them, she crossed the room and switched off the light. Heading down the corridor that led to the bedrooms, she undid the buttons on her blouse and peeled it off. She dropped it into the laundry hamper that stood in the bathroom.

Quickly divesting herself of the rest of her clothes, she stepped into the shower and turned the water on hot. Standing beneath the spray, she let the events of the day wash away down the drain. It had been a strange and harrowing day. It had been the first day of the trial. But now the day was over and tomorrow wouldn't be as bad as today. She was betting on that.

Climbing between the sheets, clean and refreshed, she felt better than she had for days. In the silence and security of her bed, a calmness descended. Though his questions had rubbed salt in all her wounds, she was certain the peace she felt in that moment had everything to do with Blake.

She reached up and touched her lips and her thoughts centered on the wonder of his kiss. Out of the blackness of her darkest hour, she felt the tiniest frisson of hope. She couldn't pinpoint when things shifted, but she no longer regarded him as the enemy. He felt badly about what had happened to her and how he'd contributed to her pain. *He'd come here to apologize, hadn't he?*

He was a good man, a kind man. A man worthy of her admiration and respect. If they'd met under different circumstances, she might already be half in love with him...

The more she contemplated it, the more she accepted he was a special person in her life. If the cloud of tragedy hadn't been swirling all around her, she'd want to get to know him better, to know what made him tick. She wondered about his family—his brother who'd taken his own life. *How had his brother's death affected Blake, the brother who'd been left behind?* She knew with a certainty that he was no stranger to pain. No one could live through such heartache and not feel its devastating effects...and empathize with others. She ought to know.

She wondered briefly if he were married. He'd worn no ring on his finger... Still, that didn't always mean a man was single... She turned over on her side and buried her face in her pillow, embarrassed and annoyed at the direction of her thoughts. They made her feel disloyal to her daughter's memory. That should be her focus at this time, not curiosity about a man who was defending her ex on a charge of murder.

Still, she fell asleep with an image of Blake in her mind and for the first time in a long time, a soft, wistful smile played around her lips.

CHAPTER 14

Blake snuck a sideways glance and moved slightly until he had a clear view of Natalie. She sat in profile, quiet and composed. Today, she wore another dark-colored suit, this one with fine white pinstripes. Her blouse was a lime green color, peeking out from her jacket. Her hair was once again contained in a bun that sat on the nape of her neck. Her hands were folded in her lap. If she was aware of his scrutiny, she didn't show it. Swallowing a sigh, he returned his attention to the front of the courtroom.

The next witness called by the prosecution was Dylan Bedford. In his mid-twenties and dressed in an ill-fitting suit and cheap tie, Bedford looked anything but comfortable. Still, that could simply be a reaction to being in the witness box. For the average person, unused to the legal system, being in the spotlight in a courtroom was daunting. After being sworn in, the prosecutor began to examine his witness.

"Were you traveling northbound on Anzac

Bridge the morning of October ninth?" Crown Prosecutor Villa asked.

"Yes. I was on my way to work," Bedford answered.

"What time was it?"

"It was nearly half-past eight. I remember because I'm normally in my office by then. I was running late."

"Tell us what you saw," the prosecutor invited.

Bedford took a breath and then blew it out before replying. "Like I said, I was running late. The traffic was heavy. It was peak hour. I was cursing the traffic because it would cause some strife with my boss if I was late again."

"Do you make it a habit of being late?" Villa asked.

The witness blushed and Blake almost felt sorry for him. He wasn't so old that he couldn't remember what it was like to be twenty-something and waking up on Monday morning trying to get over a big weekend.

"No, but it's happened more than once. I started a new job only three months ago. I... I'm trying to make a good impression."

The prosecutor nodded in acknowledgement and urged the witness to continue.

"That morning, I was impatient to get to work. There was a white, early model Toyota HiLux utility in the lane directly in front of me. He changed lanes all of a sudden."

"Did he use his traffic indicator?" Villa asked.

"Yes. But only a second or two before he switched lanes."

"Did he switch to the left or the right lane?"

"He switched to the left."

"So that's the lane closest to the steel and wire barricade, right?"

"Yes."

"Is there a pedestrian or bicycle path on that side?"

"No, it's on the other side."

"What happened next?"

"The man drove a little further forward and then braked. He came to a stop."

"You saw him pull over?"

"Yes."

"What happened then?"

"He put his hazard lights on."

"And then what?" Villa asked.

"And then nothing. I kept going. I was late for work. I didn't pay any attention to what was going on behind me."

"Did you see anyone alight from the Toyota pickup?"

"No, as I said, I saw the vehicle pull over and then I went past. I didn't look back."

"Thank you, Mr Bedford. I have no further questions." Villa turned to Blake. "Your witness."

Blake got to his feet. "Mr Bedford, you've already told us you were late for work that morning. You were concerned you'd have another black mark against your name, weren't you?"

The witness held Blake's gaze and answered cautiously. "Yes."

"You were traveling pretty fast across the bridge, weren't you, Mr Bedford?"

"No. Like I said, the traffic was heavy. I wasn't doing more than twenty or thirty miles an hour."

Blake kept his expression neutral, despite the fact he'd been hoping the witness would provide a different answer.

"You said you saw my client, Ian Johnson, use his indicator when he changed lanes, right?"

"Yes," the witness agreed, his expression still cautious.

"I put it to you that you were mistaken," Blake said. "I suggest that the traffic was too heavy and you were traveling too fast to see if Mr Johnson used his indicator."

Bedford's face took on a mutinous expression. Blake's gut clenched with dread. He wasn't going to get what he wanted.

"No. I definitely saw it. He only used it a second or two before he switched lanes, like I said. I had to brake to avoid hitting him. I blew my horn at him and I might have even followed him into that left lane and tailgated him if I hadn't been late for work."

"You also said you saw the hazard lights in use on Mr Johnson's car," Blake said.

"Yes."

Blake eyed the witness steadily. "Is that what you would have done, if you'd switched lanes and stopped on the bridge?" he asked.

"Yes. Exactly right. That's what I would have done. What any normal person would have—"

"I put it to you Mr Bedford that you're mistaken. The hazard lights were not on."

The man stared back at Blake. "Yes, they were."

Blake schooled his features into a neutral expression, disappointed he hadn't been able to shake the man. It was the first blow, but Blake didn't want the jury to see how it affected him. Keeping his gaze firmly averted from Natalie, he hoped there wouldn't be too many others.

At the invitation from the judge, Greg Villa called his next witness. Geraldine Harvey took the stand. Blake knew from her statement that she was in her late forties, though she looked a decade younger. She worked as a beauty therapist at a day spa in one of the ritzy hotels that were perched along the northern end of the harbor.

After establishing her credibility as a witness, the prosecutor got straight to the point. "Ms Harvey, were you traveling in a northerly direction along Anzac Bridge on the morning of Monday, October ninth?"

"Yes. I was on my way to work."

"Did you see anything unusual that day as you crossed the bridge?"

"Yes. I saw a car pulled over in the far left lane."

"Do you know what kind of vehicle it was?"

"No, I'm not good with cars, but it was a pickup of some kind."

"Do you remember what color it was?"

"Yes. It was white."

The prosecutor picked up an 8 x 10 color photograph and handed a copy to Colby who passed it on to Blake. It was a picture of Ian's Toyota. "No objection," Blake said, passing it back.

The prosecutor nodded in acknowledgement

of Blake's comment and turned back to his witness. "Ms Harvey, I'd like you to take a look at this picture."

The clerk of the court stepped forward and took the picture from the prosecutor and handed it to the witness.

"Is this the vehicle you saw stopped in the far left lane on Anzac Bridge?" Villa asked.

The woman picked up the glasses that hung from a fine gold chain around her neck and put them on. She looked at the photograph, lowered her glasses and then returned her gaze to the prosecutor. "Yes, this looks like the car."

"Your Honor, let the record show that the witness has identified the vehicle belonging to Ian Johnson as the vehicle she saw stopped in the far eastern lane on the date in question."

"Duly noted," the judge replied and made a notation on the paper in front of him.

"I'd like to tender the photograph," Villa said.

The judge looked in Blake's direction. "Any objection, Mr Harton?"

"No, Your Honor."

"Very well," the judge replied. "I'll mark the photograph as Exhibit A. You may continue with your witness, Mr Villa."

The prosecutor looked down at his notes and then addressed the woman once again. "Ms Harvey, when you noticed the white vehicle, did you see its driver?"

"Yes. I saw a man climb out and open the rear passenger door. He leaned in and pulled something out."

"Did you see what it was?"

"No. I kept driving past."

"Do you recognize the man you saw outside the vehicle that day?"

Blake held his breath. Geraldine Harvey turned to look at Ian. "Yes," she said. "He's sitting over there."

She pointed directly toward Blake's client.

"Let the record show that this witness has pointed to the defendant," Villa said and then regained his seat.

Blake kept his features composed. There was no point in making a scene over the witness identifying his client as the man in question. Their defense didn't rest on whether or not Johnson had committed the offense. He stood and took a moment to read over his notes, even though he'd memorized every word. He directed his attention to the witness.

"Ms Harvey, I noticed you required reading glasses to inspect the photograph. Do you wear glasses at other times?"

"No. I only need them for close-up work."

Blake nodded and continued. "And when you say you saw Mr Johnson outside his car, you weren't very close, were you?"

"No, not as close as I would need to be to require my glasses."

"I see. And when you saw Mr Johnson in those few seconds as you passed, can you tell us what he looked like?"

The woman frowned in confusion. "He looked like he does now. Brown hair—"

"I'm sorry to interrupt, Ms Harvey," Blake said. "What I mean is, did he look angry? Was he shouting? Gesticulating? Anything to cause you to think he might be out of control?"

The witness nodded. "I guess he looked angry, yes. I only saw him for a moment. He seemed to be saying something, but I had my windows up and the traffic around me was noisy. I couldn't hear what he said."

"Well, I put it to you that he was acting both angry and erratic and that in the moment you drove by him, he was no longer functioning in a normal way."

The woman shrugged and shook her head. "I don't know. Like I said, I didn't see him for long."

"When you saw Mr Johnson's pickup, the hazard lights weren't on, were they?" Blake stated.

The witness paused. A frown creased her forehead. "I don't think so. I don't remember seeing any hazard lights."

Blake nodded in relief and advised the court that he was done with the witness. At least he had someone who hadn't seen the hazard lights. The more normal behavior Ian exhibited during the offense and immediately after, the harder it would be to prove he was is a dissociative state and that was Blake's only hope of having his client avoid responsibility for the death of Lacey Johnson.

As he returned to his seat, he took care to hide his frustration. He needed at least one of the witnesses to back up Ian's claim that he was out of his mind, acting on autopilot when he chose to pull over, reach into the back seat and take his young daughter from her car seat. It seemed Blake would have to wait for the next witness and hope for a break then. At least Harvey had conceded that the hazard lights hadn't been used.

John Locke was the third eyewitness called by the prosecution. According to the statement he'd given to the police at the time of the offense, Locke was a thirty-seven-year-old salesman who worked for an insurance brokerage firm in Balmain. Like the other two witnesses, on the morning in question, he'd been on his way to work. This man was perhaps the most dangerous to Blake's client and Blake hoped like hell he could do some damage to the man's testimony. If not, they were in trouble.

"Mr Locke," the prosecutor said, "can you tell the court what you saw on the morning of October ninth?"

"I was driving north across Anzac Bridge. I saw a white Toyota HiLux pulled over in the far left lane. It had its hazard lights on."

"What else did you see?"

"I saw a man climb on top of the roof of his vehicle."

"Was he carrying anything?"

"Yes, he had a child in his arms."

Blake opened his mouth to protest, but then closed it again. *What was the point?* They weren't disputing that Ian had thrown his daughter over the side of the bridge. It was his state of mind when he'd done it that was up for debate.

"What happened next?" the prosecutor asked.

"I was almost alongside the man's vehicle by this time. I'd slowed down to get a better look. It was strange, seeing this man crouched on the roof of his car holding a child. The next thing I knew, he stood and threw the little girl over the side." The man's voice hitched, as if he was recalling the awful incident and was still unable to believe it.

"What did you do then?" Villa asked, his voice gentle.

"I kept driving. I didn't know what to do. I thought I must have been mistaken. I thought he must have tossed a doll, or something. I mean, what kind of person throws a child off the side of the bridge?"

"Yes, you're right, Mr Locke. What kind of person throws a child over the side of a bridge?" the prosecutor repeated quietly. A moment later, he closed with, "No further questions."

Blake kept his gaze averted from where Natalie sat behind the prosecutor and got to his feet. "Mr Locke, I appreciate that you saw this drama unfolding from quite a distance away. Did you see the man do anything before he threw the child?"

"No, apart from standing up on the roof of the car. There wasn't any pause. He stood and tossed her. It happened almost at the same time. And you're wrong. I wasn't quite a distance away by that point. I was driving forward the whole time. By the time I saw him toss the child over the side, I was right up next to where his pickup was parked."

Blake hid a grimace. This wasn't going well. He forged on. "You were listening to the radio at the time, weren't you?"

"Yes."

"In fact, you were listening to the news, right?"

"Yes. It came on as I was heading over the bridge."

"I put it to you that you're mistaken about the hazard lights. You were distracted, listening to the news and you simply made a mistake."

"No, I didn't make a mistake and I wasn't so distracted that I didn't notice everything about that truck. You see, my father had one of those vehicles when I was a kid. When I saw one pulled over, I took a particular interest in it. It brought back fond memories. Then I saw the man climbing onto the roof with the little girl and that was even stranger. And then he tossed the poor child over the side..."

The man shook his head and stared down at his hands. When he spoke again, his voice was softer, less certain.

"I think I went into shock for a while. I was sure it couldn't have been a kid. I began to doubt myself, but I ended up calling the police. I just had a terrible feeling in my gut. I wanted to be sure."

"How much time had elapsed from when you saw the man climb on top of the roof of his vehicle to when he tossed the child over the side of the bridge?" Blake asked.

The man thought for a moment. "Twenty or thirty seconds, maybe less. It seemed to happen very fast."

"And he didn't look sideways, up and down, back toward the traffic?"

"No."

Blake nodded in satisfaction. "No further questions." He hadn't been able to get the man to retract his evidence about the hazard lights, but he *had* managed to elicit the information that Ian had acted single mindedly when he climbed onto the roof of his car and threw his daughter over the side of the bridge and the witness had voiced what every other person in the courtroom was thinking: *What kind of person did something like that?* Not someone in their right mind, that's for sure. All Blake had to do was get the jury to believe it.

CHAPTER 15

The judge called a recess and Blake stepped out of the courtroom with a sigh of relief. The day had been a tough one, with none of the prosecution's witnesses budging from their statements and there were still three more to come, including the State's forensic psychiatrist. He hoped like hell his own expert witness would come through for him and prove his client was acting in a dissociative state at the time of the offense. If not, Blake's impressive track record in a courtroom was going to take a hit.

From the corner of his eye, he spotted Natalie where she stood on the opposite side of the waiting area outside the courtroom. He was immediately flooded with guilt. Whether her ex-husband had been acting in a dissociative state or not, there was no denying he'd caused the death of their child.

As if sensing his scrutiny, she looked over in his direction and immediately her green eyes narrowed in anger and flashed with accusation. Blake stared back at her and was flooded with guilt. The feeling annoyed him. He turned away from her and took refuge in the restrooms.

———————————

Natalie stared after Blake and wished she were any place but there, waiting outside the courtroom, waiting for the next witness to take the stand and recall the last moments of her baby's life. From what she'd heard that morning, the prosecution witnesses were holding up under Blake Harton's scrutiny. That was a good thing. The sooner they convinced the jury to convict her husband of murder, the better.

"We have two more civilian witnesses to give evidence, and provided we don't run out of time, then it will be the forensic psychiatrist's turn," Colby said quietly from where he stood nearby. "His evidence is going to be crucial."

She drew in a deep breath and closed her eyes briefly as she exhaled, praying silently for the strength she'd need to see this through.

"Are you all right?" he asked, his face a mask of concern.

"Yes. At least, I will be as soon as I have this behind me."

———————————

Blake flipped through the notes he'd written on the next witness's statement. Roger Bannon had also been traveling on Anzac Bridge that fateful day. Blake hoped the man wouldn't prove too damaging to Ian's case. From the corner of his eye, he saw Natalie and the solicitor assisting the prosecutor return to the courtroom and take their seats. He wished there was something he could say to her, some words of comfort, but there were none. The only thing he could do was get on with his job.

The knock on the door heralded the return of the judge. The usual ceremony of standing and bowing and regaining seats was carried out and then the judge asked the prosecutor if he was ready to continue.

"Yes, Your Honor," Villa replied, getting to his feet. "The prosecution would like to call Roger Bannon to the stand."

An Asian gentleman with salt-and-pepper hair and a sprightly step took a seat in the witness box. The court officer went through the procedure of administering the oath and the witness was duly sworn in. After establishing the fact Roger Bannon was a retired police officer heading to Rozelle for a medical appointment on the morning in question, the prosecutor asked him to recount what he saw.

"I was driving north along Anzac Bridge, headed toward Rozelle. I noticed a white Toyota HiLux twin cab parked in the far left lane. As I got closer, I saw a man climb off the roof of the car and open the driver's side door."

The prosecutor acknowledged the comment with a nod. "What happened next?"

"The man climbed back behind the wheel and

then the vehicle pulled back into the traffic. I was probably two or three cars behind him at that stage."

"Did you notice if the man used his indicators when he rejoined the traffic?"

"Yes, he did."

"Did you notice anything else?"

"No. Nothing out of the ordinary. He continued to drive along the bridge. I followed his vehicle all the way off it and then changed lanes to head toward Rozelle. He took a different exit."

"Did he use his indicators?"

"Yes."

"What direction was he headed?"

"Northwest."

"Thank you, Mr Bannon. I have no further questions."

Blake got to his feet. The testimony from the prosecution's eye witnesses was becoming disconcertingly familiar. Once again, he sought a way to put a dent in their evidence.

"Mr Bannon, you wear glasses when you drive, don't you?"

The man started a little in surprise, but nodded. "Yes."

"And you weren't wearing them on the day in question, were you?"

It was a guess, but Blake had nothing to lose and the question was one well worth pursuing with a witness as old as Bannon. Blake had struck pay dirt with it in the past.

The man squirmed and looked down at his hands. "Well, no. I'd broken them a couple of days before. They were in the shop getting fixed."

Blake suppressed a smile of satisfaction. "So, when you say you saw my client use his traffic indicators, you're not exactly sure, are you? In fact, without your glasses, it's quite possible you could be wrong."

The man looked uncertain. "Yes, I guess so."

"And it's fair to say, isn't it, that your vision wasn't good enough to tell anything much at all about the way Mr Johnson continued along his journey. He might have swerved, braked suddenly… In fact, he could have done any number of things without you noticing, couldn't he?"

"No, I—"

"Nothing further," Blake interrupted. He returned to his seat and prepared for the next witness.

Villa got straight to his feet, as Blake had known he would. "Mr Bannon, are you required under the terms of your driver's license to wear glasses when you're driving?"

"Well, no. My vision's been fine until recently."

"And what strength are your lenses?"

"I don't know, but they're not very strong. The optometrist told me my eyesight was good for my age and that the glasses would only make a slight difference. In fact, he told me it wouldn't matter if I didn't wear them at all."

Villa nodded, satisfied. "Thank you, Mr Bannon. Nothing further."

———————

Blake watched Roger Bannon climb down from the witness box and make his way back to his seat and released a soft sigh. He'd done a good job discrediting the man's evidence, but Villa had definitely clawed back some ground. Things weren't looking good.

The court officer called out the name of the next witness. From the corner of his eye, Blake noticed his client sit up with a start. Heather Long was a teacher at the twins' school. Ian must have forgotten she was on the witness list. The young woman had a tidy figure and wore a pale yellow blouse and a tailored white skirt. As she made her way to the witness box, her long brown hair swung gently over her shoulders.

The court officer administered the oath and the witness put her hand on the Bible and solemnly agreed to tell the truth. Greg Villa got to his feet.

"Miss Long, would you mind telling the court how old you are?"

"I'm twenty-four."

"And what is your occupation?"

"I'm a school teacher at Lilyfield Elementary."

"And do you teach Darby and Bailey Johnson?"

"No. They're in kindergarten. I teach the fourth grade."

"Do you know the Johnson twins?"

The woman smiled. "Of course. Everyone knows the Johnson twins. They're adorable."

Blake glanced at his client. Ian's expression was one of fierce concentration. His lips trembled, like he was trying hard not to cry. Blake felt a pang of sympathy.

"Miss Long, I want to take you to the morning of October ninth," the prosecutor continued. "Were you at work that day?"

"Yes."

"And did you see the Johnson twins that day?"

"Yes."

"Can you tell us about that?"

The woman took a moment to collect her thoughts. "I was on playground duty. The bell had gone and I was in the process of locking the front gates. I saw the boys' father pull up outside the school."

"Do you remember what he was driving?"

"Yes. It was a white Toyota twin cab. I'm not sure what model. I'm not very good with cars. I only know it was a Toyota because I drive a Corolla. I recognized the company insignia on the grill."

"How did you know it was Mr Johnson?"

The witness shrugged. "To tell you the truth, I didn't. I only guessed because I saw the twins and knew who they were."

"Did Ian get out of the car?"

"Yes. He walked with the boys up to the school gates."

"How far away were you?"

"Only a few yards."

"Did you speak to him?"

"Yes. I said hello."

"Did he respond to you?"

Despite the fact Blake had read the woman's statement, he still held his breath.

"Yes. He said, 'How are you?' but he didn't look at me when he said it and I could tell he was just being polite. At the time, I thought it was because he didn't know me."

Blake's breath came out in a rush that he disguised with a cough. It sounded very much like Ian had been capable of normal conversation a very short time after he'd tossed his daughter to her death.

The prosecutor cleverly paused, giving the jury time to let the last answer sink in before continuing. Blake would have done the same thing.

"Did he say anything else?" Villa finally asked.

"No. At least, not to me. He gave both boys a kiss and told them to be good. I remember thinking it was very sweet."

"Did you notice anything about the twins' behavior?"

"I remember thinking they were quiet and subdued, but it was Monday morning. A lot of kids drag their feet on the first day back at school. I didn't notice anything that set off alarm bells."

"What did the defendant do after that?"

"He returned to his vehicle and left."

The prosecutor acknowledged her answer with a nod. "Thank you, Miss Long. I have no further questions."

Blake got to his feet. "Miss Long, you've only been at Lilyfield Elementary for a couple of months, right?"

"Yes, that's right. I'm filling in for a teacher who has taken maternity leave."

"And in the two months you've been there, you

haven't taught the Johnson twins, have you?"

"No."

Blake paused. "There are several sets of twins at Lilyfield Elementary, aren't there?"

"Yes. We have another set of identical twins in kindergarten and we have a set of fraternal twins in the second grade. I believe there are also a couple of sets of twins in the fifth grade."

"The other set of twins in kindergarten are male children, too, aren't they?"

"Yes, they are."

"And they look similar to the Johnson boys."

Miss Long frowned. "No, I don't think they look similar at all. The Johnson boys have red hair and freckles, like their mom. The other twins are fair. They're quite distinct from the Johnsons."

Blake couldn't prevent a frown. It wasn't the answer he'd hoped for. It served him right for asking a question when he didn't know the answer. Recovering quickly, he continued.

"I put it to you, Miss Long that you're mistaken when you say my client spoke to you outside the school yard."

The witness shook her head, looking confused. "No, he definitely did."

Blake swallowed a growl of frustration. One step forward, two steps back. It had been the story of his entire day. "Thank you, Miss Long. No further questions."

The judge cleared his throat. "All right. Well, it's almost four. I think this is an opportune time to call an end to the day. We'll resume tomorrow morning at ten. Bail is continued."

He banged the gavel and then stood and left through the doorway behind the bench. The sheriff ferried the jurors out through another exit. Blake drew in a deep breath and let it out on a heavy sigh. The second day was over. No doubt tomorrow would be just as tough. He wondered how Natalie was faring and allowed himself a glance in her direction.

She'd remained in her seat. Colby Shearer was speaking to her in low tones. No doubt he was giving her a rundown on the day's proceedings and informing her of what would take place the next day. The day had been a good one for the prosecution, but the most crucial evidence was yet to come. Blake prayed his psychiatrist was up to the challenge. If he wasn't, Ian Johnson could kiss his freedom good-bye. It was as simple as that.

Natalie dragged herself up the steps and across her front porch. Riffling in her handbag for her house keys, her fingers finally closed around them and she fitted the key in the lock. Pushing the door open with her shoulder, she closed it behind her and dropped her keys and handbag on the table that stood in the hall. The house was so quiet without her boys.

As much as she longed to have them by her side, she didn't want them to see her like this: sad and dejected, desolate beyond anything she could imagine. It wasn't as bad as the hours and days after Lacey's death, but it was close. Monica had stepped in then, too.

Monica. Natalie didn't know what she'd do without her best friend. She'd never be able to repay her for everything she'd done, and it wasn't just about minding the boys. Monica had been there for her in her darkest hour. She wouldn't forget that.

Tugging out her phone, she dialed her friend's number. She'd taken to calling Monica in the evenings to fill her in on the day's events. She also wanted to speak with her children, to hear her sons' voices. She might not be able to see them, but at least she could talk with them and hear about their day. At the moment, it was her favorite thing to do.

To her relief, Monica answered and after a brief hello, she put Natalie through to the boys. They both spoke over the top of each other until Natalie could barely tell what was being said, but they sounded happy enough and for that, she was glad.

"When are we coming home, Mommy?" Darby asked quietly.

Natalie bit her lip against a sharp sense of longing. "Soon, baby. I promise."

"Is Daddy going to jail?" Bailey asked.

"I don't know, honey. Maybe. He did a very bad thing. He needs to be punished."

"Isn't he sorry he hurt Lacey?" Darby asked.

"Yes, sweetheart. He's very sorry, but sometimes being sorry isn't enough."

"You're right," Bailey said matter-of-factly. "He should be punished."

Tears stung Natalie's eyes. She bit her lip harder against another surge of emotion. A sob caught in her throat. *This was so wrong.* Her little boys should never have had to even contemplate the need for their father to be punished, let alone accept that it needed to be done. It wasn't fair and it was all Ian's fault. She wanted to scream with the injustice of it.

Taking a deep breath, she did her best to hold onto her control. The last thing her sons needed was to hear their mother fall apart. Blowing kisses down the phone, she ended the call with forced cheerfulness before she completely lost control. Stumbling into the living room, she kicked off her sandals and then stubbed her toe on the couch in the dark. With a strangled curse, she collapsed against the cushions. Curling up into a ball, she cried her heart out.

CHAPTER 16

Blake shot a sideways glance in Natalie's direction. Dark circles shadowed the skin below her eyes. She was dressed simply in the same suit she'd worn on the first day only this time, it was teamed with a soft blue shirt. Her hair was once again pulled back into a bun. She sat quietly, staring straight ahead, barely blinking as the prosecutor led his expert witness through his evidence.

Professor Kevin Quirk was a forensic psychiatrist of some repute. With more than thirty-five years of clinical experience, there was no doubt he was well qualified to voice an opinion on the defendant's state of mind before, during and immediately after the offense. These days, Quirk spent most of his time examining defendants, usually at the request of the crown. Most of his money now came from court appearances.

Blake had come up against him in previous cases. Quirk was a forthright and believable witness, who spoke with confidence and grace.

He had a deep, authoritative voice that resonated through the room. Juries tended to hang on his every word. His full head of thick white hair and regal bearing added to his air of authority. In short, he was a tough witness to crack. Blake had his work cut out for him that day.

After establishing the psychiatrist's impressive credentials, Villa put his first real question to his witness.

"Professor Quirk, did you examine the defendant?"

"Yes."

"On how many occasions did you meet with the defendant?"

"He came to my office three times."

"And were you able to draw a conclusion about his state of mind at the time of the offense?"

"Yes."

"Please tell the court about your conclusions," the prosecutor invited.

Quirk cleared his throat and looked directly at the jury. "I examined the defendant extensively on three separate occasions. I found him to be a normal, clear-thinking adult. At the time of the offense, I believe he knew exactly what he was doing. He was furious at his ex-wife and the recent family law court decision. He wanted to get back at both his ex-wife and the judge who'd made the decision."

There was an angry outburst from the direction of the dock, but the witness appeared unperturbed. The judge cautioned Blake to keep his client quiet and then instructed the prosecutor to continue.

"Professor, would you say that a normal person would do what society deems to be normal things?"

"Yes."

"So if I told you a man driving his car was obeying traffic rules, using his indicators to change lanes, putting on his hazard lights when he became stationary, would you consider this to be a demonstration of normal behavior?"

"Yes, I would."

"Professor, what is dissociation?"

The professor leaned back in his chair and gave the appearance that he was well versed with the concept and wanted to take his time to explain.

"Dissociation is a mental process of disconnecting from one's thoughts, feelings, memories or sense of identity. It most commonly occurs in children who have suffered some form of prolonged trauma, such as sexual or physical abuse. The stress of war or natural disasters may also cause dissociation."

"What percentage of the population suffer from such a state?" the prosecutor asked.

"About seven percent," Quirk replied.

The prosecutor nodded. "Thank you, Professor. In your professional opinion and based on your extensive examination of the defendant, at the time of the offense, do you think the defendant was acting in a dissociative state?"

"No."

Once again, there was a loud mutter of

disagreement from the dock. Blake turned and glared at Ian over his shoulder. They didn't need another rebuke from the judge.

"Why have you come to this conclusion?" Villa asked.

The professor cleared his throat. "A number of factors. The defendant told me the idea of throwing one of his children off the side of Anzac Bridge came to him as he was driving across it that morning. He used his indicators to change lanes and when he pulled over, he had the foresight to activate his hazard lights, as is the normal procedure to alert other commuters to the fact he'd come to a halt.

"There were three children seated in the back of the defendant's vehicle. When I asked him why he chose his daughter and not his sons, he explained that he realized his five-year-old boys would be too heavy to toss over the high steel and wire barricade that separated the road from the water below." The professor paused and looked straight at the jury. "Someone with such clear thinking processes was most certainly not acting in a dissociative state."

Blake kept his expression neutral. The professor's evidence had been powerful. Blake only hoped he could counteract it. He steeled himself for what was to come.

"Thank you, Professor. I have no further questions." The prosecutor returned to his seat.

Natalie eased a tense breath out between her dry lips. The crown's expert witness had come across well. He was both confident and believable. His words had resonated with the jury. She could tell it from the expressions on their faces. They'd listened closely to his testimony and they'd believed him, just like she did.

Her heart sank at the indisputable confirmation that Ian had been fully aware of his actions when he'd tossed their little girl over the side of the bridge. The dreadful knowledge devastated her all over again. Still, she held on to her emotions as tightly as she could and only a single hot tear escaped and rolled down her cheek.

She looked across at Blake and saw him organizing his notes. It was his turn to cross examine the witness. Looking tall and handsome in his flowing black robes and wig, he stood and eyed the man who had remained in the witness box.

"Professor Quirk," he began. "You said my client was a normal, clear-thinking adult who had carried out his actions for no other reason than to get back at his ex-wife and a judge. That's correct, isn't it?"

"Yes."

"It's true, isn't it, Professor, that a person in a dissociative state has disconnected from their feelings, thoughts and memories. That's what you said, right?"

"Yes."

"And that a person acting normally does normal things."

"Yes."

"You agreed with the prosecutor when he said obeying traffic rules, using indicators and the like were all signs of normal behavior."

"Yes, that's right. It's the way most of us behave, most of the time."

Blake stared at the witness. "What about when Mr Johnson climbed onto the roof of his car? Was that normal behavior?"

"Not exactly," the professor conceded.

"What about when my client tossed his little girl over the side of the bridge? Was that something you'd expect to see someone do who was acting normally?"

"No."

Blake nodded. He paused a moment before continuing. "You said that approximately seven percent of the population suffer from dissociation, but that's not true, is it?"

The professor frowned. "Yes, of course it's true."

"But that's only a guess, isn't it, Professor? Those statistics only count the people who come into contact with health professionals, don't they?"

"I... I suppose so," the professor replied.

"There are many more people who suffer from this kind of dissociative state who never come to the attention of the medical profession and who therefore go undiagnosed and uncounted, right?"

"Yes, that could be true," the professor conceded with obvious reluctance.

"So the fact you say only seven percent of the population suffer from this illness is not technically correct, is it?" Blake insisted.

"No, I guess not."

Blake nodded in satisfaction. Natalie released her breath. He'd scored a fair point.

"Professor, you said that Mr Johnson had told you he deliberately chose his daughter over his boys because they were too heavy to toss over the barricade, is that right?"

"Yes."

"I put it to you that my client didn't say that."

"You're wrong. He did."

Unperturbed, Blake plowed on. "Tell me, Professor. Dissociation can last a few moments or years, can't it?"

"Yes, that's right."

"I put it to you, Professor that during the time Ian Johnson made and acted on the decision to throw his daughter over the side of the bridge, he was acting in a dissociative state, completely disconnected from his conscience and from everything he knew to be right—and as such, cannot be held responsible for his actions."

Once again, the professor frowned. "No. No, I don't agree with that. The evidence shows—"

"Nothing further, Your Honor," Blake interrupted and returned to his seat.

The prosecutor got to his feet. "Professor Quirk, in your professional opinion, and after your extensive examination of the accused, was Ian Johnson suffering from dissociation at the time he threw his little girl over the side of the bridge?"

The professor looked directly at the jury and answered in a strong, clear voice. "No."

Villa nodded, satisfied. He looked back toward the judge. "The prosecution rests."

The judge cleared his throat and looked back at the lawyers. "All right. We'll take a short recess. Mr Harton, are you ready to proceed with your first witness?"

Blake stood and addressed the judge. "Yes, Your Honor. We are."

"Very good. We'll see you after the break."

As the jurors filed past the bar table, Blake took care to keep his expression neutral. He'd made some inroads into the professor's testimony, but there was no denying the man's evidence was damning. Coupled with Ian's admission that he deliberately chose his little girl to toss over the bridge and it was all Blake could do not to throw in the towel. He only hoped he could resurrect something from Ian's testimony—that was, if Ian agreed to testify.

Australia's legal system was a common law system inherited from England at the time of colonization. It recognized that the accused wasn't required to give evidence. If a defendant chose to exercise his right to silence in this way, it was mandatory for the judge to give the jury an explicit direction not to read anything into the fact the defendant chose not to give evidence on his own behalf.

Blake hadn't discussed the matter with his client since the first day of the trial, but the truth was, if Ian were to have any hope of getting the jury to return a not-guilty verdict, he'd have to take the stand. The jury had heard from the police, the eyewitnesses, the ex-wife and the experts and they wanted to hear from him, to hear him describe his state of mind and what the hell had been going through his head at the moment when he decided to toss his baby over the side of the bridge to almost certain death.

From the corner of his eye, Blake saw Natalie stand and make her way toward the exit. She didn't once look his way. He sighed quietly, wishing—not for the first time—that they'd met under different circumstances. With no other choice, he resigned himself to the fact that the timing was all wrong and there wasn't a damn thing he could do about it.

————

Natalie splashed water over her face and patted it dry with a tissue. She peered at her reflection in the mirror that lined the wall of the restroom and frowned at the image that looked back at her. At some point during the night, she'd made her way to her bed and had woken in the early hours reaching for her sons. They weren't there. The bed had been as empty and desolate as the emptiness that surrounded her now and in the darkness of the night, the trial in all its harrowing detail had come rushing back to her.

She longed for her children to be close by her side, safe and protected from harm. She longed for her baby, who would never be coming back.

She longed for a time when she'd been happy...

Without conscious effort, her thoughts turned to Blake who continued to look the epitome of the successful barrister—tall and commanding, handsome enough to turn the heads of most of the female occupants in the courtroom, including those on the jury. Natalie could only hope they wouldn't be swayed by his good looks and charm and would listen to the evidence and make their decision accordingly.

The prosecution had finished with their witnesses. It was now the defense's turn. That meant Ian. Colby had told her that morning when she'd arrived at court that they assumed her ex-husband would take the stand. The evidence so far had been damning. The jury wanted to hear from him. Colby told her if the accused was his client, he darn well would have been doing everything he could to convince the man he had to testify, despite the fact that a jury wasn't supposed to read anything into the fact if he chose not to.

The thought of watching and listening to Ian explain his thoughts and actions that fateful day sent a shiver of icy apprehension down Natalie's spine. *How could she sit there and listen to him talk about his decision to throw their baby to her death? How could she not?* Natalie hadn't been given the opportunity to ask Ian why he'd done what he had. This was her chance to discover the truth, to put some meaning into something that until now was totally incomprehensible. She needed to listen and hopefully accept what her baby's father had to say. She'd sit through his testimony, if it killed her.

With that grim thought, she collected her handbag from beside the sink and exited the restroom. By the time she reached the door that led into the courtroom, her palms were cold and sweaty and her heart beat double time. She forced deep breaths into her lungs and did her best to calm herself. The last thing she needed was another panic attack—right before Ian took the stand. It would only delay his testimony and she wanted this over and done with as quickly as possible. She wanted to put the nightmare behind her and wrest back some form of control over her life.

As she walked down the center aisle and made her way back to her seat, she glanced at Blake. He was looking over his notes. His expression was focused, his body language calm and composed. He gave off an air of confidence that was almost inspiring and would have been if they'd been on the same side. He was everything a client wanted in a lawyer. His reputation for being the best was well earned. She only hoped his skill didn't jeopardize the guilty verdict she longed for, no *needed,* in order to find some kind of closure.

Way before she was ready, the judge re-entered, took his position on the bench and asked for the jury to be sent in. When they were seated, he directed Blake to call his first witness. Natalie's belly clenched with dread.

Dressed in the same cheap suit and tie he'd

worn the previous two days, Ian stood and made his way to the witness box. After taking the oath and swearing to tell the truth, he settled himself in his seat and waited for the questioning to begin.

Blake stood and went through the same routine questions the prosecutor had done with her. They established that her ex-husband was a thirty-year-old, self-employed plumber. He was divorced and the father to three children, one of whom was the victim at the heart of the murder trial. Not giving the jury time to dwell on that fact longer than necessary, Blake hurried on.

"Mr Johnson, you were married for nearly seven years. Was it a happy marriage?"

Ian shrugged. "Happy enough for most of the time. It was only toward the end that things turned sour. It just didn't work out."

"What about your children? Can you tell the court about them?"

Ian's expression relaxed into a smile. Pride shone from his eyes. "I have twin boys, Darby and Bailey. They're five. I love them with everything I have."

"And what about Lacey?" Blake asked gently.

Natalie couldn't help but admire his courage for addressing the elephant in the room head on. Everyone present knew her father had thrown her to her death. Everyone in the room was waiting to hear why.

Ian's eyes welled up with tears. He looked down at his hands that were clenched in his lap. "Lacey. What can I say?" he replied quietly. "She was my princess, my sweet baby girl. I loved her so much!" His voice choked on a sob, but he managed to continue through his distress. "I can't believe what I did! I can't believe she's gone! I'm so sorry, baby! Daddy loved you so much! I'm so sorry!"

Huge sobs shook his shoulders and he buried his face in his hands. The courtroom was deathly silent. Not a single person listening to the testimony was unmoved. Tears stung Natalie's eyes, but she made no effort to wipe them away. Several of the jurors were also crying. Giving Ian time to compose himself, Blake was slow to ask his next question.

"Mr Johnson, it's obvious how deeply you feel about your children. When you and your wife separated, did you seek primary custody?"

Ian swiped at his eyes with the back of his hand, sniffed and nodded. "Yes, of course I did!"

"Was it because you thought your ex-wife was a bad mother?"

"No, never! She was a great mom! She's still a great mom!"

He looked in Natalie's direction and her eyes once again filled with tears. Her chest tightened on a surge of emotion she was powerless to control.

"It was never about my wife's limitations as a mother. It was more about my need to have my children living with me, learning and growing with me by their side, every day." He shrugged and then added. "It's hard when a couple separates." He eyed the jury. "If any of you have been there before, you know what I mean. You want your kids and so does your ex. Both of you can't win. Unfortunately for me, I was the one who lost."

"You fought for them in the family court?" Blake asked quietly.

"Yes. I spent every penny I had on lawyers. Why do you think I drive that piece of junk HiLux? I sold my brand new Ford Ranger to help finance my legal costs. The court case dragged on for two years."

Natalie swallowed a quiet sigh. She'd also spent most of her savings on legal fees.

"When was the final decision made?" Blake asked.

"The Friday before Lacey's death. I can't remember the date, but I'm sure you do."

"Friday, October sixth," Blake supplied.

Ian shrugged. "I believe you."

"On that day, the judge handed down his decision in your long-running family court case, correct?"

"Yes."

"Who was given primary custody of your children?"

"I already told you. The judge gave custody to my ex-wife."

"By your ex-wife, you mean Natalie Johnson?"

Ian flicked a narrow-eyed glance in her direction and then answered Blake's question. "Yes."

"You were given access to them?"

"Yes. Every other weekend."

The words were uttered without inflection, but Natalie caught the bitterness in her ex-husband's eyes. She marveled that he could control himself so well in this courtroom. He hadn't shown any such restraint in the family court.

"How did that make you feel?" Blake asked quietly.

Ian blew his breath out on a heavy sigh. "I was furious," he admitted. "I raged like a wounded bull. I'm embarrassed to admit I narrowly escaped being charged with offensive conduct that day."

Blake nodded sympathetically. Natalie's hands clenched into fists. Ian was doing a good job of convincing the jurors he was genuinely contrite. She hoped they'd see through his ruse. Then again, maybe he was? What did she know? He was like a stranger to her these days.

"Why were you so upset at losing custody of your children, Ian?"

"They were my kids! I had as much right to them as Natalie! I loved them and they loved me!"

"What did you do after the court handed down its decision?" Blake asked.

"I left the courthouse and called my brother."

"What's your brother's name?"

"Keith Johnson. I called him and told him what happened. I let off some steam. He calmed me down, told me it would be all right. I walked around for a while and tried to get my head straightened out. After that, I stopped by Natalie's house. It was my weekend to have the kids."

"Were they happy to see you?"

"Yes, they were always happy to spend time with me. Lacey kept asking when I was going to move back home and live with them."

Once again, Blake shot his client a look filled

with understanding and sympathy. Natalie clenched her jaw against a burst of anger. She and Ian had made an effort to keep the difficulties in their relationship from their kids. It wasn't Lacey's fault that she didn't understand her parents were through with each other and that her daddy would never live with them again.

"What did you do over the weekend?" Blake asked.

"On Friday night, we watched a movie at home. I think it was *Beauty and the Beast*. I made popcorn. Over the weekend, we went to the zoo and to the beach. It was warm enough to swim. We had ice cream and pizza." He shrugged. "We had fun."

"Were you still angry?"

"No."

"But at some point, you did get angry again, right?"

Once again, Ian sighed. His shoulders slumped despondently. "Right."

"Tell us what happened."

"It was Monday morning. I overslept. We were running late and it was mayhem trying to get the kids up and dressed and ready for school. I was supposed to take them back to their mother's place. The kids wanted to stay with me. They were upset when I told them no. I started to explain that the judge had decided they were to live with their mom permanently, but they didn't understand and I didn't have time to get into it with them. They had to get to school."

Natalie started in surprise and sat up straighter

in her seat. This was the first she'd heard of her children not wanting to return home. She narrowed her gaze at Ian and wondered if he was telling the truth. Short of quizzing her sons, there was no way to know for sure. The surge of anger she'd forced back earlier, rekindled.

"Is that when you started getting angry?" Blake asked.

"I guess so. I got mad all over again about the judge's decision. It wasn't fair. He had no right to choose Natalie over me. He didn't even know us and he didn't know my kids! The more I thought about it, the angrier I got. Then I received *another* call from Natalie."

"What did she say?"

"She chewed my ass out for being late and accused me of doing it on purpose. I just lit up. I saw red."

"What did you say?"

"I told her I'd take the kids to school so no one would be late. She calmed down and accepted my offer. We ended the call."

"What happened next?"

Natalie's fingers dug into her seat and her stomach went cold with dread. The next few moments were going to be the hardest. She steeled herself against what her ex-husband was about to say.

"I was driving the kids to school. We were going across Anzac Bridge. I live in Glebe. It's west of the city. The kids live with their mother in the northern suburbs. They go to school in Lilyfield. It was out of my way, but I'd told Natalie I'd do the school run. I kept thinking about her—Natalie—and how she was always mad at me for something; how the judge sided with her; how she got to see our kids almost every day. And when I did have them, she kept calling… It didn't seem right and it definitely wasn't fair. The angry thoughts I'd experienced the Friday before, resurfaced.

"I remember my hands tightening around the steering wheel as the anger kept growing in my head. I wanted to do something to hurt Natalie, like she'd hurt me. She could have let me have our children. She could have agreed to be the one with the weekend visits. Instead, she fought me every step of the way and in the end, she won."

"So, you were on the bridge and you were growing increasingly angry. What happened next?" Blake asked.

"I remember looking in the rearview mirror at the kids who were sitting in the back. Bailey was on the far side and Darby was behind me. Lacey was in her car seat in the middle."

"Is it true that you told Professor Quirk that you chose Lacey because she was the lightest of the three and therefore easier to carry?"

Ian shook his head in adamant denial. "No, I didn't tell him that."

Blake stared at his client. "You're sure?"

Ian held his gaze without flinching. "I'm certain."

Natalie's mouth fell open. The professor had given evidence that Ian had said just that. One of them wasn't telling the truth. She had a terrible feeling it was her ex. She glanced at the jury for their reaction. Most appeared to pick up on the inconsistency and were looking at Ian with a mixture of surprise, doubt and speculation.

"What else do you remember?" Blake asked.

Ian shook his head. "I don't remember anything after that. I saw the kids...saw Lacey... That's all. The next thing I remember is getting *another* call from Natalie. She asked me where Lacey was. I told her... I told her Lacey was gone."

"What did you mean by that?"

Ian shrugged and stared down at his hands. "I don't know. I guess that she was dead."

Natalie whimpered and pushed a fist against her mouth in an effort to hold back a sob. Every word of that conversation was seared into her brain and the agony of it hadn't eased. Several of the jurors looked shocked. One of the older men glared at Ian with narrowed eyes.

"Did you tell your ex-wife that you'd dropped your sons off at school?"

"No, we didn't mention the boys. She only wanted to talk about Lacey."

Natalie gasped. Now she knew for certain Ian was lying.

Blake cleared his throat. "Do you remember changing lanes and pulling over on the bridge?"

"No."

"Do you remember taking Lacey out of the car and climbing onto the roof of your truck?"

"No."

"Do you have any memory of throwing your daughter over the side of the bridge to her death?"

"No."

Once again, she was filled with rage that came from the certainty her ex-husband was lying. He'd *told* her he'd tossed their daughter over the side of the bridge. There was no way he hadn't been aware, right from the very beginning and for a long time afterward, of exactly what he'd planned.

Natalie stared at Blake. *Surely he knew his client was lying?* Wasn't it his job to find out the truth? Or perhaps he didn't want to know? Even though the rational part of her accepted that he represented her ex-husband and it was his job to do everything he could to secure an acquittal, she couldn't bear the thought that a win was more important to him than the truth.

With her gaze still narrowed on him, she watched him nod in response to his client's answers, as if satisfied with them. He glanced up at the judge. "I have no further questions."

Chapter 17

Blake returned to his seat. He didn't dare look in Natalie's direction. He hoped he'd done enough and was relieved Ian had managed to keep his cool throughout the examination. They'd talked about it during the break. It was okay for the jury to see an upset father who was angry at losing his kids. That was understandable. What was less acceptable was an angry ex-husband who had deliberately set out on the most awful course of revenge.

Blake hoped Ian's circumstances would resonate with those members of the jury who'd experienced the breakdown of a marriage. Given that there were twelve of them, the odds that at least two or three were separated or divorced were in his favor, despite the fact the ones that had made such admissions during questioning had been struck out during the jury selection process. Not everyone was prepared to air their dirty laundry in public. Sometimes, jurors weren't quite forthcoming with specific details of their personal lives. It was just the way it was and it was what he was counting on.

Blake had been surprised and disconcerted by the fact Ian had denied any memory of tossing his daughter off the side of the bridge. There had been that phone call to his wife, after all and Ian had talked about climbing onto the roof of his car with Lacey during the first interview Blake had with him. The knowledge that his client might be lying under oath didn't sit well with Blake, but short of requesting that he be excused from the trial, there was nothing he could do. If he refused to represent Ian at this late stage, a mistrial would be declared. Johnson would be obliged to find another barrister and the whole sorry trial would start again. Natalie would be forced to testify all over again, to relive the horrific moments again and again. It would never be over.

No, his only recourse was to hope Villa did his job properly and caught on to the fact that the defendant hadn't told the truth. Blake returned to his seat with dread churning in his gut. Greg Villa got to his feet and Blake braced himself in anticipation of the prosecutor's cross examination.

"You were angry when your ex-wife called you that morning and demanded to know why you were late, weren't you?" Villa began.

"Yes. Like I said, she was always calling wanting to speak with the kids or chewing me out about something."

"You were still at your home when she called, right?"

"Yes. I overslept. We were running late."

"How long did it take for you to get the children ready and get on the road?"

Ian thought for a moment. "Twenty-five minutes or so, I guess. I don't know exactly."

"I assume in that time you got the kids out of bed, dressed, breakfasted, repacked their overnight bags. If they're anything like my kids, you hunted around for lost shoes and missing clothes, right?"

Ian chuckled. "Right, that's exactly what it was like. Lacey couldn't find her sandals."

The prosecutor smiled in response. "Did you find them?"

"Yes. But it took awhile. That was one of the reasons I offered to take them to school. They were dressed and ready to go."

Villa acknowledged Ian's comment with a nod. Blake's gut clenched with nerves. Ian was being far too chatty, offering up more information than was asked. They'd talked about keeping his answers brief. It appeared he'd forgotten those instructions. Blake hoped it wouldn't be his client's downfall.

"So on the morning of Lacey's death, you got your children up and dressed, found lost shoes, packed up bags and got them all out the door and ready for school, right?"

"Yes, that's right."

"And this took about twenty-five minutes, correct?"

"Yes."

"So twenty-five minutes after the phone call from your ex-wife who was annoyed at you for being late, you finally got out the door?"

"Well, no, it was more like ten, maybe fifteen. We were already up and dressed when she called. We just weren't quite ready to leave."

"And during that ten or fifteen minutes, you were still angry, weren't you?"

The brusque words were stated more than posed as a question, but Blake's client answered all the same.

"Yes, of course I was. I was annoyed that Natalie had picked a fight with me over something so trivial. She accused me of being late on purpose. She said I was doing it out of spite. It was bullsh—I mean, it was nonsense. Of course I didn't do it on purpose. The very idea is ludicrous!"

"Ian..." Blake murmured under his breath, willing his client to hold his temper in check.

The last thing they needed was to let the jury get a hint of the anger Ian kept hidden deep inside. Blake had glimpsed it in his office. He didn't need to see it again and neither did the twelve people who held the outcome of Ian's trial in their hands. Then again, given what he knew about Ian's less than truthful testimony, perhaps it was for the best. Under the cover of his black robes, Blake's hands clenched into fists and a fresh wave of nerves rushed through his gut.

"So, you got the kids into the car and headed over the bridge. You were taking them to school, right?"

"Yes."

"And still, you were angry."

"Yes."

"It was peak hour, wasn't it?"

"Yes."

"The traffic was heavy."

"Yes."

"You were traveling slowly."

"Yes."

"And all the time you were thinking about your ex-wife and the court decision and the tough hand you'd been dealt."

"Yes."

"And somewhere along the way, in the middle of all that morning traffic, you decided to get back at your ex-wife, to show her who was boss. That's what happened, wasn't it?"

"No, it wasn't like that." Ian practically snarled.

The prosecutor's eyebrows lifted in surprise. "Oh, so you remember that much of the morning, do you? Sorry, I'm getting a little confused about when exactly your memory started to fail."

Ian's expression darkened and lines furrowed across his brow. Once again, Blake tensed.

"Mr Johnson, before you got on the bridge, you went through at least a dozen traffic lights. You didn't run any red lights, did you?"

"No."

"And when you were driving along Anzac Bridge in heavy, peak hour traffic, you obeyed the traffic rules, didn't you?"

"Yes."

"In fact, at least one witness saw you use your indicators to change lanes. Do you deny doing that?"

Ian shrugged. "I don't remember."

"That's very convenient of you, Mr Johnson."

Blake leaped to his feet. "Objection, Your Honor! The prosecutor is badgering the witness."

Villa waved his hand in the air. "Withdrawn."

Blake scowled. The fact that Villa withdrew the question was hardly recompense. The jury had already heard the cynicism in the prosecutor's tone. At least some of them would be thinking the same thing.

Villa cleared his throat and stared balefully at Blake's client. "Let me put this to you, Mr Johnson. See, I think you knew exactly what you were doing from the time you ended that call from your ex-wife. You were mad. In fact, you were furious—at your ex, at the judge, at life. You'd just lost a two-year battle to keep your kids and once again, your ex-wife was giving you a hard time. You piled the kids in your car and you kept stewing every mile that you drove. You looked in your rearview mirror and a plan began to formulate; a plan to get back at your ex-wife. You put on your indicator, switched lanes and pulled over into the lane nearest to the steel barrier. You'd already decided to throw one of your children off the bridge. You realized it would be easiest to toss your daughter. I'm right, aren't I?"

Ian shook his head, his expression adamant. "No, you're wrong! It wasn't like that!"

The prosecutor plowed right on, his voice rising in volume and intensity. "With your mind made up, you climbed out of the car and grabbed your little girl. You deliberately chose her because you realized the barrier you needed to clear in order to throw her into the water was high—at least ten foot—too high for you to toss one of your sons over. So, you took Lacey—sweet baby Lacey who was only three years old—you took her in your arms, you climbed onto the roof of your vehicle in order to get the height you needed. And then, without pause, you tossed that poor baby to her death."

"No! No! No!" Ian shouted, his face flushing with anger. "That's not how it happened! That's not how it was!"

"How do you know, Mr Johnson?" Villa said smoothly. "You don't have any memory past the time you looked in the rearview mirror, remember?"

"I didn't mean to kill my little girl! I swear it!" Ian cried, his breath coming fast.

The prosecutor remained unperturbed. "I put it to you, Mr Johnson that you're lying when you say you didn't tell Professor Quirk that you made a deliberate decision to take Lacey because she was light enough to toss."

"No! I didn't say that!"

"Mr Johnson, after you got rid of Lacey, you returned to your vehicle and continued across the bridge, didn't you?"

"I don't know."

"You dropped your sons off at school. You had a brief conversation with one of the teachers and kissed the boys good-bye. When your ex-wife called a little while later, you told her you'd taken your sons to school."

"No, I didn't say that," Ian insisted, his jaw thrust out stubbornly. "We only talked about Lacey."

"I put it to you that you *did* talk about the boys. That's the reason why your ex-wife telephoned their school."

Ian glared at the prosecutor. "No, you're making things up," he denied heatedly.

"That might be your opinion, Mr Johnson, but we've heard testimony from other witnesses who recall exactly that. All very normal behavior; don't you think?"

Once again, Blake got to his feet. "Objection, Your Honor. The prosecution's own expert agreed that a dissociative state can last for as little as a few moments. It is the defense's position that by the time my client returned to his car and drove across the bridge that he'd returned to some degree of normality, enough that he could function in a normal way."

The judge nodded. "Sustained."

Villa smiled like a cat that had gotten the cream. Blake froze. He'd made a mistake. He was sure of it. A moment later, the prosecutor confirmed it.

"Mr Johnson, do you agree with what your lawyer just said? That by the time you returned to your vehicle after tossing your child over the side of the bridge, you'd come out of your state of funk and were more or less back to normal?"

Blake's client hesitated and Blake silently willed the man to disagree.

"Yes, I guess so."

"So, you *do* remember getting off the bridge, dropping your boys at school?"

Ian frowned in confusion, obviously uncertain about what to say. "I...I don't think so. No, I don't remember going to the boys' school."

"How else then did your sons arrive at school?"

Ian's brow furrowed in confusion. "I don't know. I guess I must have dropped them there. But I don't remember doing it and I definitely didn't talk to any teacher."

"And yet we've heard testimony from independent witnesses who said you did just that and appeared to be acting in a normal manner."

Ian shrugged. "If you say so."

"Because someone who was truly out of their funk would realize the enormity of what they'd done and would call the police, wouldn't they?" Villa stated, his voice pure steel.

"Yes, I guess so."

"And you didn't."

"No."

The prosecutor paused and shuffled through the papers in front of him. Blake knew it was a ploy to give the jury time to ponder the last few statements. He'd used the same tactic many times himself. A moment later, Villa looked up at Ian.

"You told us during your questioning that you didn't know what you meant when you told your ex-wife that Lacey was gone and it was only after Mr Harton prompted you that you agreed that you probably meant she was dead, but that's not true, is it, Mr Johnson?"

"Yes, it is!"

"I put it to you that you didn't just tell your ex-wife that Lacey was gone. You told her you'd thrown your daughter off the bridge. There could have been no doubt in your mind at that moment that your daughter was dead. There was simply no guessing about it. You knew she couldn't have survived that fall and that's exactly what you intended!"

"No! No! That's not right! I didn't know! I didn't mean it!"

The prosecutor plowed on. "Mr Johnson, you say this anger of yours, this anger that drove you to the point where you lost complete control over your senses and threw your baby to her death, arose from a family court decision that didn't go your way. Is that correct?"

"Yes. That's correct."

"And yet, the judge gave you generous access to your children, did he not?"

Ian's face turned an angry red and even from the distance that separated them, Blake could see his client's whole body tense. Blake's gut clenched. Villa was goading Ian into losing his temper and from what Blake could see, it was working.

"Generous, my ass!" Ian exploded and spittle flew from his mouth. "Two days every fortnight!" he screamed. "Two *fucking* days! You call that *generous?*"

Blake kept his gaze fixed on the bar table, not game to look any of the jurors in the eye. He was sure they were all staring at his client in horror. In a few short seconds, Ian had gone from a man who was understandably upset about losing a custody battle to one who was almost foaming at the mouth. All of a sudden, the extent of his anger over the custody dispute became crystal clear and Blake was sure there wasn't a single person on the jury who doubted his client was capable of murdering his child as a payback to the woman who, in his mind, had stolen his children away.

Blake risked a glance in Natalie's direction and swore under his breath. Her beautiful green eyes were pools of pain. Tears rolled down her cheeks. He'd never seen her looking so desolate. He wanted to go to her, to take her in his arms. He wanted to wash away her heartache and make everything better.

But he couldn't do any of those things—and in fact he had to represent her ex to the best of his ability—and the knowledge ate at him. All of a sudden, he was done with this trial, done with Ian Johnson. He wanted to throw in the towel, storm out of the courtroom, leave his client to whatever was to come.

And then reality reared its ugly head and he slumped down in his seat. He didn't walk out on things when they were headed in the wrong direction. No, he was Blake Harton Junior. When the going got tough, he got tougher. He'd built his reputation on that very motto and it had seen him through some difficult situations. Some just as difficult as this one. He still had his expert witness to come. Hopefully the learned Professor Jackson-

Lane would salvage the car wreck his case had just become.

Once Ian was excused from the witness box, the judge took a short adjournment. All too soon, the parties returned to the courtroom and the judge invited Blake to call his next witness. He stood. "The defense calls Professor Albert Jackson-Lane."

The door to the courtroom opened and a small, elderly gentleman with a shiny, bald head strode down the aisle and took his place in the witness box. After swearing an oath to tell the truth, Blake started with the preliminaries.

In short succession, he established that Professor Jackson-Lane was a man with impressive credentials in the field of psychiatry and more than forty years of experience in the field. The man still had an office in the city and continued to service his regular clients. No one in the courtroom could dispute the professor's expertise in his field. He was the perfect candidate to offer a professional opinion on the state of mind of the defendant at the time of the offense. Blake was counting on him to blow the jury away.

"Professor, you've heard of the term dissociation?"

"Yes, of course. It is a recognized medical condition."

"Can you tell us what it is?"

"Dissociation can be defined as disruptions in aspects of consciousness, such as identity, memory, physical actions and the environment."

"And what symptoms might a person suffering

dissociation experience?" Blake asked.

"Well, the specific signs and symptoms can vary depending upon the type of dissociative disorder the person's experiencing."

"So, it's a disorder, is it?" Blake asked.

"Yes, it certainly can be," the professor replied. "When a person experiences severe dissociation symptoms, they may be diagnosed with a dissociative disorder. Some of the symptoms can include a major inability to remember personally relevant events that goes beyond mere forgetfulness. People can experience confused and dazed wandering; they can also have two or more identities or personality traits within them, also known as split personality. Some people experience a feeling that objects in the external world are changing in shape and size or feeling that people around them are automated or inhuman."

"Professor, this is fascinating stuff, but I wonder how this relates to Ian Johnson. You examined Ian on several occasions, didn't you?"

"Yes. Ian visited my offices four times over the course of a number of weeks. We spoke for an hour at a time."

"And over the course of these four hours of consultation, were you able to draw any conclusions about my client's state of mind at the time of the offense?"

"I was. You see, I listed for you the most common symptoms of a severe dissociation disorder, but there can be other signs that someone is suffering from a dissociative state."

"Can you please elaborate, Professor?"

"Of course. Mental health problems such as depression, anxiety and suicidal thoughts and actions are a classic sign of dissociation. More importantly, feeling a sense of detachment from oneself, like seeing one's life as if they're watching a movie is another symptom of the condition."

Blake nodded. He'd been over the professor's testimony. There were no surprises. The evidence was being relayed as rehearsed.

"Professor, when you examined Mr Johnson, what conclusions did you draw?"

"I spoke to your client at length about his thoughts and feelings leading up to the offense, and afterwards. He told me about feeling like he was outside his body, like he was viewing what was happening from a distance and though he could see what was going on, he was helpless to stop it. As a result, I came to the conclusion that at the time of the offense, he was suffering from a dissociative state."

"That's your professional opinion?" Blake asked.

"Yes, Mr Harton. That's my professional opinion."

Blake nodded, satisfied with the answer. "Can this kind of dissociative state come without warning?"

"Sometimes."

"One more thing, Professor. In your professional opinion, is a person who suffers a dissociative state responsible for their actions?"

"It depends upon the symptoms they're experiencing, but in the case of Mr Johnson where he was suffering what we commonly refer to as 'an out of body experience,' my answer is, no. I don't think someone in that state can be held responsible for their actions."

CHAPTER 18

Natalie looked down at her fingernails and realized she'd chewed them to the quick. She'd listened to the testimony given by Blake's expert and felt even more confused. On the one hand, people saw Ian acting normally right up to, and including, the moment he'd thrown Lacey to her death and afterwards. On the other hand, a reputable psychiatrist was convinced Ian had been acting outside of his usual mental state and couldn't be held responsible for what happened. But her ex's claims were full of holes. Did he remember throwing their daughter over the bridge, or did he really not recollect what happened? Surely it couldn't be both. What was the truth? She sighed quietly and waited for the prosecutor to begin his cross examination. She didn't have to wait long.

Greg Villa got to his feet, looking stern and commanding. "Professor Jackson-Lane, you said that this kind of dissociation can come without warning, didn't you?"

"Yes, that's correct."

"But that's unusual, isn't it?"

"Yes, it is."

"In fact, most sufferers of this kind of disorder suffer for many months or years, correct?"

"Yes, that's correct."

"And in fact, the number of diagnosed sufferers equals about seven percent, right?"

"Yes. Those are the official statistics."

"Do you disagree with the statistics, Professor?"

The professor flushed. "No, but I've been a psychiatrist for many years. In my experience, there are many others experiencing these kind of symptoms that go undiagnosed."

"Be that as it may," Villa continued, "the only statistics we have reveal that a mere seven percent of the population suffer from this kind of disorder, correct?"

"Yes, that's correct."

"Tell me, Professor, when someone is experiencing the kind of dissociation you say the defendant was experiencing at the time of the offense, is it likely they'd follow rules such as stopping for red lights, keeping to the speed limit, using indicators to change lanes—that kind of thing?"

The professor shifted in his seat and looked uncomfortable. "No," he said reluctantly.

"Professor, in all your years of attending clients in your psychiatric practice, have you ever known someone suffering from this kind of disorder to present with no symptoms prior to the event?"

Once again, the witness looked uncomfortable. "No."

"Professor, you say that the defendant told you he experienced an out-of-body state while this terrible event was unfolding, right?"

"Yes, that's how he described it to me."

"Would it surprise you to know that today, the defendant gave sworn testimony to the effect that he couldn't remember *anything* past the time he first drove onto the bridge?"

The professor nodded slowly. "Yes, that would surprise me."

"It's contrary to what he told you over the course of several meetings, isn't it?"

"Yes, it is."

"Tell me, Professor, do you think the defendant was lying then, or now?"

Blake shot to his feet. "Objection! Your Honor, this isn't a question this witness can answer."

The judge looked sternly down at Blake. "It's a fair question, Mr Harton and one you should have given some thought to before you put your client on the stand. I'll let the question stand and I direct the witness to answer it."

Blake dropped back into his seat. With a gargantuan effort, he kept his emotions from showing on his face. He focused his attention on the bar table in front of him.

The professor cleared his throat. "I'm not sure I can properly answer that question."

"But you agree, don't you, Professor, that the two statements are in direct conflict with one another, right?"

"Yes. If one has no memory of an event, it's impossible to recall how one felt during that event."

The prosecutor nodded with satisfaction. "Professor, I put it to you that the defendant, Ian Johnson, wasn't in a dissociative state when he made the decision to throw Lacey Johnson over the side of Anzac Bridge."

"That is not my professional opinion."

The prosecutor shot him a look of disbelief. "Despite what you just heard?"

The professor looked at him, a stubborn expression on his face. "Yes."

The prosecutor merely shook his head. "Professor Jackson-Lane, I put it to you that contrary to what you might have us believe, the defendant, Ian Johnson, knew exactly what he was doing when he acted on his decision to toss his daughter over the side of the bridge."

"I disagree."

The prosecutor eyed the professor steadily before eventually lowering his gaze. He looked up at the judge.

"Nothing further."

The judge glanced at his watch and then at the lawyers who sat at the bar table. "I note the time and I think it's appropriate to take a break. In fact, I have another small matter to deal with, so we'll adjourn until the morning."

The judge brought the gavel down and the court officer ordered everyone to rise. Once the judge and jury had departed, Blake returned to his seat with a sigh. His expert witness had been shot down in flames and there was nothing he could do about it. Tomorrow, he'd call his character witnesses, for all the good that would do. He only hoped Johnson realized the damage he'd done by giving false testimony.

Still, it wasn't in Blake's nature to give up. He hoped like hell Ian's brother and work colleague would come through. Blake was exhausted, both mentally and physically, and it wasn't over yet. He glanced across and noticed Natalie was still in her seat. As her legal team packed up their papers and prepared to leave, she stared off into the distance, looking sad and alone. A few wisps of hair had come loose from her sensible bun and now curled around her ears. Her mascara had smudged in the corners of her eyes and tears had dried on her cheeks. The sight of her distress tore at his heart. He wanted to go to her and apologize, to reassure her this wasn't personal. He wanted to wipe away her pain. He wanted...

But he couldn't do any of those things. At least, not there.

Natalie closed and locked the front door behind her and her shoulders slumped on a weary sigh. It had been a long and emotional day in court and she was glad it was over. Dropping her handbag on the hall table, she continued down the corridor and into the kitchen. She'd left in a rush after oversleeping and there were still dirty breakfast things in the sink. A plate used for the piece of toast she'd tossed in the trash and a coffee mug that had only been half-drunk were evidence of her attempt to eat before she left.

She'd known the day would be a tough one. Colby had warned her it was the defense's turn to call their witnesses. Sitting there and listening to Ian talk about the days leading up to the tragedy... And then the description of the tragedy itself...

It was too much. Even now, hours later, her eyes welled up with tears. She bit her lip against a sob, forcing it back, even though she wanted nothing more than to throw herself down and have a good cry. The kids were still at Monica's. There was no one around to see. No one around to witness her pain.

She'd barely cried since Lacey's death. Not the kind of all-out howling she wanted to do. Having the boys close by made that impossible. She needed to stay strong, to keep up the façade that her life hadn't irrevocably altered or that at any moment, she might shatter into so many pieces she'd never get put back together again.

Yes, that's exactly how she felt. Like the slightest thing would break her, and that would be the end of her. She'd lose her boys; she'd lose her job, her house. The life she had would never be the same again.

She let out a bark of laughter. *Ha! Who was she kidding?* Broken or not, her life would never be the same again. Period.

A knock on the door caught her attention and broke through the blackness of her thoughts. She frowned. It wasn't late, but it was unusual for her to get visitors. For a few days, probably most of the first week after Lacey's death, the house had been crowded with people. Friends, work colleagues and distant relatives—some of them she barely knew. Then there'd been the media camped outside her door: She hadn't even been able to look out the front windows without seeing reporters and cameramen.

Eventually, they'd lost interest, or perhaps something bigger hit the news. She didn't know. From the moment she realized her baby had been tossed to her death by her father, she'd lost touch with the day-to-day happenings in the world, felt numb to it all.

Gradually, all but Monica and Natalie's sons had departed the rooms of her home and she'd been left in near-blessed silence. No outsiders enquired about her state of health or whether she'd like a cup of tea. No one hovered just out of sight, uncertain whether to approach, to speak, to move.

In those dark days, she'd hugged the boys often and long and told them over and over how much she loved them. Before Monica had taken them to her place and while her sons slept, she'd sit quietly on the couch, staring into the distance, with Lacey's pink blanket and teddy bear squeezed tightly between her fingers. Tears had leaked almost constantly from her eyes, but she couldn't allow herself to let go of the stranglehold she had on her emotions for fear she might fall apart in front of them, sob her heart out, cry and never stop.

The knock came a second time and this time, it was accompanied by a voice.

"Natalie? It's Blake."

Blake.

Her ex-husband's lawyer; the man defending the unforgivable. *What was he doing at her door again? She'd cried in his arms the last time, but that was before this courtroom drama had begun to unfold so painfully… Did he really expect her to talk to him? To let him in now?*

She should have kept her distance. He was the enemy and she'd let him under her defenses, invited him in. Then, afterwards, in the courtroom, he'd looked as somber as everyone else when Ian had recounted his story and she'd realized there was no joy in the case for him, either. With a quiet sigh, she walked down the hallway and unlocked the front door.

He stood with his hands in his pockets a few yards from the door. He was dressed in a charcoal-gray suit and tie, although the latter had been loosened. She imagined he'd worn it to court, beneath his black barrister robes. As the door opened, he looked up at her and the sadness in his eyes tugged at her heart.

"May I come in?"

She stared at him. As much as she longed to curl up on her bed and cry herself to sleep, she didn't want to be alone. With the boys staying with Monica, the house was so quiet—abnormally so. It felt like the room she'd been taken to at the funeral home. She'd sat in the dim silence, staring at pictures of caskets and flower arrangements and answering a myriad of questions, all the time trying not to think about why she was there.

In response to Blake's quiet question, she finally

offered him a reluctant nod. Turning her back on him, she headed toward the kitchen, leaving him to close and lock the door. She filled the kettle and set it to boil. He appeared in the opening to the room and slowly moved toward her. He came to a halt on the other side of the counter. He was close enough that she could see the fatigue lines around his eyes and mouth. He'd had a tough day, too.

"Would you like a cup of coffee?" she asked.

He shifted his weight from one foot to the other. "Natalie, I... I wanted to apologize. I... I can't imagine how it must have been for you today."

She compressed her lips against a surge of emotion and thought back to Ian's testimony and that of his psychiatrist. "Yes. It was hard to listen to. I... I appreciate your apology, but you're representing Ian. You don't have to apologize for doing what he's paying you to do."

He grimaced. "For what it's worth, I took his case on pro bono. After listening to his testimony today, I wish I'd stayed right away from it."

"He lied under oath," she stated.

Blake held her gaze. "Yes, he did."

"When did you realize?"

"When he denied talking to you about the boys. After you told me about that phone call, I asked him about it. He told me you had called him. He told me about telling you about Lacey and the boys and today he denied that. He also told me about climbing onto the roof of his pickup with your little girl, yet today he apparently had no memory of any of it after the time he entered the bridge."

She stared at him. "What are you going to do?" she asked quietly.

"This late in the trial, there's not a lot I can do. If I withdraw my representation, the judge will declare a mistrial and—"

"We'll have to start all over again," she finished.

He nodded. "That's the last thing I'd wish on you." He sighed and scrubbed at his short hair, his frustration evident, and then he sighed again. "Greg Villa hammered him on cross. Let's hope it's enough."

"Do you believe your psychiatrist's testimony?" she asked quietly. "Do you believe Ian was in a dissociative state?"

Blake looked thoughtful. "I thought I did," he said slowly. "In fact, during the initial interview I had with Ian when we spoke about what happened, it's the first thing that came to mind."

"And now?" she asked softly, aware of his inner struggle from the look of distress on his face.

"Now, I'm not so sure. Given that Ian lied about what he did and did not remember..." His voice drifted off and he followed the admission with another grimace.

A fresh wave of anguish washed over her. It was like a physical pain. Though she'd always been convinced her ex had known exactly what he was doing when he tossed their baby to her death, it didn't make it any easier to bear. To accept that, meant it was likely his crime was premeditated and *that* was simply unthinkable; beyond horrific; completely unimaginable. That would mean Ian had planned her baby's death.

The father of her children was a monster...

The thought exploded in her head like shattered glass and spread to every corner of her brain. She couldn't get the idea out of her mind. The noise in her ears started as a rush of blood that quickly turned into a roar. She put her hands up to block it out, but the noise only got louder. A keening wail of pain and anger echoed through the room.

She wasn't aware she was screaming until she felt Blake's arms go around her and pull her against his chest. She tensed and then began to struggle, pushing him away.

"*Shh*, Natalie. It's all right," he murmured, his hands stroking up and down her back.

Slowly, his words of comfort penetrated the pain and devastation in her head and she relaxed against him. Tears continued to pour down her cheeks. She sobbed for her broken marriage; she sobbed for her little boys; but most of all, she sobbed for Lacey, her sweet baby girl who didn't deserve to die and was now gone forever.

"How can I forgive him?" she rasped on a fresh wave of pain.

She buried her face against the softness of Blake's shirt and tried hard to control the deluge of sobs. His arms felt warm and reassuring. From a distant part of her mind, she registered the tenderness in his touch as his hands continued to stroke her back. He repeated his words of comfort. Slowly, her sobs decreased in volume and strength.

She lifted her head and looked into his eyes. He

stared down at her, his expression filled with sadness and compassion. His hand came up to cup her cheek. With the pad of his thumb, he wiped away her tears. She bit her lip against the fresh surge of emotion and did her best to swallow another sob.

Blake continued to hold her gaze and all of a sudden, the world narrowed to just the two of them, like it had that first night. The noises from the street outside faded away. The walls of the kitchen disappeared. Her world consisted of her and Blake and no one else.

Her senses became attuned to the smallest of things. She heard his soft intake of breath and felt the tremor that ran through his body. She saw his eyes flare with awareness and a different kind of emotion. Her heart skipped a beat and then took off at a gallop, pounding against her chest.

Blake's head lowered, until there was barely a whisper of air between them.

Involuntarily, she opened her mouth. A moment later, his lips touched hers. It was the briefest of contact, but it was like a torch had been lit and the heat of it raced along her veins. It was all so wrong, but it felt so right and she couldn't get enough. Her hands came up and cradled his head, holding it firmly in place.

She kissed him like she was famished and he was a mile-long buffet. She released her hold on his head and slid her hands through his hair and then moved lower. She laced her fingers around the back of his neck and drew in a deep breath. The smell of his cologne reached her nose. She arched her back and pressed against the hardness of his body. He reacted by bringing his arm around her and pressing her closer, as close as she could get.

She clung to him, kissing him ferociously and he returned her kisses in kind. His hands cupped her buttocks, drawing her ever closer. Her breasts were crushed against the hard muscles of his chest and she relished the contact. He felt so warm, so strong, so *alive*.

With her mouth still fused to his, she undid his tie and tossed it away and then fumbled with the buttons of his shirt. When she was done, she spread the fabric wide. Her breath came fast as she stared at his perfectly sculpted chest.

Well-defined pectorals dusted with golden hair, rose and fell in time with his rapid breathing. Unable to help herself, she reached out and ran her fingers over his warm skin. His muscles felt as firm as they looked and contracted beneath her touch. He exhaled sharply. She sighed in wonder.

"You're beautiful," she breathed.

He flushed and ducked his head and looked a little uncomfortable. She couldn't believe he was so modest about his physical attractiveness. His humility endeared him to her, but she didn't have the time to contemplate it for more than a second or two. She wanted to forget about thinking for a while and do nothing but feel. With that thought in mind, she reached for his belt. He stilled her hands with his.

"Natalie, I'm not sure this is a good idea."

She shook her head. "You think too much."

His gaze remained on hers, somber and serious. "We don't have to do this. We could wait."

She eyed him steadily. "*I* have to do this. I *need* to do this. Now. Please, Blake. I need to block out the pain that never goes away. I need to forget about the court case. I need to forget about Ian, about Lacey, about...everything."

His eyes glinted with compassion and understanding. He released her hands and drew her back into his arms. His lips came down on hers and he kissed her with such tenderness, a lump formed in her throat.

Like it had before, his touch ignited a fire inside her and she returned his kiss with a passion that surprised her. She barely knew him. He was her ex-husband's lawyer. There were so many reasons why she should stop kissing him and walk away. But in that moment, not one mattered.

He was good and kind and...sexy, and right now, there was nothing and no one she wanted more. She splayed her hands across his chest. His bare skin felt wonderful. She pulled back and tugged at the buttons on her blouse. He watched her, his eyes dark with emotion.

"Are you sure?" he asked quietly.

She held his gaze and nodded. "Yes."

As if that was all the permission he needed, he brushed away her hands and attended to her buttons. As the blouse fell away, his fingers went to the clasp of her bra and a moment later, he released it. Her small breasts bounced gently. He looked his fill.

She reached once again for his belt. At the

same time, he slid his hands around her waist and went to work on the zipper of her skirt. She slid his down and he slid hers down and they shimmied out of their remaining clothes until they stood naked, admiring each other.

Natalie wanted to cover herself. It had been more than a decade since a man who wasn't her husband had seen her naked and she was far thinner than she wanted to be, but she resisted the urge to shield herself and distracted herself by fixing her gaze on Blake and looking her fill.

If she thought he looked beautiful with his bare muscled chest, the rest of him didn't disappoint. Long, muscular legs that were lightly covered in fair hair were framed by a pair of narrow hips. At the juncture of his thighs, his cock stood thick and proud amidst a nest of pubic hair. The sight of it, huge and erect, sent a renewed surge of desire flooding through her and heated her way down deep inside. Blocking her mind from all thoughts but the man who stood in front of her, she reached for him.

His arms came around her and she clung to him. They kissed with a ferocious need. Fire burned through her veins, flooding her pores with heat. Blake bent his knees and scooped her up in his arms and headed down the hall. He hesitated at the first door.

"Second door on the right," she murmured and he continued on.

A moment later, he switched on the light, entered her bedroom and deposited her gently on the bed. Natalie sent a silent prayer of thanks heavenward that she'd remembered to make it. And then Blake bent his head and suckled her nipples and all other thoughts dissolved.

His mouth was warm and wet and left a needy tug in her lower body. She yearned to feel him inside her, filling her, making her forget. She moved restlessly beneath him and even tried to lift his head, but he would have none of that. Instead, he shifted to the other breast and gave it the same attention. Need tingled deep inside her.

"Please, Blake. Make love to me."

He lifted his head and gazed at her, his eyes dark and tumultuous with desire. "Are you sure?"

In some far place in the recesses of her mind, she appreciated the fact that he kept asking, but right now, she wanted nothing more than to get on with it and quench the fire that burned inside her. She dragged his head up to hers and kissed him with all the passion she felt inside. When they finally pulled apart, both of them were breathing hard.

Blake moved and positioned himself between her thighs. At the last minute, Natalie thought about protection.

"Do you have a condom?" she asked and then blushed.

Blake stared down at her as if nonplussed, but then nodded. "Yes. Of course. In my wallet." He climbed off the bed and disappeared.

Natalie lay on her back, staring at the ceiling, refusing to contemplate what they were about to do. It was madness. They'd probably both regret it, but right now, she didn't care about tomorrow or even later that night. She wanted him and he wanted her and she knew with certainty that he was someone who could make her forget—even for a little while.

A moment later, Blake rejoined her and pulled her back into his arms. He kissed her and stroked her and held her close before once again, positioning himself between her thighs. With his cock now sheathed, he eased his way inside. She thrust her hips upward impatiently. Taking her cue, he surged forward until he was buried inside her. She gasped at the feel of him.

And then, she was clinging to his shoulders and meeting his thrusts head-on. Harder and harder, higher and higher, the passion and need built inside her. Her breath came fast, her heart pounded and still he stroked in and out. Long and deep, short and fast, he changed it up until she couldn't stand it a second more. Cresting on a wave of desire, she reached the pinnacle and with a cry of relief, went free-falling over the other side.

Her orgasm seemed to last forever as her inner muscles tightened and released around his cock. It had been so long since she'd climaxed with a man. It felt so good. It felt *unbelievably* good. Gasping for breath, she fell back against the sheets. Blake leaned down to kiss her and she eagerly kissed him back.

"Now it's your turn," she whispered and was rewarded with a slow, sexy smile.

"I hope you're ready," he said in a voice that was rough with desire. "You're in for a wild ride."

She was still replete from her orgasm, but even so his words sent a thrill of excitement arcing through her. She threaded her arms around his neck and pulled him down hard against her. With her breasts crushed against his chest, he moved his hips and returned to his rhythm. His strokes started out slow, but quickly built up speed. His face was a picture of concentration.

Harder and harder, faster and faster, he thrust deep inside her core. She clung to him, loving the way he abandoned himself to the act. And then his body tightened beneath her fingers and his breath came harsh and fast. He pumped harder, grunted, then groaned and collapsed against her as he found his release.

A few minutes later, he lifted his weight off her and rolled onto his back. Natalie peeked at him, suddenly unsure of herself. Now that it was over, cold reality was setting in. He was her ex-husband's lawyer. He was also a man she barely knew.

"Wow," he said quietly and reached for her hand.

Taking her hand in his, he threaded his fingers through hers and squeezed. The action was so simple, but it touched her deep inside. All of a sudden, it didn't matter who he represented or how long she'd known him. He was a good man, a special man. A man she could fall in love with.

The thought startled her. *What was she doing? How could she think about love?* She'd only just buried her baby. There was nothing more important in her life than that. Lacey's sweet face swam before her and guilt hit her, heavy and hard. She was supposed to be thinking about her baby and the monster who'd stolen her life.

She didn't have time to seek out love, no matter how much her lonely heart yearned for someone who cared. Her life centered around the loss of Lacey and it would be that way for a long time to come. Maybe forever. She pulled her hand from his.

"Are you all right?" Blake asked softly.

A surge of emotion tightened her chest and tears burned behind her eyes. After all the tears she'd cried, she wanted to be done with them, but there seemed to be an endless supply.

"Y-yes," she managed, but Blake wasn't fooled.

He rolled onto his side and faced her. "Please don't tell me you regret what we just did."

She forced herself to look at him and was taken aback by what she saw. His expression was stark and needy. Vulnerability shone in his eyes. It hadn't occurred to her how he might feel about their lovemaking. It was obvious this was more to him than a casual coupling. The thought filled her with equal parts joy and fear that he might read more into this than what she was ready or willing to give.

"Blake..."

"Yes?"

"I... Thank you." The words were totally inadequate, but she didn't know what else to say. She peeked at him once again and this time, his expression was as dark as a thundercloud.

"You're *thanking* me?" he asked, his voice dangerously calm.

She shook her head and tried to explain. "I don't mean it like that. It's not like I'm grateful for you having sex with me. It's just..."

She shrugged and his frown deepened.

"It's just what?" he asked.

"It's not what you're thinking," she replied hurriedly and once again shook her head. "I'm not doing a very good job of this, am I?"

As if taking pity on her, he sighed and pulled her close. "What we just did together was amazing," he said quietly. "It's never been that way for me before. You have no reason to believe me, but it's the truth. The circumstances of our meeting are all wrong, but I can't pretend that I don't like you, Natalie. I like you a lot. I like you way too much. If I wasn't your ex-husband's lawyer, I'd have asked you out already."

She stared at him and finally offered him a brief smile. "And if you weren't my ex-husband's lawyer, I might have said yes." She sighed softly. "The court case kind of complicates everything. There's no denying it."

This time, his sigh was heavier. "You're right, but I'm not sorry about what we did. The trial's almost over. I tried to stay away from you, but I couldn't. After the day you had—the day we both had—I needed to make sure you were all right. I needed to talk to you, reassure myself that what went on today hadn't overwhelmed you, gotten you down."

"Did you think I'd do something stupid?" she asked quietly and couldn't help but think of his brother.

He shook his head slowly, but his words weren't quite so certain. "No, not really. But I wasn't sure. After all, we don't know each other very well. I'd known my brother all my life and I still didn't see it coming. I guess I wanted to make sure that someone else I cared about wasn't suffering the same way."

The look on his face was heartbreaking and all Natalie wanted to do was kiss his pain away, but his tragedy had happened months ago. There was nothing she could do about that now. Still, she was curious about how it had happened and knew firsthand how talking about sad events could sometimes help and—

Hang on a minute, had he just said he cared about her? The idea warmed her through. She took his hand in hers and laced their fingers together.

"Tell me about your brother," she said quietly.

Chapter 19

Blake closed his eyes and concentrated on the softness and warmth of Natalie's hand. It was small and slim and though her nails were well-shaped, the red polish on them was chipped and the nails had been chewed short. Given the horror of what she'd endured over the past six weeks or so, he understood their condition; a visit to the beauty salon was probably the last thing on her mind.

He cast his mind back over the past couple of hours and couldn't remember when he'd felt so good. Despite the difficult day, she'd given herself wholeheartedly to their lovemaking and while it had been fast and furious at times, it had also been slow and sweet and tender.

What would it be like if they were given the opportunity to explore a relationship? Despite the fact his professional allegiances lay firmly in her enemy's camp, they had an indefinable connection, a spiritual awareness that had been there right from the beginning. It was the reason he'd dropped everything and gone to her in the hospital mere hours after meeting her. She'd needed him and he needed to be with her, to make sure she was okay. And not because either was weak or faint of heart.

It was a feeling he'd never experienced before, even in his youth when he'd fallen head over heels in love with Marjorie-Leigh Albright who was in the sixth grade. He'd vowed to love her until the day he died. Now he could barely remember what she looked like.

But with Natalie, it was different. *He* was different. He wanted to be kinder, gentler, funnier. He wanted to be the best man he could be and it was all because of the way she made him feel. It was a little frightening, this control she seemed to have over him. Even more so, when he didn't know if she felt the same way. They'd just made sweet, sweet love, but the truth was, they barely knew each other.

"Blake? I'm sorry... Did I say something wrong?"

Her voice was filled with uncertainty and the tone penetrated the thoughts that filled his mind. He blinked and remembered she'd asked about David. He turned to her and offered her a quick smile of reassurance. He didn't talk about his brother with anyone, but with Natalie, it seemed all right. He wanted her to know about his brother and the tragic end to David's life. He wanted her to understand the reasons behind his need to represent her ex-husband. He needed her to understand it wasn't about her, it was all about *him*.

"David was three years older than me. He was married with two little kids. Harry and Josie. They're six and four... I still can't believe he left them."

"He hung himself, didn't he?" she asked quietly.

"Yes." Blake was overwhelmed with images of his brother. David's ex-wife, Harriet, had been the one to find him swinging from a steel beam in his garage. She'd made the fatal decision to call on him the same afternoon the family court had handed down its final decision awarding her sole custody of their children. When he'd failed to answer his phone or return her messages, she'd gone to his home to collect some of their things and confirm the future arrangements. She'd called Blake right after the discovery, hysterical with shock and grief. It was Blake who'd arrived at his brother's house minutes before the police.

In the time it had taken the first responders to get there, Blake had found a sharp knife from the kitchen and cut his brother down, unable to bear the thought there wasn't even the slightest possibility David might still be alive. He immediately checked for a pulse, but there had been nothing. In the back of his mind, he registered that the police might take issue with the fact he was interfering with a potential crime scene, but Blake was never in any doubt that his brother had taken his own life.

"Looking back," he continued quietly, "the signs were there for everyone to see. David had been depressed over the divorce and then the battle over his kids. Like you and Ian, it was bitter. The court had given interim custody to Harriet and though the decision wasn't unexpected given the age of the children, it still devastated David. He began drinking heavily and often failed to turn up at work."

"What did he do for a living?" Natalie asked.

"He was an architect. He was a partner in Reynolds and Ashcroft, a large firm of architects in the city. He loved his job, but it wasn't enough to get him through the loss of his family."

Natalie's expression filled with compassion and understanding. "That's why you took on Ian's case, wasn't it?"

Blake looked at her and nodded grimly. "Yes. The first time I met him, he told me about the divorce and the battle he'd been having over his kids. He told me the court had handed down a final decision and they were to live with their mother at least until the age of sixteen. It killed him to know that his contact with his children had been reduced to a couple of days every fortnight. It sounded so much like my brother's story. I understood Ian's anger and his grief."

Natalie's eyes flashed and she withdrew her hand from his. "Even if it doesn't seem fair, that doesn't excuse what he did!" she said.

Blake held her gaze steadily. "No, it doesn't. But at the time I agreed to represent your ex-husband, I strongly believed that at the point he threw your daughter to her death, he was in a state of dissociation. I mean, what other explanation was there? What person in their right mind throws their child off a bridge? It seemed impossible to consider anything else."

Blake scrubbed a hand through his hair in an

effort to ease his frustration. He was still finding it difficult to accept the expert evidence that suggested otherwise. The more he heard about his client's rational, normal actions in the moments before the tragedy occurred, the more he was forced to acknowledge the potential for an alternate truth: *Had Ian Johnson been of sound mind and deliberately tossed his little girl over the side of the bridge?*

Natalie rolled on her side, away from him and dragged the sheet up over her shoulder. A moment later, he heard the unmistakable sound of her crying. Blake's heart tripped over with sadness, and emotion was a tight band around his chest. He reached over and stroked her hair.

"I'm so sorry, Natalie. I'm so sorry. When I took on this case, I didn't know… I didn't know."

She rolled back to face him and the agony on her face nearly tore him in two.

"He did it to hurt me, Blake!" she cried. "He wanted to get back at me for getting the kids! I know it! You know it! I just hope the jury knows it, too. Nothing will bring back Lacey, but I pray to God Ian's forced to pay. If he spends the rest of his life in jail, spending every waking moment thinking about what he's done, it won't be enough."

Her voice hitched on a sob and fresh tears filled her eyes. Blake pulled her close and was relieved when she buried her face against his chest. Her sobs weren't as noisy and out of control as the first time, but they broke his heart just the same. This woman had been through so much—too much. *How was anyone expected to bear such pain?*

He'd thought his brother's suicide was hard to accept, and it had been, but they were talking about the callous murder of a young child. It simply didn't compare. He clenched his jaw at the thought of standing before the twelve men and women who had the job of deciding his client's fate to deliver his final address. He was the defendant's lawyer. It was his job to convince the jury to set his client free; to accept that Ian Johnson had been mentally impaired at the moment he did what he did and therefor couldn't be held responsible for his actions.

Knowing what the prosecution's psychiatrist had said about the man's mental state, coupled with Ian's lies, Blake didn't know how he was going to do it. *How was he going to make the jury believe his closing arguments when he didn't believe them himself?* And yet, he had no choice. He'd agreed to represent the man and he'd see it through to the end, if it killed him. *Would the woman who cried quietly in his arms understand if her ex walked free?* He could only hope.

———————

The public gallery in the courtroom was full to bursting. It seemed everyone in Sydney wanted to be there on the last day of the trial of the man who'd tossed his baby daughter over the side of Anzac Bridge. The judge had yet to appear for the morning session and the murmur of voices filled the room. Natalie stole a glance in Blake's direction and blushed when he caught her gaze. Quickly, she looked away.

It was one thing to lay her heart open before him in the privacy of her bedroom. It was quite another to come face to face with him on opposite sides of a courtroom. She no longer thought of him as the enemy, but it was difficult to sit there knowing he represented her ex-husband and was going to do everything he could to convince the jury to return a not guilty verdict.

The first character witness Blake called was Ian's brother. Keith Johnson was five years older than Ian and admitted he had never liked Natalie. It was apparently an attitude shared by all the members of Ian's family. Along with Keith, Ian also had two younger sisters. His parents, Bill and Mavis, were still alive, but they might as well be dead for all the time they spent with Natalie and their grandchildren. It had been that way even before the divorce. Natalie had done her best over the years to convince them she was worthy of their son and brother, but it had all been for nothing. She eventually gave up. She'd maintained a civil relationship with them only for Ian's sake and for the sake of their kids.

Blake went through the usual preliminaries and established the relationship between Ian and Keith. Ian's brother told the court he worked as a security guard for a bank.

"What is your relationship with Natalie Johnson?" Blake asked.

Keith shot her a look that barely concealed his

contempt. "She was married to my brother. She's my ex-sister-in-law."

"Were you aware your brother and Ms Johnson were going through a difficult custody dispute?"

"Yes. Ian often called me about it."

"What did Ian tell you?"

"That his ex was trying to take his kids; that she was playing for keeps."

"I want to take you to Friday, October sixth. Did you receive a phone call from your brother that day?"

"Yes."

"What was the call about?"

"Ian had just come from the family law court. The judge had made a final decision on his custody case. The decision had gone against my brother. He'd lost his kids."

Blake acknowledged the comment with a slight nod. "How was Ian's mood?"

"He was fu—I mean, he was very upset."

"What did he say?"

"I'm not sure I remember the exact words, but he was angry and upset and I could tell it was a struggle for him to hold it all together."

"Did you offer him any advice?"

"Yes, I told him this wouldn't be the end of it. That there were always ways to appeal. I tried to calm him down."

"Were you successful?"

"Yes, I think so. By the end of our conversation, he was much more rational and sounded more like himself. He told me it was his weekend to have the kids. He wanted to make the most of it."

"Did you speak to your brother during the course of that weekend?"

"Yes, a couple of times."

"Did the court decision come up again?"

"Yes, once or twice. Ian was still angry and was trying to work out what to do."

"When you heard about what your brother had done to Lacey, what did you think?"

"I was shocked and sad."

"Were you surprised?"

"Yes and no. I had no idea Ian was thinking about doing anything so drastic, but it made a terrible kind of sense. He was hurting and he wanted others to hurt, too."

"Has Ian ever snapped like that before?"

"No."

"So, would you say his behavior was out of character?"

"Definitely."

"Mr Johnson, does Ian love his children?"

"Of course he does! He's a great father! He plays with them, takes them to soccer practice. He taught the twins to ride pushbikes. He loves those children more than anything and he loved Lacey most of all. She was his little princess, his little baby girl."

Blake looked at his witness and nodded. "Thank you, Mr Johnson. I have no further questions."

Blake returned to his seat and the prosecutor got to his feet. Natalie braced herself for the cross examination.

"Mr Johnson, you love your brother, don't you?"

"Yes, as much as anyone does, I guess."

"And you'd do anything to help him, wouldn't you?"

"Yes."

"You've helped him out in the past. You'd given him advice; provided him with an understanding ear."

"Yes."

"In fact, it would just about kill you to see your brother go to jail, wouldn't it?"

"Yes. And he doesn't deserve to be there. What happened to Lacey wasn't his fault. The court shouldn't have given his kids to his ex. It wasn't fair."

"You're right, Mr Johnson. Sometimes life isn't fair." Villa glanced at the jury. "It doesn't mean we have the right to toss our children over the side of a bridge to their certain death and then go on our way, though. Does it?"

Keith looked like he wanted to argue, but grudgingly shook his head. "No."

The prosecutor checked his notes and then looked back up at the witness. "Mr Johnson, you said your brother was looking to hurt someone the way he'd been hurt, you're talking about his ex-wife, aren't you?"

Keith stole a glance at Natalie and then quickly averted his gaze. She narrowed her eyes at him and willed him to tell the truth.

"Yes," he replied finally.

"You don't like Natalie Johnson, do you?"

"Not particularly."

"And you sympathized with your brother when the judge found against him, didn't you?"

"Yes. Like I said. It wasn't fair. Those kids belong to Ian as much as they belong to *her*." Keith's lips turned up in a sneer.

Natalie felt the heat of anger and embarrassment rise in her cheeks. She worked hard to hold on to her temper and keep her feelings from showing.

"Mr Johnson, you said that though you were shocked at what happened to Lacey, you weren't surprised. You realized your brother was in a bad way that Friday afternoon, didn't you?"

"You've got that right. He was furious."

"So furious, in fact, that you weren't surprised that he wanted to do something awful to hurt his ex-wife. He wanted to get to her in a way she wouldn't forget. One thing more important to her than anything else in the world was her children. What better way to hurt her than to hurt them, or at least the one he could carry and hoist over the barricade?"

"No, I didn't mean—"

"You said your brother loves his children and that he loved Lacey most of all, but that's not true, is it, Mr Johnson?" Villa interrupted.

"Yes, of course—"

"We don't hurt the people we love, Mr Johnson. We don't throw them over a bridge to their certain death and then tell anyone who'll listen how much we loved them."

Keith opened his mouth and looked like he was going to argue, but once again, Villa cut him off.

"No further questions, Mr Johnson."

The judge excused Keith from the witness box

and then asked Blake to call his next witness.

"The defense calls Adam Croft."

Natalie watched one of Ian's work colleagues make his way to the stand. Adam and Ian had done their plumbing apprenticeship together more than a decade earlier and had remained friends. Like Ian, Adam also ran his own business.

Natalie had always gotten on with Adam and he'd spent many evenings in their home. He was a regular visitor to barbeques and other family occasions. He wasn't married and had no children and had become another uncle to their kids. The boys especially loved their Uncle Adam.

In quick succession, Blake established the relationship between the men. Adam gave Ian a glowing character reference as far as his work ethic went and his ability to be a good father and friend, but nothing could disguise the fact that this prince among men had tossed his daughter to her death.

Natalie almost felt sorry for Blake. He'd been charged with a near impossible task. As if sensing he was making very little ground, a few moments later, Blake finished his questioning and returned to his seat. Villa didn't bother to cross examine. No matter how many of Ian's friends tried to sugarcoat what had happened, it wasn't going to change the jury's mind about what he'd done or make them forget.

Finally, Blake got to his feet and announced that the defense rested. The trial was all but over.

CHAPTER 20

The judge brought the gavel down and announced a short adjournment. He stood and left the courtroom, along with the jury. Natalie sighed. She was so tired, she could hardly hold her head up. She snuck a look at Blake. He caught her gaze and held it. It took all her effort to look away. A faint headache had made itself known behind her eyes. She hadn't slept properly for more than six weeks and was looking forward to the time she could close her eyes and think of nothing but sleep. The trial couldn't be over soon enough.

And now, it almost was. The barristers would present their closing arguments to the jury and that would be the end of it. The jury would go off to wherever they were sent to deliberate and decide on Ian's future. She was quietly hopeful they'd heard enough to convince them he was guilty, but it was always possible that one or two would hold out and refuse to side with the others.

The thought that Ian might be set free, might

not be held accountable for his actions because of one or two rogue jurors, filled her with icy dread. Her stomach clenched in response and her heart rate quickened. She concentrated hard on her breathing in an effort to hold off a panic attack. *Please, God, let this nightmare be over.*

Colby had explained earlier that Greg Villa would make his closing arguments first. The crown prosecutor had assured her upon her arrival at court that morning that he was confident of a win. The jury were maintaining eye contact with him and that was always a good thing. He was certain they believed the prosecution's expert testimony and the evidence of the other witnesses who told of the way Ian acted before and after the crime. Villa had certainly been convinced by the evidence and he was sure it would convince the twelve men and women who were responsible for deciding Ian's fate. Natalie prayed that would be so.

Testifying about the breakdown of her marriage and the subsequent battle over the kids had been one of the hardest things she'd ever done. And then to sit there before Ian, knowing what he'd done, hiding her hurt and pain and heartbreak so she didn't give him the satisfaction of witnessing how much his actions had destroyed her. It was beyond difficult, but she'd managed it. And now, with the end in sight she hoped and prayed her efforts hadn't been in vain.

A loud knock caught her attention and then the court officer asked all present to rise. They did so as the judge made his way through a rear entrance and returned to the bench. Once seated, he cleared his throat and asked for the jury to be returned.

Natalie stared at each and every one of them as they entered the courtroom and took their seats. Over the past few days, she'd memorized their features. The grandmother with the salt-and-pepper hair; the young lady with the colored braces and the mole on her cheek; the man who'd worn the same suit and tie each day; and the girl with the purple hair and the piercings in her nose and chin. These and eight others were the ones who got to decide if Ian was jailed or set free.

After the jury was settled, the judge turned to Villa and invited him to make his closing remarks. Natalie stole another glance at Blake, but he appeared to be absorbed in his notes. As the crown prosecutor began to speak, her stomach tensed with nerves.

"Ladies and gentlemen of the jury," Villa started in his mellow baritone. "You have before you a man who was a dedicated family man, a good husband and father... And then, things began to go off course. It's a sad fact of Australian society that one in three marriages end in divorce. Some of you might have already fallen victim to this. We're not here to judge the accused on his failed marriage or the subsequent battle he fought for his children. We're here to determine whether, in a moment of madness or in a cold and calculated move to spite his ex-wife, he murdered his daughter. Little Lacey Maree Johnson, a child who was just three years old."

Natalie swallowed hard. This was going to be just as tough as listening to Ian's testimony. She clenched her hands into fists until what few nails she still had dug into her skin. She welcomed the pain.

"Now, Mr Johnson and his legal team would have you believe that it was all a terrible accident. That at the moment the defendant made the decision to throw Lacey off the bridge he was suffering mental incapacity, an impairment that affected his brain to such an extent that he can't be held responsible for his actions. Mr Harton would have us believe his client's actions were as a result of a fluctuating madness, a dissociative state." He paused briefly. "I beg to differ and I think after hearing the evidence, you do, too."

The prosecutor let the words hang in the air. The room was still and silent. Natalie held her breath, along with what felt like every other person present. She stared in the general direction of the jury, not brave enough to look them in the eye, to gage their reaction to Villa's words. Once again, she tightened her hands into fists.

"You see," Villa continued, "the evidence just doesn't support the defendant's theory. He says he has no memory after driving onto the bridge, that from that moment until sometime after the tragic event, he was dissociating and yet you heard from several witnesses how the defendant not only obeyed road rules, but he also had the presence of mind to use his traffic indicators, to change lanes, to pull over onto the far side of the bridge, to use his hazard lights, to choose his smallest and lightest child, to climb onto the roof of his truck in order to get the height he needed to ensure Lacey cleared the wire fence. In fact, contrary to what the accused would have you believe, his actions appeared very normal and rational prior to and after he tossed his baby off the bridge.

"You heard from the reputable forensic psychiatrist, Professor Kevin Quirk. You heard him speak about a dissociative state and how someone suffering from such a condition isn't capable of acting normally and making rational decisions. And yet, the defendant did so, many times over. In fact, he told his wife what he'd done, shortly after he murdered their daughter.

"You heard the testimony of the young teacher, Heather Long, and how she was there when the defendant arrived at his sons' school. She called out to him and he returned her greeting before kissing his sons good-bye and heading on his way. I suggest to you that all of these actions demonstrate a man who is far from being in a dissociative state. In fact, as you heard from the detectives, it wasn't until the police interview that Ian Johnson began to show signs of mental distress and I'm sure, given the enormity of what he'd done, every single one of you would understand how, at that point, shock might have set in."

The prosecutor paused and took his time to eyeball each of the jurors before speaking again. "Shock. Distress over the death of a child. Normal responses to a tragic event. Normal responses for a man who might suddenly feel remorseful for his monstrous act, an act so horrendous, so unfathomable that we can scarcely comprehend it.

"Don't let your shock over the defendant's actions cloud your judgment. Make no mistake, this man knew exactly what he'd done. He knew at the time he formed the plan to get back at his ex-wife. He knew at the time he switched lanes and pulled over in the lane beside the steel barricade. He knew when he opened the door and reached in for his little girl. He knew at the time he climbed onto the bed of his truck with her in his arms. He knew when he climbed onto the roof, still holding his little girl, and braced himself for what he was going to do next. And he needed all his strength.

"You see, the steel barrier is at least ten feet high. Even standing on the roof of his vehicle, it was a fair distance to throw. If the defendant misjudged, his baby would have hit the barricade and probably fallen back in his truck. She might have been injured, even seriously, but the odds are she would have survived the fall. It wasn't good enough, because this man, this little girl's father, was determined to end her life.

"He held her tight and then threw her with all his might. He had to, in order to make sure she cleared the barrier and hit the water below. That's the shocking truth and nothing the defendant can say will change the facts. That's the reason he chose Lacey. He told Professor Quirk just that, and even though he denied it here in the courtroom, you and I know the truth. He had three children in the back of his car. He chose the smallest, lightest one. It doesn't take a genius to figure out why."

Once again, the prosecutor paused. The air in the courtroom was so thick, it was stifling. A band of ice tightened around Natalie's chest until she could barely draw breath. Her poor baby. She prayed desperately for the nightmare to be over. And then Blake got to his feet. She steeled herself against what he might have to say.

"Ladies and gentlemen of the jury," Blake began. "Let me start by thanking you for your presence and for your courage in listening to what has been a most difficult trial. You heard harrowing evidence that a father threw his child to her death. You heard expert evidence how these actions can only be considered as rational because of the behavior Ian Johnson had exhibited immediately before and after the tragic event. And yet, I challenge each and every one of you to think, just for a second, how anyone in their rational mind could do such a thing? How could a father toss his little girl over the side of a bridge to her death? It's beyond our imagination. We can't conceive of how such a thing could happen. And yet it did.

"There's no denying Mr Johnson loved his children. He fought long and hard in the courts, spent every cent he had in an effort to gain custody of his sons and daughter. No one does that if they don't care. And it was the very fact that he cared so much that caused the awful tragedy that resulted in the loss of his daughter's life.

"You heard Mr Johnson talk about the final family court hearing that didn't go his way. He'd spent all his money. Tried his hardest for fair treatment in the courts—and then lost his fight for his children.

"Yes. Awarding his wife full custody, with only twice monthly weekends with his children was a savage blow. One might even say that final court decision had been the catalyst for what this father did, even though a weekend separated the decision from the morning he lost control of his faculties, it didn't matter. Mr Johnson spent the weekend in deep disappointment and anger at what had happened, was irritated by the constant calls by his ex-wife and then he woke late and fought with her. A stupid argument about punctuality, but it didn't matter. The anger that had been simmering all weekend came to a head.

"Now, no one's excusing his actions. My client accepts he did an awful thing. Mr Johnson doesn't deny he caused his daughter's death. That's not in issue. What you need to decide is whether his actions were the result of mental impairment—dissociation, if you like—or if he deliberately planned and murdered his child."

Blake paused and glanced at the notes on his desk. Natalie was sure it was a deliberate ploy to allow the jury time to consider his words. The prosecutor had employed the same tactic to good effect.

A moment later, Blake cleared his throat and continued. "You heard evidence from the learned

Professor Quirk that Ian Johnson couldn't possibly be suffering from dissociation because his actions prior to and immediately after what happened were the acts of a normal, rational man. Then renowned psychiatrist, Professor Jackson-Lane said the exact opposite. You heard him testify to the fact that dissociation can come upon someone without warning and can last a few moments, a few weeks or much longer. Professor Quirk also conceded this point."

Once again, Blake paused a moment before continuing. "So, ladies and gentlemen of the jury, when you consider who the man and father was by all accounts—never before a threat to his children—and then examine that man's actions, there is only one possible, sensible conclusion you can draw: You must come to the conclusion that no normal human being, no rational father, thinking with a clear head, could possibly throw his daughter to her certain death. And when you realize this, you understand that Ian Johnson was acting under some form of mental impairment, some kind of dissociative state when he did what he did and ended his little girl's life—and therefore he cannot be held responsible. You have no choice but to find my client, Ian Johnson, not guilty."

Blake returned to his seat and there was an audible sigh that rolled like a wave across the courtroom. It was almost like the entire group of people gathered there had released a collective breath. Natalie included. Her hands trembled and her stomach still churned with nerves, but underneath the stress and trauma of the trial, was a fledging feeling of relief. It was over. Now it was up to the jury.

Taking a deep breath, she lifted her gaze and scanned each and every one of their faces, wanting them to see her, to remember her and to think about her when they were in the jury room deliberating. Prior to going to court, Colby had explained that the decision had to be unanimous. If they couldn't agree, the judge would declare a mistrial and the legal teams would have to start all over again, including calling the witnesses. She couldn't bear that.

Please, God, let it be over. Let them come to the only decision they can and let this be done.

She bowed her head, tired beyond belief, and whispered the desperate prayer under her breath.

CHAPTER 21

Blake looked up and down the street, checking for the presence of reporters or cameramen before sneaking another peek at the soft golden lamplight that glowed between a tiny gap in the curtains that hung in Natalie's front room. Her car was parked in the driveway, but apart from the light, he hadn't seen any other evidence that she was home. He'd gone back to his office after the judge brought the trial to an end and the members of the jury were sent out to begin their deliberations. Apart from a brief glance in Natalie's direction in the course of his departure, there hadn't been any opportunity for them to speak.

Not that he would have, anyway. He was the head of the defense team. She'd given evidence for the prosecution. It was best they kept their distance until the jury made their decision. The wait while the jury was deliberating was often agonizing and Blake anticipated this one would take longer than most. To some of the jurors, it would be a clear-cut decision. To others, it would be far more complicated. He was in a similar quandary.

Though he'd come to accept his client had probably premeditated—to some degree—his plan to toss his child off the bridge and likely remembered far more than he'd admitted, part of Blake still struggled to accept that any sane person, let alone the child's loving father, could throw his innocent baby to her death. No doubt some of the jurors would struggle too, and that meant it could be days, even weeks before they reached a decision. *If* they reached one. Not all juries could agree.

The thought of a hung jury made him groan aloud. Though there was always a chance the Director of Public Prosecutions wouldn't ask for a retrial, Blake held out little hope that would be the case here. A child had been thrown to her death by her father. Justice would be served. The public would accept nothing less, and rightly so.

He snuck another peek at Natalie's front door and cursed softly under his breath. What was he doing, sitting in his car outside the house of the woman he had no right to care about like this? It was ludicrous and probably a little unethical—at least until after the trial, although he could honestly say in good conscience, he'd done his very best for his client. Even knowing and caring for Natalie, his professionalism hadn't been impeded. He was proud of that fact and wouldn't have had it any other way.

Blake's thoughts turned toward the jury who were even now deliberating on Ian Johnson's fate. If he was found guilty, Blake would have failed him. If he was found not guilty... Blake couldn't bear the thought.

Natalie would be devastated. She blamed her ex for her baby's death and was convinced he'd done it on purpose. The more evidence Blake heard during the trial, the more he believed she was right. He was just glad it was over. As soon as the jury made a decision, he could put it behind him and get on with his life.

Is that what he wanted? To forget all about the Johnsons and move forward with his life—a life that didn't include Natalie? He'd only known her six weeks, but that short time didn't seem to matter. He couldn't remember not having her in his thoughts and not wanting her in his life. Some people would think it was too sudden and some of them might be right, but that's not how he felt.

So what was he doing, hiding out in his car? Why didn't he just stride up the garden path and knock on her door and tell her how he felt. Was he afraid of how she might react? Was he afraid she'd laugh in his face? Was he afraid that as much as this felt right, it might go very wrong? There were children involved. She had two sons. Was he ready to take them on? He was smart enough to realize any relationship with their mother would also mean a relationship with them.

He'd always steered clear of serious relationships, especially after his brother's messy divorce. David and Harriet had been high school sweethearts. Blake had never seen two people more in love. But they hadn't made it past five years. They'd been divorced twelve months when David decided he'd had enough.

It was a sad and tragic circumstance, and one that didn't foster tender feelings toward marriage and long term commitment. Natalie and Ian were another example. She'd testified that the two of them had once been happy and then they'd fallen out of love. They'd gone from a presumably comfortable relationship to the point where one of them murdered their child in order to hurt the other—in a way so horrific most people couldn't even contemplate it. And yet, it had happened.

Was he willing to take the risk, with his heart, with his life? Could he and Natalie beat the odds? Not all marriages ended in divorce. In fact, the odds were still in their favor. Was he brave enough to discover if they were in the winner's circle, or would fear of failure hold him back?

Was it necessary to come to a decision right now? All he wanted was to say hello to her and maybe hold her, feel her softness against him, draw strength from her goodness, just for a little while. Before he could change his mind, he opened the door of his Roadster and shut it behind him. Locking the car with his remote, he hurried across the grassy verge, opened her gate and strode toward the front porch.

Determined to follow through, he knocked briskly on the door. A few moments later, it was answered by a tall, attractive blond wearing white jeans and a tank top that fit her like a glove. He stepped back in surprise.

"Oh, hi. I'm sorry. I was looking for Natalie."

"And who are you?" the woman asked, her manner definitely cool.

"I'm Blake Harton. I'm a fr—"

"You're that lawyer!" the woman interrupted. "The one defending that scumbag. I saw you on the news. How could you? Don't you know what he did? Don't you *care*?"

Her voice had risen along with her anger. She looked like she was ready to slam the door in his face. Blake took another step backwards. This had been a bad idea. He didn't know who the blond was, but she was definitely in Natalie's camp. This wasn't the time to have a heart to heart with the woman, no matter that he was halfway in love with her.

He held up his hands in a sign of surrender. "I'm sorry. I'll come back another time. I—"

"Monica, who is it?"

Blake heard Natalie calling from somewhere inside the house. He looked at the woman, presumably Monica, and remembered Natalie telling him about her friend. The woman had been taking care of the twins during the trial. Unmindful of Natalie's query, she continued to glare at him.

"It's no one, Natalie. Just some bottom-feeding lawyer."

Blake's face flamed with a mixture of embarrassment and anger. This woman didn't even know him and yet she was judging him. He bet she'd scream the house down if he dared to pre-judge her. She—

Blake's thoughts were interrupted by the appearance of Natalie in the open doorway. Monica moved slightly to one side to allow her friend some room.

"Blake. What are you doing here?"

"Hi. I…just wanted to say hello." It sounded so lame, he blushed again and wished he could speak with her in private, but from the dark frown on Monica's face, it was obvious Natalie's friend wasn't going anywhere.

But after a long moment, Natalie stood back to allow him to enter. Not giving her time to change her mind, he strode across the porch and stepped inside, brushing past Monica as he did so. The woman made a sound of annoyance in the back of her throat and he had to stifle a grin. She reminded him of an overprotective Alsatian. The knowledge that Natalie had such a good, fierce friend pleased him. Everyone needed a friend like Monica to watch their back.

"Hey, aren't you the man with that cool car?"

"What are you doing here?"

The questions were fired at him almost simultaneously and he walked further into the open-concept kitchen and living area to find the twins staring at him from the couch with identical expressions of curiosity. From the corner of his eye, he saw Monica come in behind him.

"Hi, boys." Blake played it safe. There was no way he was going to identify them by name. Though he remembered one of them was Bailey and the other one was Darby he had no way of determining which one was which, short of asking them and seeing as they were dressed in identical school uniforms, there was no guarantee he'd get it right the next time.

"What are you doing here?" the second twin asked again, his expression much less friendly than his brother's.

"I dropped by to see your mom. Is that all right?"

"I guess so," the little boy replied uncertainly.

"Did you bring your car?" the other twin asked.

Blake smiled at him. "Yes, I did. Would you like to see it?"

"Yes!" the same boy cried and darted off the couch. He was off and running toward the door before Blake had a chance to blink.

"Darby James Johnson! Come back here!"

Natalie's voice rang out through the room. The boy pulled up short and slowly turned around.

"Oh, Mom! I just want to see it!"

"Darby, it's dark out already. You won't see a thing. Besides, it's time for you and your brother to get into the shower and clean up before bed. You have school in the morning."

Darby groaned. "But, Mom! Can't I—?"

"Darby..."

Natalie's voice held a note of warning and the little boy's shoulders slumped in defeat. He slowly dragged himself back toward the couch. Blake couldn't help but feel sorry for him.

"Hey, buddy, don't worry. I'll bring it around another time. Perhaps we could go for another ride." He looked over at Natalie. "Would that be all right with you, Mom?"

He grinned and was relieved when he caught the sparkle of amusement in her eyes. After the awful hours they'd endured in the courtroom, it was good to see she found something within her to smile about.

"Of course. That sounds like fun, doesn't it, Darby?"

"Yes!" Darby punched the air triumphantly, his grin stretched wide.

"Can I come, too?"

The quiet request came from Bailey who had gotten up off the couch and now approached them.

"I don't see why not," Blake replied. "We've fitted in there before." He looked at Natalie. "As long as it's okay with your mom."

"Of course," she said.

Bailey's grin was slow in coming, but when it did, it lit up his face. Blake's heart pounded at the sight of it, pleased beyond reason. He couldn't imagine the boys had had too much to smile about in the past little while. It made him feel good to know he was part of the reason behind the lift in their spirits. And theirs weren't the only spirits that had lifted. Blake couldn't believe how much better he felt being around them. *Maybe he was ready for fatherhood, after all?* The thought sobered him. His smile disappeared.

Natalie noticed his change in demeanor and frowned. Determined not to spoil the moment, Blake forced a smile.

"Well, I guess I'd better get going. I can see you have your hands full," Blake said and headed toward the door, ignoring Monica who still stood with her arms folded across her chest leaning against the wall. Natalie followed him out.

Blake opened the door and stepped onto the porch.

"Thanks for stopping by," Natalie said quietly. "It was nice of you."

She reached out and laid her hand lightly against his chest. His heart skipped a beat and then took off at a gallop. Memories of their night of lovemaking bombarded him from every side. He wanted nothing more than to pull her in his arms and kiss her senseless. But this wasn't the time or the place. She had her boys inside, as well as her guard dog.

And then she surprised him by pulling him into the shadows and coming up on tiptoe and pressing a soft kiss against his lips. It was sweet and tender and lingered on his skin long after she'd pulled away. He burned to feel her naked, their limbs tangled in the sheets, but it wasn't going to happen while her house was filled with children and a less then friendly guest. Then there was the trial to consider. With the decision still hanging over their heads, neither of them would be putting it behind them anytime soon. If ever.

———————

Natalie closed the door behind Blake and took

a moment to steel herself against the inevitable barrage of questions that was sure to come her way. She was relieved to note the boys had departed for the shower. True to form, Monica started in on her the moment she stepped back into the kitchen.

"Blake *Harton*? Are you out of your *mind*?"

Natalie shrugged, buying time. She didn't know how Monica had sensed there was something between her and her ex-husband's lawyer, but it was obvious she knew something.

"He's a nice guy," she replied, trying hard not to sound defensive.

"A nice guy! Are you *kidding*? He's defending your ex-husband! The man who murdered your child! How can you even *talk* to him, let alone invite him into your home! I don't understand!"

Natalie sighed. Walking over to the kitchen, she filled the kettle and set it to boil. She would have preferred a glass of wine, but she'd sworn off alcohol until the trial was over. She refused to obliterate her troubles that way. It wasn't healthy and she was a little scared that if she allowed alcohol to be her crutch, she might never be able to give it up when this nightmare was finally over, as surely it would be soon.

"Would you like a cup of tea or coffee?" she asked quietly.

Monica sighed and shook her head. "Coffee... But are you even *listening* to me? Honey, I know you've had it tough—God knows, you've had it worse than anyone should ever have to deal with, but *Blake Harton?* How can you fraternize with the enemy?"

Natalie spooned instant coffee into two mugs and then added cream and sugar to Monica's. When the kettle boiled, she poured in the water and stirred both mugs with a spoon. Handing one to her friend, she took a seat upon the couch before replying.

"I understand how you feel, Mon. Believe me I felt the same way. The softening of my attitude toward my ex-husband's lawyer didn't happen overnight. In fact, I'm still a little confused about how I feel, but I've learned Blake Harton's a decent man with a kind and generous heart. He's also a great lawyer who happens to be representing my ex-husband."

"He's not just representing him, Natalie! He's *defending* him! He's making excuses for what that bastard did! Doesn't that *matter* to you?"

"Of course it matters," she replied and then took a sip from her mug.

"Well, it didn't look that way to me," Monica replied, her tone accusatory.

Natalie bit her tongue against a quick retort. Monica's heart was in the right place. She was like a sister and only wanted to protect her from harm. Natalie understood and appreciated where Monica was coming from, even if her love life was none of her friend's business. But she didn't want to lie and she didn't want to send her friend off not understanding. Because without Mon, she had no one. Still, it wasn't fair to let her friend think Blake was nothing more than a lowlife lawyer who took pleasure in defending the indefensible.

"Don't judge him without knowing him, Mon. Being a defense lawyer is only a tiny part of who he is. Yes, he's defending my ex-husband, but what you don't know is that his brother committed suicide earlier in the year over a messy custody battle."

Monica gasped and her face lost color. "Oh, Natalie! How awful!"

Natalie compressed her lips. "Yes. It only happened about seven months ago. The wounds are still raw. It's part of the reason he agreed to defend Ian."

Monica blew out her breath on a heavy sigh and shook her head slowly back and forth. "Shit. This world is so fucked up."

Natalie thought of Lacey, her sweet little girl and then she thought of Blake. She was filled with an overwhelming sadness.

"Yes."

There was nothing more she could say.

CHAPTER 22

Blake crushed up a ball of paper and tossed it toward the bin. It had been more than a week since the jury retired and everyone was on edge. Each time the phone rang, he jumped, expecting it to be Judge Chamberlain's clerk advising him the jury was back in. Four times, the jury had returned with questions, mostly revolving around the issue of mental health. It was obvious there was a struggle going on in the jury room. Blake had hoped that by now they'd reached a unanimous decision. The only good thing to have come from the days that had passed at a snail's pace was that he'd managed to spend more time with Natalie and her children.

Two days' earlier, they'd gone on the promised ride in his Roadster and when he'd put the top down and the wind had blown through their hair, the boys had squealed in delight. They'd gone to the beach and eaten ice cream and he'd barely cringed when they'd dripped it all over his custom leather seats.

The truth was, he was falling hard and fast for both Natalie and her boys and though the thought of making any kind of permanent commitment still scared him, it didn't instill the abject terror it would have done as little as a month earlier. He'd even surprised himself and done some online research on suitable family SUVs. He was definitely making progress in the relationship department and he had Natalie and the twins to thank for it.

He'd made other pleasing progress too, by taking the first steps toward reconnecting with his niece and nephew. The phone conversation with his ex-sister-in-law, Harriet, had been difficult, but she'd agreed to let him stop by. They'd arranged a meeting early the next week. In the meantime, he'd set up trust accounts in the name of Harry and Josie that would mature when they turned eighteen. He wouldn't let his brother's children suffer financially from the loss of their father. Not if he could help it. And now he was also determined to help them emotionally.

For a long time, he'd kept his distance, even before David's death. The divorce and ensuing custody battle had been long and bitter and he'd been forced to take sides. David would often end up passed out on his sofa after drinking heavily and filling his condo with awful stories about what was happening between him and his ex-wife. All Blake could think about was how grateful he was that he'd remained single and childless and that's why he'd silently vowed to stay that way for the rest of his life.

But that was then, when everywhere he looked there was darkness and pain. Ever since Natalie had entered his life, the darkness had been lifting, letting the light slowly but surely back in. And she seemed to feel it, too. It was like the two of them were helping each other erase their painful pasts. One day at a time, they were smiling more and crying less and there finally appeared a glimmer of light at the end of the long black tunnel. And he was glad.

———————

Natalie moved through the list of numbers printed on the page beside her and entered them into the spreadsheet she had open on her screen. It was fortunate she was so good at her job because her concentration was shot this past week since the jury had retired and she'd returned to work. The crown prosecutor had promised to call her as soon as he had any news. The wait was killing her. She wondered how Blake was faring.

She'd spent the last evening with him. He'd come over for dinner, and afterwards, had played Twister on the living room floor with her boys. They'd laughed and squealed and shouted, all the time sounding like normal kids. It warmed her heart to know that they were improving, that they were slowly putting the tragedy behind them. They were still receiving regular counseling and she was hopeful they'd pull through healthy and whole.

She wasn't quite as confident about herself, but she was in a much better place and she had Blake to thank for that. Monica still thought it strange that she was dating her ex-husband's lawyer, but Natalie knew him well enough now to see beyond his career and the connection to her ex, and find the man behind the job. He was a good man, a kind man and he treated her and her boys well. There were times when she felt almost happy—or at the very least, at peace.

It was a good feeling and one she would hold on to for as long as she could. There were plenty of dark days still ahead of her, but somehow, the thought of them felt more manageable with Blake by her side. Every time she thought that way, she shied away from it. The knowledge that she was falling in love with him frightened her more than she could say. She'd been in love once and it hadn't worked out. *Was she brave enough to try again?* She didn't know.

The phone at her elbow peeled, interrupting her thoughts. Distractedly, she reached over and picked up the phone.

"Baker and Carr Construction, this is Natalie."

"Natalie, it's Greg Villa."

At the sound of the crown prosecutor, Natalie's belly somersaulted with nerves. There could only be one reason for his call.

"Mr Villa. W-what can I do for you?"

"I wanted to let you know the jury's back. I understand they've reached a decision."

Natalie's lips went dry and her palms went damp. Her pulse pumped loudly in her ears. She could barely hear the rest of the prosecutor's conversation.

"Would you like to be there?" he asked.

A thousand thoughts flew through her head and with them her nerves multiplied, but there was really never any doubt about her response. "Yes."

"Good. Can you be at the supreme court in an hour?"

"I'll be there."

Not trusting herself behind the wheel, Natalie spoke to her boss, then took a bus from her office downtown to the courthouse. The conversation and noise of the traffic around her blurred and dissolved into nothingness as she concentrated on what was about to happen. The jury had reached a decision. One way or the other, this nightmare was coming to an end. She prayed the verdict was one she could live with. Either way, this was it.

She stepped off the bus and made her way inside, putting her handbag on the scanner. After walking through the security station, she gathered her things on the other side and made her way to the courtroom. A crowd of reporters stood outside the door. They flew into action when they saw her.

"Ms Johnson, do you think the jury will find your ex-husband guilty?"

"What will you do if they set him free?"

"Are the twins at school?"

"When was the last time your sons saw their father?"

"Will you be disappointed with a not guilty verdict?"

The questions kept coming, but she ignored them. Keeping her head down, she opened the door to the courtroom and shut it behind her. Inside, it was mercifully quiet, even though a fair number of the seats in the public gallery were already full. *How had they found out the jury had arrived at a decision?* She assumed someone connected with the court or the police had spread the word.

She didn't blame them for their interest. The case had captured the horrified attention of most of Sydney. She hadn't been able to switch on the television or open a newspaper without seeing or reading some commentary on the case. She was sure she and her family were the subject of many conversations around water coolers and tearooms throughout the city and probably even the state and would continue to be for a long time to come. That was just the way it was.

She looked around for Blake, but he wasn't there yet. She assumed he'd attend and not leave it to his instructing solicitor. She hoped so, anyway. She wanted to see him again.

As if her thoughts had conjured him up, the door to the courtroom opened and Blake strode down the aisle. He glanced at her and sent her the briefest of smiles by way of greeting. She understood. Their interaction in the courtroom was dictated by their roles, the fact they were on opposing sides, the solemn occasion, and the silent expectations of the members of the public and media that crowded the room.

And then there was a flurry of activity as the

crown prosecutor and Colby and two other lawyers who flanked Blake filled the seats along the bar table. The judge had continued Ian's bail during the jury deliberations, but when he appeared in the courtroom, he was closely followed by two corrections officers. Natalie took comfort in their presence and hoped they'd be shortly leading him out in handcuffs.

Her gaze went to her ex. His hair was disheveled and he looked like he needed a shave. It was almost like he'd decided to forgo any kind of personal hygiene during the time he'd been away. He returned Blake's brief nod of acknowledgement and then took a seat in the dock. Shortly afterwards, there was a sharp rap on wood and the door behind the bench opened.

Judge Chamberlain appeared in the opening, his scarlet robes fluttering as he walked. His expression remained grim as he took a seat and then turned to address the court officer.

"Please, send the jury in."

The man nodded and exited through a side door. A short time later, the door opened again and the twelve men and women who comprised the jury solemnly filed in. When they were seated, the judge addressed the foreman who was a middle-aged man who'd spent the entire trial staring at the bar table with a frown on his face.

"Mr Foreman," the judge said, addressing the man by his position, as was the custom. "Has the jury come to a decision?"

"Yes, Your Honor."

"And is your decision unanimous?"

Natalie held her breath. Her nails dug into her palms.

"Yes, Your Honor."

Her breath escaped on a rush. The pressure around her chest eased, but it wasn't over yet.

The judge read out the charge of murder that had been filed against her ex. It seemed to take forever.

"How do you find the defendant, Mr Foreman? Guilty, or not guilty?" the judge finally asked.

Once again, Natalie's breath caught in her chest. Everything inside her stilled. The courtroom, the jurors, the lawyers, all of it turned fuzzy. Every fiber of her being concentrated on the man who addressed the court.

"Your Honor," the foreman replied. "We find the defendant, Ian Johnson, guilty."

A loud cheer went up from the public gallery. Natalie gasped and cried out in relief. Tears poured down her cheeks unheeded as she tried to take it in.

Guilty.

He was guilty! Guilty of taking her baby's life. Guilty of doing an act so cruel and spiteful it was beyond the comprehension of any normal human being; completely and utterly unfathomable. Then Ian started yelling and it was all the corrections officers could do to keep him restrained. The judge rapped his gavel on the bench in an effort to restore order.

"You bitch!" Ian screamed, looking straight at her. "This is all your fault! You made me do it! You're the reason Lacey died. You—"

"For Pete's sake, get him out of here!" Blake snarled and the corrections officers finally took charge. They manhandled Ian out of the dock, across the courtroom and through yet another doorway. Natalie did her best to stop shaking.

"Are you all right, Natalie?"

She looked up and found Colby staring down at her, a worried expression on his face. With an effort, she took a deep breath and eased it out between taut lips.

"I'm fine," she assured him, trying to focus on the good thing that had happened. Ian had been found guilty. He was going to be punished for taking the life of her child. And she was glad. If that made her an awful person, then so be it.

Blake watched Natalie leave the courtroom surrounded by her legal team. They were in high spirits and Blake didn't blame them. He, on the other hand, was totally drained, physically and mentally. The trial had taken its toll. He'd barely slept while it had been going on and the week of waiting for the verdict hadn't been any better. He was relieved it was all over and though the verdict hadn't gone his client's way, Blake was satisfied with the result.

Guilty.

He should be feeling sorry for Ian, but the truth was, he was relieved the man's actions wouldn't go unpunished. It would mean some kind of closure for the family Lacey had left behind and Blake wasn't unhappy about that.

The judge had stood the matter over for sentencing. More psych reports would be ordered. It would be six weeks or so before they met again in the courtroom for the judge to hand out his punishment. Fourteen years non-parole period was what Blake expected, but who knew how this might pan out? The case had touched the psyche of Sydney. The city would never forget.

He thought of Natalie and longed to go to her, to share in her relief, but she'd be busy with her lawyers and no doubt with the media. There would be time enough later for them to talk. At least, he hoped so.

Now the trial was over, would she still want anything to do with him? Perhaps she'd want to cut all connection to her ex-husband and the tragedy that had unfolded, including the court experience. Blake was part of that, even indirectly. *Would she fear he'd remind her of all the things she was trying so hard to forget?*

All of a sudden, he felt uncertain. They'd been growing closer over the days and weeks since they'd first met, but were they close enough? Could their burgeoning feelings continue to grow and flourish now that the trial was over?

What if the media discovered their closeness? Would it matter to her if they turned on her for finding love with someone else, and not just anyone, but the man who'd defended her ex-husband on a murder charge? Would it matter to *him?*

Blake didn't know, but all he could do was talk to her, put his heart on the line and after that...hope.

———————

Natalie heard the knock on her front door and grimaced. She hoped it wasn't another reporter. She'd done enough interviews to last her a lifetime. No doubt there would be more to come, but right now, she wanted to be left alone. The phone hadn't stopped ringing since she'd arrived home and she'd finally given up answering it. She'd set her message bank to kick in after the first ring and that suited her just fine.

Peeking through the curtains in the front room, she was surprised and relieved to see Blake standing on her porch. He was dressed in the suit she'd seen him in earlier. With her pulse picking up its pace, she opened the door and glanced around to make sure there were no lingering reporters. Though she didn't care what they thought of her relationship with her ex-husband's lawyer, she'd had enough media attention for one day.

"Hi," she said and then looked away. Things between them felt different now that the trial had come to an end. The reason for bringing them together had suddenly disappeared. It threw her off balance.

"Hi," he said and looked just as uncomfortable.

"Would you like to come in?" she asked, belatedly remembering her manners.

"Yes. Thank you. That would be nice."

Natalie closed the door behind him. It was only two in the afternoon. She probably should have returned to work, but after the jury's decision had been handed down and she'd dealt with the subsequent deluge of emotion and barrage of questions from the press, she'd thought of nothing more than escaping the crowds and had taken refuge behind the walls of her house. She wasn't sure how Blake had guessed she was home. Perhaps he'd tried to contact her at work and had been told she wasn't there? No matter, he was there now and she was glad.

They hadn't been intimate since that first time, more than a week ago. It wasn't because of a lack of desire to repeat the magic of that night; it was more because of a lack of opportunity and an unspoken need to take things slow. At Natalie's request, Monica had dropped the boys back home after the last witness had given evidence. Natalie had been excited and thrilled to see them. Though she was glad they hadn't been around to witness the evenings when she'd cried half the night away, it had been lonely and far too quiet without them.

Blake looked around the empty kitchen. "Where are the twins?"

"At school."

His eyebrows rose slightly and he nodded in acknowledgement. "What will you tell them?"

"About today?"

"Yes."

She sighed softly. "I guess I'll tell them the truth.

They understand their dad did something terrible to Lacey and they know that bad deeds must be punished. I'll tell them that their dad's being punished for hurting Lacey. I'm sure they'll understand. I'll make certain their therapist is brought up to date."

Blake shook his head back and forth, his expression filled with sadness. "I'm so sorry, Natalie. There are no winners here."

She closed her eyes briefly against a surge of emotion. "No."

"I wish I could do something to help," he said, shrugging helplessly.

"I wish you could, too. I wish you could wave a magic wand and all of this would go away. I wish you could turn back time, back to when my family was happy, back to when Lacey was still alive. I remember when she was born." She shook her head and smiled softly. "She was laughing right from the start. That sounds impossible, but it wasn't for my Lacey. It didn't matter if the sun was shining or if there was clouds and driving rain, she was my little bowl of happiness. Everyone who met her loved her..."

Her voice drifted off and a band of emotion went tight around her chest, making it difficult to breathe. She crossed her arms in front of her and tried to hold on to her emotions. "Why, Blake? Why did it have to happen? Why Lacey? Why was it *my* little girl?"

Despite her efforts, she choked on a sob and her voice hitched. Tears burned behind her eyes. It never ceased to amaze her how the tears could keep coming. She'd cried an ocean of them over the past couple of months. And yet, they continued to flow, just like they did now. When Blake moved to draw her into his arms, she buried her face against his chest. He felt so strong and warm and dependable. A safe harbor in the midst of a turbulent storm. His expensive cologne filled her nostrils and she breathed in deeply, loving the spicy, familiar smell.

They'd only known each other a couple of months, but it felt like forever. She thought she'd been in love with Ian, and she had been, but those feelings couldn't compare to the way she felt when she was with Blake. Their connection was so effortless, so real. It was like Blake spoke to her without words, understood her like no one else ever had. She couldn't explain it, but there was no denying it was there. She just hoped he felt it, too.

As if reading her mind, he tilted her chin up with his fingers and tenderly brushed her tears away. The pad of his thumb moved lower, across her lips and rubbed the plump flesh. Heat trailed in its wake. She stared up at him, her lashes still wet with tears and it was then she knew she'd fallen in love with him.

It had come out of nowhere, surprising and inexplicable. In the midst of hurt and anger and unimaginable sorrow, she'd found something wonderful. It was so fragile, so special she worried that it might not last, might not survive the pressures of everyday life.

Was their connection strong enough to matter? Only time would tell.

Sliding her hands around his neck, she drew his head down to hers. Their lips met in a kiss so sweet and tender, it brought fresh tears to her eyes.

"Why are you crying?" he whispered, his forehead pressed against hers.

She could only shake her head again, beyond words, but she answered him with another kiss. His lips were firm and masculine and felt amazing beneath hers. She kissed the corner of his mouth, his cheek, the tip of his nose. Her lips explored him with a mixture of wonder and awe. *How had she found this good man? Would he be prepared to hang around?*

The thought sobered her. After all, it wasn't just her and her needs she had to think about. The boys liked him and appeared to enjoy his company, but were they ready to accept another man in their lives? Was she? It was so soon. Lacey had been dead barely two months. But Natalie had been lonely for so long. The divorce had been a long time in coming. Her relationship with Ian had died many months before she'd taken that final step...

She yearned to be held, to be comforted, to be cherished...to be loved.

Did she deserve such joy? Did she deserve to feel loved and adored, like so many others? A surge of emotion went through her. Yes, she deserved it. By God, she deserved it. She was a good person who tried hard to live a good life. She did her best to raise good children who were thoughtful, kind and had good manners. She went to work; she ran her household; she made sure there was plenty of time for cuddles. Her kids loved her and she loved them...but she needed more, something they couldn't give. Something that only Blake could.

Taking his hand, she led him to the couch, thankful that she'd tidied up the toys and books that had been spread across it before she'd left for work. With a gentle push, she forced Blake to sit. He stared up at her, his eyes flaring bright with emotion.

"I want to make love to you," she whispered and ran her finger slowly down his cheek.

Across his lips, over his nose, she traced the lines and planes of his face. His skin was bronzed from the sun. A faint five o'clock shadow darkened his cheeks. His hair glinted blond from the light that shone in through the sliding door to the backyard. She ran her fingers through its thickness, massaging his scalp.

He groaned and reached up and circled her hips. With his legs spread wide, he dragged her further forward. She kneeled, putting them almost at eye level. His gray jacket had already been discarded. She reached up and tugged at his navy-blue tie. Once it was loose, she slid it from his neck and tossed it to the floor. Next, she went to work on the buttons of his shirt. The fine cotton fabric felt soft and luxurious to the touch. His clothes were as costly as his cologne. He wore both of them well.

With the last of his buttons undone, she spread his shirt wide and looked her fill. He was just as beautiful as she remembered. His pectorals gleamed in the golden light, firm and well defined. She scraped over his chest with her fingernails. When she flicked over the dark nub of his nipples, he sucked in his breath.

A surge of powerful desire rushed through her and she reveled in the way it made her feel. This man commanded a courtroom and yet he was like putty in her hands. It was a heady feeling. Following through, she leaned forward and stroked his nipples with her tongue, first one, then the other. He tasted warm and masculine. He tasted wonderful.

Over and over, she sucked and licked and nipped and Blake moaned with pleasure. He moved until he lay sprawled against the couch and she followed him down.

Pressed against her, his hard cock nudged her. She rubbed against it, craving the indescribable pleasure of the pressure of his erection against her mound.

Need burned inside her, but she wasn't ready to surrender to its call. Reaching for his belt, she undid it and slipped it from the loops of his pants. With her gaze holding his, she undid his button and eased down his zipper. All the time, he stared at her, his breath coming fast.

His underwear was silky and soft beneath her touch. The bright green fabric was printed with cartoons. It was so surprising, so incongruous, it brought a smile to her lips.

"Donald Duck?" she asked teasingly, with a raised eyebrow.

He grinned back at her, unashamed. "Who doesn't like Donald Duck?"

She chuckled and the feel of it sent a fresh wave of joy rushing to her heart. She couldn't remember the last time she'd laughed. It felt foreign. It felt good.

With renewed enthusiasm, she ran her hand over the thickness of his erection, caressing it through the satin of his boxers. It was thick and hard and inviting. She squeezed her legs against another surge of desire.

Easing the fabric down over his hips, she pushed the elastic lower until his cock sprang free. Encircling it in her hand, she squeezed it rhythmically and then stroked it up and down. A tiny drop of fluid leaked from the head of his cock. She bent over it and swiped at the moisture with her tongue. It tasted salty and warm.

Opening her mouth, she took all of him in and sucked until her cheeks hurt. Blake's groans got louder. His fingers plowed through her hair, holding her head in place. With his cock still in her mouth, she reached lower and fondled his balls. Full and firm, the feel of them sent another wave of desire surging through her.

Needing to feel more of his naked skin, she tugged at his suit pants. He lifted his hips to assist her to rid him of the rest of his clothes. His boxers and pants slid over his thighs. She pushed them the rest of the way off his legs.

Her hand caressed his knee and then her eyes widened in surprise. A scar, pale and thick, crisscrossed his left leg, just below it. She ran her finger over it, curious as to how he'd gotten it.

"An unfortunate run-in with a tree in Centennial

Park when I was a kid," Blake explained with a wry smile. "I was trying to fly a kite while riding my pushbike. Mom kept telling me to watch where I was going. Too bad I didn't listen."

"Did it hurt?"

He grinned. "Like hell. Mom took me to the emergency department. I got six stitches. I think the local anesthetic hurt even worse."

Natalie smiled. She'd once had a small skin cancer cut off her back. One of the disadvantages of having fair skin and freckles. She knew all about the pain of a local anesthetic.

Blake kicked off his pants and underwear and drew her closer. He nuzzled her neck. "Where were we?"

"I think I was sucking your cock," she replied saucily.

His eyes darkened with desire. "You were indeed, and doing a mighty fine job."

She giggled and blushed. She couldn't remember ever being so naughty. Sex with Ian had been enjoyable in the early days when they were in love, but even then, it hadn't been fun. There had never been any lighthearted banter. In fact, she didn't think they'd done much talking at all. Having her mind engaged in the act as much as her body was a new experience and one that she wanted more of.

"It's time you got rid of these clothes, woman," Blake muttered, interrupting her thoughts.

He reached up and undid the buttons on her white blouse and then made short work of her lacy white bra. Her gray pinstripe skirt soon followed, along with her matching white underwear. Within moments, she was just as naked as he.

"Come here," Blake ordered, tugging her by the hand.

He lay back on the couch and she followed him down. She stretched out on top of him and they both gasped at the feel of skin on skin. Where he was all hard muscle and sinew, she was soft and pliant. Though she worked hard to stay fit and healthy, the stress of the divorce and subsequent nightmare battle over the custody of her children had left their mark on her body. She was skinny and angular where once there had been curves, but it didn't seem to matter to Blake. He drew her close, tightening his arms around her and burying his face in her neck.

"You smell so good," he murmured.

She nipped at his shoulder. "So do you."

His lips found hers and together, they shared the sweetest of kisses—long and slow and tender. And then the kiss deepened, mouths opened, tongues entwined. Heat flared between her thighs. She moved against him and he growled against her throat.

"I want you," she whispered.

CHAPTER 23

Blake's blood pounded through his veins. The effort of holding back and burying his cock deep inside Natalie was taking its toll. When she took him in her mouth, he thought he was going to explode. She felt so good, so right in his arms. His earlier doubts and fears seemed like a lifetime ago and from the sound and feel of it, Natalie wanted this as much as he did.

In one swift movement, he rolled over and took her with him until she was lying beneath him on the couch. Her chest rose and fell rapidly. She stared up at him in surprise.

"Wow," she chuckled.

He grinned down at her, unrepentant, loving the sound of her mirth. He could count on one hand the number of times he'd heard it. The knowledge that she felt good enough to laugh with him warmed him all the way inside.

"That's better," he replied. "Now I have you at my mercy."

She smiled back at him and reached up and

splayed her hands across his chest. Her fingers found his nipples through the scattering of chest hair. He stilled their movement.

"Oh no, you don't," he said. "This time, it's all about you." With that, he cupped her breasts and squeezed them. With the pad of his thumbs, he stroked her nipples. They hardened beneath his touch. He bent his head and replaced his hands with his mouth. He laved her nipples with his tongue, just like she'd done to him.

She moaned and moved restlessly beneath him, but he was a long way from being finished. He slid lower, making sure he dragged his erection across her body. She squirmed and twisted her hips, as if searching.

"Please, Blake. I want you."

"You already told me that," he replied, flicking her nipple once again with his tongue.

She groaned and reached for him, but he moved out of the way. "Uh, uh. No you don't. All in good time, babe. I let you have your wicked way with me. The least you can do is repay the favor."

His grin was pure wickedness and he laughed when she poked out her tongue. The glint of amusement in her green eyes told him she was as into their love play as he was. Satisfied, he slid his body lower still, until he was kneeling on the carpet. Pulling her toward him, he spread her thighs wide. Before she could protest, he buried his face between her legs and breathed in her sweet scent.

"Blake!" she squealed.

He looked up. "What? Don't you like it?"

A faint blush stained her cheeks. "I... I don't

know. I... I've never had anyone do that to me before."

Blake hid his surprise. He never imagined she hadn't engaged in oral sex with her ex-husband. *Perhaps Ian wasn't as into that as other guys?* Blake didn't know, but he was inexplicably pleased he would be the first man to give Natalie that kind of pleasure.

"I want to taste you, babe, like you tasted me. Will you let me?"

Her blush deepened, but she nodded. He grinned at her. "This is going to blow your mind. Lie back and see."

She shot him a dubious look and he could see that she didn't quite believe his claims. No matter. He'd show her. With that, he positioned himself between her open thighs and licked her silky folds. Long, slow strokes from top to bottom, side to side and back to the top again.

Natalie gasped in surprise and her hands fisted against the couch, but she didn't tell him to stop and so he licked her all over again. This time, he parted her folds with his tongue and delved into her secret places. He found her little nub and stroked it lightly, rhythmically until she squirmed beneath him.

He lifted his head and stared at her. Her eyes were closed and her mouth was parted. Her breath came out in little pants. "Do you like that?" he asked.

"Yes," she breathed.

Spreading her lips wide with his fingers, he thrust his tongue in as far as it would go. Imitating the movement of his cock as he plunged in and out of her entrance, he made love to her with his tongue.

"Please," she gasped, tilting her hips up toward him.

"Please, what?"

"Please, Blake. I need you inside me."

He slid a finger into her warmth, first one and then two. She pushed herself against him and made little whimpers of need. Blood pounded in his cock. He felt like he was going to explode. But this was about Natalie and her first experience. He'd make it memorable for her if it killed him. And it might very well do that. Still, he couldn't think of a better way to go.

With his hand hard against her mound, he worked his fingers in and out. She was warm and wet and slippery. Her desire coated his fingers. He pulled them out and tasted them before plunging back inside her again. She responded with another whimper of need.

And then her hands tightened in his hair and her body tensed against his. Her breathing quickened, her cries became more frantic. He pumped his fingers and flicked at her nipples with his free hand. Her hips twisted and lifted and then she gasped and her eyes flew open and she let out a shout. It was filled with wonder and relief. She stared at him in amazement. Spread before him, her face flushed with her orgasm, she'd never looked more beautiful. A surge of possession rushed through him. She was his. No ifs, ands or buts.

———————

Natalie floated in a warm and balmy ocean, her body weightless. She couldn't remember the last time she felt so free. It was as if Blake, through his gentle lovemaking, had washed away all of her troubles, all the torments of the past couple of years. Her body tingled from what he'd just done to her. Her legs were heavy and weak. She sank into the soft leather of the couch, loving the way it cradled her tired body. She felt truly sated, more relaxed than she could ever remember being, and didn't ever want to move.

"Hey, sleepyhead. Have you forgotten something?"

Blake's teasing question penetrated the fog of her euphoria and with reluctance, she opened her eyes. His smile was soft and tender. He sat on the edge of the couch with her feet in his lap, just inches from his erection. Her eyes widened at the sight of it and she blushed. She couldn't believe she'd forgotten he'd chosen her pleasure over his.

"It looks like you have a problem." She grinned and touched his cock with her toes.

He grinned back at her. "I'm hoping you might have a solution."

She cocked an eyebrow and pretended to think. "*Mm*, I might."

"What do you suggest?" he asked.

Natalie gently batted his cock again with her foot. "It looks awfully swollen. Perhaps I could get you some ice."

Blake choked on his laughter. "*Hm*. No, I don't think I need ice."

"Maybe I could put some pressure on it?" she suggested. "I've heard that's good for swelling."

"Pressure, hey? What did you have in mind?"

Natalie sat up and on her hands and knees, crawled to the end of the couch. She reached for his pants and found his wallet and removed a condom. Sheathing his cock, she moved to straddle his legs and then maneuvered herself until she was seated over his hard length. Inch by inch, she slid lower until the whole of him was nestled deep inside her. The feel of him, the length and breadth of him buried in her warmth stole her breath. He felt so good, so right.

Holding on to his shoulders and staring into his eyes, she rocked her hips slowly forward. The feeling was like nothing she'd ever experienced and from the expression of concentration and wonder on his face, it appeared like he hadn't either.

"You're so beautiful," he whispered. His arms came around her and crushed her against his chest.

Rising and falling, she maintained her rhythm and slowly picked up her pace. Blake's breath came faster. His arms dropped from around her shoulders and tightened on her hips, urging her onward.

"That's it, Natalie. God, you feel so good. Don't stop. That's it."

The murmured words of encouragement fueled her to greater heights of passion. The spark that she thought had been well satisfied ignited back to life and fire once again surged through her veins. She moved against him, breathing harder with exertion.

The feel of Blake's cock inside her, his obvious enjoyment of their lovemaking, the total connectedness she felt with him sent her spiraling out of control. She tensed, close to the edge and when Blake got there before her, it was enough to send her toppling over the other side.

Her cry of release mingled with his and together, they collapsed, Blake against the sofa and Natalie against him, utterly spent. It was official: She was in love with Blake Harton.

———————

Blake greeted Esther with a smile and a jaunty wave on his way past her desk.

"You seem awfully cheery for a work day," she grumbled.

Blake lifted his hands in a sign of surrender. "Hey, what can I say? The sun's shining, the birds are singing, the trial from hell is over."

Esther frowned. "But you lost. Your client's on his way to jail."

He winked at her. "Right you are, Esther. That's why I pay you the big bucks."

She rolled her eyes. "I still don't get it."

"That's okay. You don't need to get it. Just know that I'm thankful you made me take that case. I'd never have met Natalie if I hadn't."

Esther's eyes widened in sudden comprehension. "Oh, I see. *Natalie.* Now I get it."

Blake smiled again. Just the thought of Natalie filled him with happiness. *Careful*, he silently warned himself. It was still early days. Last night, they'd acknowledged their feelings, but there was more at stake than the two of them. They needed to take things slow, let the boys get used to the idea. Let *all* of them get used to the idea...

Blake opened the door to his office, the smile still on his face. He pulled up short at the sight Ben Fitzgerald. Blake's work colleague and friend was seated behind Blake's desk, idly playing with a paperweight.

"Where have you been? It's past nine," Ben said by way of greeting.

"Yeah. I overslept," Blake replied and his mind immediately filled with memories of Natalie in his arms, tangled amongst the sheets.

The day before, after making love, Blake had gone with Natalie to collect the boys from school and had then returned with them to her place. He'd helped the boys with their readers and then the four of them had enjoyed a hearty home-cooked dinner before watching some TV until the twins went to bed.

Natalie hadn't wanted them to find him there in the morning, so he'd snuck out in the early hours and had returned to his condo. He'd gone back to bed and had promptly fallen asleep. With all that had been going on, he'd forgotten to set his alarm.

"You look far too jovial for someone who overslept," Ben grumbled.

Blake acknowledged his comment with a nod.

Until now, he'd been careful to keep his fledgling relationship with Natalie a secret. She had enough going on and so did he. But now, the trial was over. It would be six weeks or more before the psych reports would be ready for presentation at Ian's sentencing hearing. Six weeks. He couldn't stay silent about his love for that long. Not now he knew Natalie felt the same way. He was relieved when she agreed they could at least tell their family and friends.

He looked at Ben. It wasn't that long ago that Ben had been a single man, footloose and fancy free. Now he was happily married to the girl of his dreams. If anyone was going to understand Blake's sudden change in heart, it would be him.

Blake moved toward the desk and took the chair opposite his friend. "Remember how you were when you fell in love with Abby? You didn't walk, you bounced, and you couldn't stop smiling."

Ben chuckled. "Yeah, I remember. It still feels like that."

Blake smiled back at him and then drew in a deep breath. "Well, I met my Abby," he said quietly.

Ben's expression registered his surprise. He sat up straighter in his seat. "Wow! That's great."

Blake nodded and smiled again. "Yeah, it is."

"Who's the lucky girl?"

Blake cleared his throat, buying time. This was where it was going to get a little tricky. "Her name's Natalie Johnson. She's—"

"Holy shit! You've gotta be kidding! She's the mother of that little kid. The one whose father threw her over Anzac Bridge. It's been all over the news."

"Yes."

Ben gaped at him in shock and shook his head. "I don't understand."

"Yeah, it's a bit hard to take. Let's just say, we didn't plan to fall in love."

"Hang on, you represented the father. Her ex."

"Yes." Blake looked away. "To tell you the truth, I don't know how it happened. It was just one of those things. We met and somehow we connected. We fell in love."

Ben regarded him uncertainly. "I'm really happy for you, mate. Truly, I am, but... Are you sure? I mean..."

His voice drifted off. Blake understood his friend's concerns. They were similar to his own—concerns he probably still had, if he were honest.

Ben's frown deepened. "She has a couple of other kids, doesn't she?"

"Yes. Twins. Darby and Bailey. They're five."

"I thought you didn't do commitment? She must be really something if you're prepared to take on a wife and step-kids."

Blake thought of Natalie and once again, his smile stretched wide.

"Oh, yes, she is."

Epilogue

Two months later

Natalie climbed up the small stepladder and stretched so that she could place the glitter-covered angel at the top of the Christmas tree. She twisted so that she could see her sons who were busy placing the final decorations lower down.

"How does it look, boys?" she asked.

"It looks great, Mommy!" Darby squealed.

"It needs to go a little bit more that way," Bailey said, pointing to his left.

Natalie adjusted the angel. "How's that?"

Bailey's face lit up in a smile that matched his twin's. "Perfect."

Natalie climbed off the ladder and stood back to survey their handiwork. They'd purchased the fresh spruce Christmas tree from the Christmas tree farm way out at Dural, at least an hours' drive west of Sydney. She'd been relieved when the salesperson had assured her they could deliver.

The tree had arrived that morning and they'd spent most of the day decorating it.

Natalie had Christmas carols playing softly in the background. She'd always loved Christmas. It was a special time of year. Before her parents had died, they'd enjoyed nearly every Christmas together.

Her thoughts turned to Lacey, as they often did. Her therapist had helped to reassure her that thinking about her daughter was healthy and she ought to accept that there was nothing wrong with remembering her little girl. She'd been a part of their lives. She'd always be there on some level.

It was going to be the first Christmas without her. The thought dimmed Natalie's joy. There would be other firsts she wouldn't get to enjoy with her little girl. This was only one of many. She had to be strong and accept the sadness that would never completely go away. At least she could take comfort in the fact her ex-husband was being punished.

Natalie had attended the sentencing hearing in the city. It had taken place a fortnight earlier. Everyone had been shocked when the judge handed down the sentence: Thirty-two years non-parole period. It far exceeded the normal length of sentence for a child killer. Ian would be in jail a very long time. Natalie was glad. Though she was working on forgiving him, she hadn't gotten there yet. There was a chance she never would.

The sound of a car horn outside her front door snagged her attention. She frowned. She wasn't expecting any visitors. Blake had told her he'd be caught up at the office most of the weekend attending to a pile of work. She'd spoken to him on the phone the previous evening, but she hadn't seen him since Friday night when he'd come over for dinner and had ended up staying the night. Every now and then, he had a sleepover.

The twins appeared to accept his presence. In fact, they hadn't even questioned why he was at their breakfast table. It probably had a lot to do with the fact Blake had given them another quick ride in his Roadster. The boys thought it was the coolest thing. With summer holidays almost upon them, there would be plenty of time for other trips. She'd have to talk to Blake about his thoughts on getting some car seats.

Natalie was relieved the twins had taken to Blake so quickly and without any drama or fuss. She'd told them about their father and the sentence he'd been given. They both expressed their relief that he'd be locked away for a long time to come. It saddened Natalie that it was unlikely Ian would ever repair his relationship with his sons, but then again, did he deserve to have a relationship with them, after what he'd done? Probably not.

The beep of the horn sounded again. She turned to Darby. "Darbs, can you have a look out the front window and tell me who it is?"

Darby took off with Bailey close on his heels. A moment later, she heard their excited squeals coming from the other room. Curious, she left the living room and headed toward the front door.

"Mommy! Quick! Come and see!" Darby shouted. Bailey just jumped up and down, grinning widely.

"What is it?" she asked.

"Quickly! Come and see!" Darby repeated impatiently.

Natalie parted the curtains wider and peered out into the street. She started in surprise and then a smile tugged at her lips. Blake sat behind the wheel of a shiny, black SUV, grinning from ear to ear.

"Can we go out and see him, Mom?" Bailey asked excitedly.

"Can we?" Darby echoed.

Natalie laughed. "Of course."

She opened the front door. The boys pushed past her and ran across the porch and down the steps. They hurtled down the garden path, jumped over the gate and didn't pause until they pulled up short beside Blake.

"Did you buy a new car, Blake?" Darby asked, his eyes wide.

"Yes. Do you like it?"

"What happened to your silver car? The one with the roof that comes off?" Bailey asked.

"Did you sell it?" Darby asked a little worriedly.

"No, buddy. I didn't sell it. I just bought this one, too. I thought we needed something a bit more family friendly to get around. What do you think?"

The boys opened the rear passenger side door and scrambled into the back. Natalie moved closer and leaned in through the open window opposite the driver's seat. The car was bright and shiny and smelled new. Pale gray leather interior added to the sense of luxury. Music played softly on a state-of-the-art sound system.

She glanced toward the boys and noticed the matching car seats that were fixed in place in the back. Her heart tripped over with love. She looked back at Blake and smiled tenderly.

"Car seats?" she asked.

He shrugged, but smiled back. "We need them, right?"

"Right," she agreed. "And the new car?"

He shrugged again. "We're a family. We need a family SUV."

His casual words filled her with a happiness so enormous she could barely contain it. She'd never expected to feel so content again. When she smiled at him a second time, she had to blink back tears.

His expression softened. He leaned over and tenderly cupped her cheek.

"Hey, don't cry. It's all right. I've reconciled myself to driving this beast around more often than not. Besides, the car seats were never going to fit in the Roadster."

She laughed and cried tears of happiness. She swiped at them with the back of her hand. Coming around to his side of the vehicle, she cradled his head in her hands and kissed him softly on the mouth. It was a kiss full of tenderness and love, a promise for the future. A future that included him.

Hours later, with the boys tucked in for the night, Natalie curled against the warmth of Blake's naked body. Spooning with the man she loved, she said a silent prayer of thanks for her blessings. Out of unimaginable horror and pain had come a love so tender, so special it took her breath away. She'd cherish it and him, close to her heart forever, along with her memories of Lacey, her sweet, sweet baby girl. Gone, but not forgotten. Always loved.

NOTE TO READERS

I do hope you have enjoyed reading Blake and Natalie's story. If you've enjoyed this book, please feel free to leave a review for At the Hand of Her Father at Goodreads and your favorite digital retailer. Every review is very much appreciated.

Receive a free book when you sign up for my newsletter if you would like to receive news on upcoming stories, release dates, book launches and other snippets. I love to receive feedback from my readers. Please feel free to contact me at chris@christaylorauthor.com.au

A Woman Scorned is the next book in The Sydney Legal Series.

Here's a sneak peek:

A

Woman

SCORNED

BOOK TWO OF THE SYDNEY LEGAL SERIES

CHRIS TAYLOR

Hell hath no fury...

Chinese-born Australian lawyer, Sally-Ann Li spent her childhood defending herself from false accusations based largely upon her race. Now an adult with a successful career in the highly reputable Sydney Legal law firm, she's relieved to have put the trauma of her youth behind her.

Detective Constable James Shepherd loves his job and he's good at it. He prides himself on playing fair, but he also likes to win. He has an enviable success record among the members of the City of Sydney homicide team and he wants to keep it that way. When a man is discovered brutally murdered in a dark city alley, James relishes the challenge of finding the person responsible and taking another bad guy off the streets.

Sally-Ann is shocked to discover her ex-brother-in-law has been murdered. She's even more shocked when she realizes she is one of the prime suspects. When the good-looking detective questions her about the murder, she's at once thrown back to the nightmare of her childhood. Underneath her veneer of confidence still lies the scared little girl who was repeatedly forced to bear the brunt of unjust accusations and the detective's visit brings all of her insecurities to the fore.

Despite this, she finds herself inexplicably drawn to the handsome detective and can't help but wish they'd met in different circumstances, but the truth is, he's determined to put her away for murder and she's just as determined to prove her innocence...

PROLOGUE

The night was well upon her. It was even blacker in the close confines of the alleyway where she hid. The foul odor of rotten food, dank drain water and a myriad of other offensive smells burned her nostrils, but she couldn't leave yet.

With the back of her gloved hand, she pushed at the damp strands of hair that were plastered across her forehead. A faint breeze tinged with the scent of salt and summer drifted through the narrow opening. Instead of relief, the air brought only another wave of stench and she swallowed convulsively.

Where the hell was he? He should have been there by now. In all the time she'd known him, his routine never changed. This was his favorite bar, his regular haunt. In ten minutes, it would be closing time. He never stayed past the call for last drinks.

The back door that led from the bar into the alley opened with a noisy protest. Light spilled out onto the dirty pavement and glinted off the barrel of the gun in her hand. She flattened herself against the wall. Her fingers tightened reflexively around the trigger.

A drunken patron stumbled through the doorway and stepped onto the uneven surface. He tottered and for a moment, she thought he would fall. She stared hard at his shadowed face, but knew even before she registered the heavy beard and long hair that it wasn't the one she sought.

Keeping to the shadows, she remained still and quiet and waited for the man to depart. Without looking in her direction, he stumbled out of the alley and onto the street. She let out her breath on a tense sigh. The gun felt heavy and awkward, as if it could sense her evil intent. Her heart thumped slow and heavy. Now that she was there, she wanted to get it over with; do the deed and then simply disappear into the blackness, never to be seen again. Just another unsolved crime on the streets of Sydney...

But first, she needed a victim...

CHAPTER 1

Detective Constable James Shepherd reached across his desk and pulled a fresh stick of gum from the packet that sat near a stack of files he'd tossed there hours earlier. Wishing it was a cigarette but determined not to break the forty-six days straight he'd managed to stay away from nicotine, he shoved the gum into his mouth and hoped it would provide sufficient distraction until the wave of cravings eased. He'd known it would be hard to quit. This wasn't the first time he'd tried to give up the smokes. He just had to keep reminding himself of the health benefits and the money he'd save.

It was times like this that were the hardest. He was doing the graveyard shift. The clock on the wall told him it was a little past two. Four more hours to go. The night had been uneventful. He'd even managed to file most of the paperwork that sat in piles on his desk. Sometimes a night behind the desk was a relief, but it meant the time dragged on. And then he started thinking about smoking again and how much he'd kill for a cigarette...

With a grunt of disgust, he forced his attention back to the paperwork.

"What is it?"

James looked across at his colleague who sat a short distance away behind a similarly overcrowded desk. Detective Constable Hung Wang had been with the City of Sydney detectives for the best part of six months. Long enough for James to realize the man had no interest in being friends or even being friendly. Taciturn to the point of rudeness, to Wang, it was all about the job.

The man regularly worked eighty-hour weeks and was among the first to volunteer for a double shift whenever they were short staffed, which occurred with regular monotony, like that night. Despite the man's standoffishness, James felt a reluctant admiration for his fellow detective who worked so hard. Then there was Wang's enviable success rate. In the short time he'd been there, Wang had solved more than half a dozen cold cases. There was no arguing the man was a dedicated and clever investigator.

The phone at James' elbow pealed, breaking the silence. Reaching across, he answered it.

"City of Sydney Police Station. This is Detective Shepherd."

"Detective, this is dispatch. We've received an emergency call. Suspected homicide in an alleyway off Bathurst Street. First responders are already on their way."

After taking down the details supplied by the dispatcher, James hung up the phone and turned to Wang. "There's been a shooting near Bathurst Street."

Wang immediately looked interested. James didn't blame him. So far, the night had been slow.

"Guess we'd better get over there, then," Wang said and pushed away from his desk.

"Guess so," James replied and followed his colleague out of the squad room.

James breathed in through his mouth in an effort to avoid the stench of rotting garbage, dank storm water and God knows what other filth that lined the broken pavement either side of the narrow alleyway that ran between two tall, crumbling buildings on Bathurst Street in downtown Sydney. The bright blue and red and white strobe emergency lights from both police and paramedic vehicles filled the night sky and bounced off the walls of the buildings. He pulled out his flashlight and directed the beam through the darkness in front of him. A rat scurried away into the shadows.

"What do we have?" he asked, approaching one of the uniformed officers who had helped secure the scene and was now standing watch over a body that lay on the ground.

"White male, mid-thirties. Shot through the head with a single .22 caliber bullet."

"Did we recover a shell casing?"

"Yes. Right beside the body. It's been bagged already. I gave it to your colleague."

The officer indicated with his head in Wang's direction. James saw a plastic evidence bag in his partner's hand. He returned his attention to the officer. "Anyone see what happened?"

The officer shook his head. "No. All we have is the woman who called it in. She'd just stepped out of the bar next door and heard a gunshot. She saw someone dressed in black and riding a motorbike come out of the alleyway shortly afterward. She noticed something lying on the ground and went to take a closer look."

James acknowledged the officer's information with a nod. "What's her name?"

"Jo-Beth Gregson. She's just over there."

James looked over in the direction the uniform indicated and saw a petite, dark-haired woman who barely looked legal. Sheer, tattered black stockings encased pale, skinny legs. A short black leather skirt barely covering the essentials was teamed with an equally brief sleeveless midriff top. Heavy makeup made her look older than she was. If he had to guess, he'd put her about the age of his younger sister.

The woman stood hunched against the concrete wall of one of the buildings. Her hands were jammed in her pockets. She stared at her feet. *Why wasn't she tucked up safe and sound in bed instead of out on the streets in the middle of the night, turning tricks and now a witness to murder? Where were her family, the people who cared?* James bit back a sigh and looked back at the officer. "I guess I'd better go and talk to her. Do we have an ID on the vic?"

"We found his wallet on him. Still had sixty bucks in it, so we can probably rule out robbery as a motive. Driver's license says he's Douglas Hanley. Lives in Granville. Thirty-six years old."

Once again, James acknowledged the officer's comments with a nod of thanks. Pulling out his notebook and pen, he moved over to where the witness stood. She looked even younger up close.

"I'm Detective James Shepherd. I understand you heard a gunshot."

The girl's dark eyes were huge in her small, pale face. Black mascara had run down her cheeks, like she'd been crying. After a decade in the police service, James had become immune to violent crimes scenes, but he wasn't so insensitive to realize the average civilian didn't react quite so calmly to the presence of a dead body within close proximity, not to mention the shock of the realization that if she'd exited a few moments earlier, she might have been a witness to his death.

The girl gave a hesitant nod, her fear evident.

James did his best to put her at ease. "It's Jo-Beth, right?"

"Yes," came the soft reply.

"What can you tell me, Jo-Beth?"

"I… I already spoke to the officer over there. I told him everything I know."

James nodded. "I'm sure you did, but I'd like to hear it again. You came from the direction of the bar, right?"

She shot him a furtive glance and he couldn't help but wonder if she was over the legal drinking age. Still, he wasn't there to bust her over underage drinking or being inside a licensed premises under the age of eighteen. His concerns lay only with the man who'd bled out on the filthy street.

"Look, Jo-Beth," he said. "I don't care if you were in the bar turning tricks or whatever it was that you were doing downtown in the middle of the night. All I'm trying to do is solve a murder. Got it?"

She flinched. His tone was harsher than he'd intended, but time was ticking away. The longer it took to gather the information, the more time the perpetrator had to get away, hide evidence, disappear. Swallowing a sigh, he did his best to curb his impatience and tried again.

"Where were you when you heard the gunshot?"

"I... I'd just stepped out of the bar. The bartender had called last drinks. People were getting ready to leave. I was hoping someone might—"

She broke off. James didn't need her to spell it out. "You were hoping to pick up a john, right? I get it. So, you stepped outside. Were you alone?"

She grimaced. "Yes. The guy I'd been chatting up decided he had to go home to his wife."

"How many shots did you hear?"

"Just the one."

"What else did you hear?"

"A few moments later, I heard the sound of a

motorbike. One of those really loud ones, or maybe it just sounded that way because the streets were so quiet and the buildings are really close. Sometimes that can magnify the sound. Then the bike came out of the alleyway, all black and shiny and rumbling."

James made some notes and then continued. "What else did you see?"

"The figure on the motorbike was dressed all in black, including the helmet."

"Could you tell if it was a male or female?"

"No. It was too dark and I only saw them for a few seconds. I still didn't realize someone had been shot."

"Could you tell anything about them? Were they tall, short?"

"Not tall, I don't think. Their legs didn't seem too long."

"What about their build? Broad, narrow? Thin? Fat?"

The girl scrunched up her face in thought, like his sister did when she was thinking hard. It made her look even younger. "Average build, I guess. Not skinny, but not fat, either."

Once again, James noted her responses before returning his attention back to her. "Anything else?"

"No."

"What about the motorbike? What do you remember about that?"

"Just that it was big and black and shiny. I don't know anything about motorbikes."

"What about paintwork? Markings? Any kind of badge?"

"No, I'm sorry. It happened so fast. I heard the gunshot and was still processing that when this motorbike roared out of the alleyway. It took me a few minutes to realize there was a man lying on the ground and that he'd been shot."

"It's all right, Jo-Beth. You've done well. Can you tell me which direction the bike took once it cleared the alleyway?"

"Yes. It turned left, but Bathurst Street is a one-way street, so there wasn't much choice unless it wanted to go against the traffic and I guess that would have drawn unnecessary attention."

James nodded in agreement. In the back of his mind, he acknowledged Jo-Beth's summation and wondered again how she'd ended up on the streets. It was obvious she wasn't stupid and she spoke like someone who'd received a reasonable education at some point in her life. *Where had it gone off track?* It saddened him to know she was just one of many young people living on the streets after life had taken an unexpected turn. He wished there was something he could do to help her, but right now, he had bigger problems to solve.

Reaching into his jacket, he pulled out his wallet and handed her his card. "Thanks for talking to me, Jo-Beth. If you think of anything else, give me a call."

She took the card and slipped it inside her shirt. James' gaze swept over her skinny form. "You eaten tonight?" he asked.

She shook her head. Once again, he reached inside his wallet. This time, he pulled out a couple of ten-dollar bills and handed them to her.

"Go and get something in your belly."

The money went the same place as his business card. She sniffed and he caught a glint of tears.

"Thanks," she said.

He brushed off her gratitude. "Do me a favor," he replied, his voice gruff. "Call home. Let them know you're okay."

She grimaced. "I don't have a home. There's no one."

James sighed. After taking down her contact details, he turned away. The late hour, coupled with the hopelessness of the young girl's situation had worn him down and he still had a murderer to catch. He and Wang returned to the station.

Dragging his keyboard toward him, James opened a new file in the name of Douglas Michael Hanley. Once they'd located his family, a formal identification would be made, but for now, the driver's license would suffice. The vic looked enough like the photo on his identification to satisfy James they had the right man.

To his surprise, the victim was listed in their database. Douglas Hanley had a handful of minor assaults and three DUI's. The most recent one was only a few weeks earlier. According to the police database, he lived with his mother. James didn't relish being the one to bring her the bad news.

He glanced at the clock on the wall. It was going on for five. He thought of Jo-Beth and then thought of his sister. Lizzie had been staying with him for the past few days. Feeling the sudden need to message her, he sent her a text.

Thinking of u. xx

A moment later, his phone *dinged* with an incoming text. He glanced at the screen. It was from Lizzie.

That's what I love about u, big brother. Ur always looking out 4 me. Xx

He shot back a reply. *Ur meant 2 b asleep.*

He didn't have to wait long for her response. *Ur meant 2 b at work.*

I am, he texted.

Then why r u texting me?

A reluctant smile tugged at his lips. *Just checking ur ok*, he texted.

I'm fine.

Good, go back 2 sleep.

Yes, Dad.

He bit his tongue. He could almost hear her snarky tone. He sent off another reply.

Hey, ur the 1 who wanted 2 stay with me. I can always send u home.

The reply was swift and short.

No!

James sighed. She was barely seventeen. It wasn't like she could hang out at his place forever. He said as much in his next text.

Please, James! Mom and I need some space. I'll behave. Promise.

He bit his lip. He wasn't that old that he didn't remember what it was like to be seventeen— no longer a kid, but neither an adult. It was a difficult time filled with conflicting emotions. Coupled with the fact their father had remarried six years previously and Lizzie and Anita didn't exactly see eye to eye... He sighed again and sent off another text.

All right. U can stay a couple more nights. Now, go back 2 sleep. U have school in the morning. I'll b home in a couple hours.

Can u bring bagels???

He read her text and shook his head with a smile and then replied.

Ur incorrigible!

???

Once again, he smiled.

CHAPTER 2

Sally-Ann Li swiped a brush through her long, straight hair and left it loose. Though she normally tied it back into a sensible bun, or at least a braid, after sleeping past her alarm she didn't have time for anything else. A slash of red lipstick, a spray of her favorite perfume and she was almost ready. Hurrying back into her bedroom, she riffled in the bottom of her closet for her shoes and finally found the ones she wanted.

The silver ones with the four-inch heels were cute and oh-so-stylish, but they were much too uncomfortable to wear to work. She had to be in court for most of the day, which meant a fair amount of time on her feet. The black suede wedges would be a far more sensible choice. Decision made, she pulled on the shoes, collected her phone from the nightstand and headed into the kitchen. She was just reaching for the oatmeal when her phone rang.

Glancing at the screen, she answered it. "Hi, Aimee. What's up?" Her greeting was met with silence and then the unmistakable sound of a sob. The realization that her older sister was crying sent a shard of panic straight to her heart.

"Aimee? What's the matter? Is everything all right? Oh, God! It's Mom, isn't it?" Sally-Ann held her breath, dreading the answer. Their mother had been suffering with a serious bout of influenza. Sally-Ann feared it had moved to her lungs.

"No, no! It isn't Mom. She's fine. Well, she's still got that cough, but otherwise she's okay. At least, she was when I spoke to her yesterday."

Sally-Ann let out her breath and then realized she still hadn't been told why her sister was upset. "Then what?"

"Oh, Sal! It's Doug!"

Sally-Ann frowned. "What about Doug?"

"I just received a call from his mother. He's... He's dead!"

Sally-Ann gasped. It was the last thing she expected her sister to say. "What do you mean, he's dead? Was he in an accident?"

"No! He's been...*murdered!*" Aimee let forth with another round of sobs.

Sally-Ann shook her head slowly back and forth in confusion and disbelief. "Murdered? Who'd want to murder Doug?"

"I don't know! He was found shot in an alleyway in the city. His mother's accusing me!"

"You? That's ridiculous! You've been divorced for years! Why would she think you had anything to do with it?"

"I don't know, but she told me she's already pointed the police in my direction! She said I never forgave Doug for putting me in a wheelchair. She said I've had it in for him all this time!"

"She's crazy!" Sally-Ann replied, still shocked her ex-brother-in-law was dead.

"Absolutely, but what am I going to do? What if the police come asking questions? What will I tell them?"

"You'll tell them the truth, of course, that you had nothing to do with Doug's death. Besides, you haven't seen him for years."

Silence greeted her on the other end of the phone. She frowned. "Aimee? It's true, isn't it? You haven't seen Doug since the divorce settlement."

"Y-yes. N-no," Aimee stuttered.

Sally-Ann's frown deepened. "Which is it, Aimee? Yes or no?"

Her sister sighed heavily in her ear. "It's true, I hadn't seen him for years, not since the judge handed down his decision, but a few weeks ago, Doug called me. It was straight out of the blue. I nearly fell over when I realized it was him."

"What did he want?" Sally-Ann demanded. Dead or not, her ex-brother-in-law had been a loser through and through. He'd never deserved her beautiful, sweet-natured sister, then or now. Sally-Ann had been pleased to see the back of him.

"He wanted to see me. He... He told me he still loved me, that he was sorry. He... He wanted to know if there was a chance we might get back together."

"*What?*" Sally-Ann practically yelled the word down the phone.

"I know what you're thinking, Sal, but until the

accident, we were happy...really happy."

"He ran off with your nurse from the rehab ward! Did you forget that?"

"No, of course not and he hurt me very much when he did that, but we'd just been told I was a paraplegic. I was never going to walk again. It was a lot for him to take in. Too much."

Sally-Ann shook her head, aghast. "I can't believe you're making excuses for him! That lowlife walked out on you and your marriage when you needed him most! And to make matters worse, *he* was the reason you were *in* a wheelchair!"

"It was an accident, Sal. Even the police agreed. He was never charged, remember?"

Sally-Ann made an impatient sound of disgust in the back of her throat. "And you know exactly how I felt about that, how I *still* feel about that!"

Aimee sighed quietly. "It happened so long ago, Sal. You need to let it go. I have." She paused and then added softly, "It was nice to speak with Doug. He was so excited. Now...he's dead."

"Hang on a minute, didn't he marry that little tart he ran away with?"

"The nurse? Yes. Apparently things didn't work out. They split a few months ago."

"Oh, Aimee! Surely you didn't give him any hope that you and he...?"

"No, of course not, but... I did meet with him." She paused and in a voice that was ragged with emotion, continued.

"You don't understand what it's like, Sal. Most everyone I meet won't even look me in the eye and those that do often look at me with pity. Doug knew me, knew the woman I was, from before. He didn't see a woman in a wheelchair. He saw *me*."

Aimee's voice broke and Sally-Ann's heart clenched with pain. She couldn't imagine what life was like for her sister. She wanted to think that Aimee was living a life just as happy and fulfilled as she had prior to the accident, but she knew she was kidding herself that was the case. For one, Aimee had lost her mobility and with it, a fair portion of her sense of self. She'd been a talented gymnast. She'd been good enough to one day qualify for the Olympics. Instead, she'd gone to college and studied psychology and sports science and had met Doug Hanley there and fallen in love. Dreams of being an Olympian had faded, but she'd still maintained her fitness and had volunteered at a local sporting complex close to where she lived, teaching and encouraging other young kids to achieve their dream.

Now that she was a paraplegic, she'd never walk the beam or swing off the high bars again. That part of her life was over forever and it wasn't the only major upheaval she'd faced. It was easy for Sally-Ann to feel aghast over the fact her sister had been civilized toward her ex-brother-in-law. It wasn't Sally-Ann whose life had been turned upside down.

And now Doug was dead...murdered.

"Do the police know for sure it was murder?" she asked.

"He was shot in the head at close range. I don't know all the facts, but apparently they've ruled out suicide." Her voice hitched. "It's just so *sad!* I can't believe it! Who would want Doug dead? It doesn't make sense! I only saw him the other day. We met for coffee. I barely recognized him. He'd lost a heap of weight."

"Two divorces down might put you off your food," Sally-Ann said dryly.

"It was more than that," Aimee insisted. "He'd changed in other ways. He was nicer. More gentle. He was so sorry for what had happened. For the first time, he actually apologized."

"Well, that's big of him. The son of a bitch ought to be sorry. He's the reason it happened."

Aimee sighed again. "Oh, Sal. No one's forgotten how I came to be confined to a wheelchair, least of all me, but I've long since forgiven him for the accident. Even so, I told him it wasn't ever going to work out between us, no matter how sorry he was. That part of my life's over."

Sally-Ann blew her breath out on a quiet sigh of relief. She'd always thought her sister could do better than Doug Hanley. The accident hadn't changed that.

"How did he take it?" she asked.

"Not very well. He actually got a bit teary. Told me again how sorry he was, how I was the only woman he'd ever loved, etc etc."

"I still don't understand why his mother would think you'd have anything to do with his death."

"She never liked me. We all knew that. I'm sure

she thinks I've been biding my time since the divorce, just waiting for the opportunity to seek revenge."

"She didn't know you very well if she thought like that," Sally-Ann commented dryly.

"That's the problem," Aimee replied. "She didn't know me at all. From the first moment Doug brought me home to meet her, she treated me coldly. She didn't want her son to be married to an Asian girl."

Anger rushed through Sally-Ann at her sister's words, fueled by the knowledge that what Aimee said was true. While Australia prided itself on being a multicultural country, there were still many people who harbored racist attitudes. Sally-Ann had often been subject to such narrow-minded attitudes in the school yard. Her high school years had been sheer hell.

With an act of will, she forced the nightmares away. She refused to be dragged back down that path, helpless and weak, voiceless, accused of crimes she didn't commit. It was the reason she'd become a lawyer and worked in the children's court. She wanted to champion the causes of some of society's most vulnerable; be their voice during their hour of need.

"Sal? Are you listening?"

Sally-Ann blinked and concentrated on her sister. "I'm sorry, Aimee. What did you say?"

"I said that Doug's mother told me I was the last person he called on his phone. That's another reason why she thinks I had something to do with his death."

Sally-Ann frowned. "I thought you said you met with him a few days ago? Surely he's made other calls since then?"

"You'd think so, but that's what his mom said."

"Do you think she's telling the truth?" Sally-Ann asked.

"I don't know. I certainly didn't notice a missed call from him and the last time I spoke to him was the day we met for coffee when I told him—hang on, there's someone at the door."

Sally-Ann poured oatmeal into her bowl and added milk while she waited on the line. She was just about to spoon some into her mouth when Aimee spoke again. This time, her voice sounded panicked.

"Oh, God, Sal, it's the police. They want to come in and talk to me. What do I do?"

"Aimee, take a breath and let it out. Stay calm. You've done nothing wrong. Let them in and talk to them. They're just doing their job."

"What if they think I had something to do with it?" she wailed.

Sally-Ann heard the increasing panic in her sister's voice. She understood Aimee's reaction. Her parents had fled China sixteen years earlier in fear of their lives, hunted by the Chinese authorities for crimes they didn't commit. They'd instilled in both of their girls a healthy fear and distrust of the police.

Over the years, in her capacity as a criminal lawyer, Sally-Ann had learned how to deal with the police and often came into contact with them in the course of her job. Aimee was a psychologist. She'd probably never had cause to speak with law enforcement officers. No wonder she was freaked.

"Do you want me to come over?" Sally-Ann asked.

"Would you?" Aimee pleaded.

Sally-Ann thought of the work piled up on her desk and the hearing she was meant to be fronting up to the court that morning. Perhaps she'd be able to deal with her sister's crisis and still make it to the courthouse in time. She'd try her hardest. The worst that could happen was that she'd have to call in a favor at work and ask someone else to attend the hearing. Her friend and colleague, Abby Fitzgerald, might be free...

The thoughts rushed through Sally-Ann's head. At the end of the day, her loyalties lay with her family and always would. She found herself responding to her sister in the affirmative.

"All right. I'm on my way. Don't say anything until I get there."

"But I didn't *do* anything!" Aimee cried.

"It doesn't matter," Sally-Ann replied, her mind now firmly committed to helping her sister. "Just tell them you're waiting for your lawyer."

James Shepherd stared down at the petite Asian woman in the wheelchair who looked at him with an expression part fear, part defiance. Douglas Hanley's mother had made mention of the fact her son's ex-wife was Asian, but she hadn't revealed the woman was in a wheelchair. James wondered if it were a permanent affliction, or if she'd injured herself temporarily. He noticed the woman held a cell phone in her hand.

"Mrs Aimee Hanley? I'm Detective James Shepherd."

"That was my lawyer," the woman said in response, indicating the phone. "She advised me not to say anything until she arrives."

James' eyebrows flew up in surprise. They were merely making preliminary enquires and had said as much to the woman when she'd demanded to know who they were and what they were there for. He would have been taken a little aback by her forceful attitude if he hadn't spied the flash of fear in her dark eyes. Now she was lawyering up. *What the hell was going on?*

"Mrs Hanley, we're just here to ask a few questions," he said in a conciliatory tone.

"My name is Aimee Li," she shot back. "My husband and I divorced five years ago. I no longer go by the name Hanley."

James nodded. "That would be Douglas Michael Hanley, correct?"

"Correct."

Wang stepped forward. James moved aside to allow his partner a little room. The woman still hadn't invited them in.

"Miss Li, I'm Detective Hung Wang. I work with Detective Shepherd. We're here to talk to you about your ex-husband. Douglas Hanley was found murdered last night. In fact, it was the early hours of this morning."

The woman didn't look surprised. "You've heard already," James stated.

She looked at him and nodded. "Yes. His mother rang a little while ago with the sad news."

Wang shot her a quizzical look. "Is it? Sad news?"

"Of course," the woman replied smoothly. "Just because Doug and I fell out of love and I chose to go back to my maiden name doesn't mean I'm glad he's dead. In fact, I still find it very difficult to believe."

James eyed her solemnly. She appeared to be genuine. Still, the mother of the deceased was adamant her son's ex-wife was involved. James' thoughts circled back to the wheelchair. If the injury were genuine, this woman obviously wasn't the shooter. Still, she could have arranged the hit...

"How long have you been in a wheelchair?" he asked.

"Five years. I'm a paraplegic," she stated flatly.

Once again, her response surprised him. "Five years... The same time you've been divorced. Is there a connection?"

Her mouth twisted into a grimace. "I was injured in a boating accident. My ex-husband was behind the wheel. Our marriage didn't survive my injuries."

James frowned. He couldn't recall any such notations about a boating accident in Hanley's file. He kept his gaze on her. "Was he charged over the incident?"

She lowered her gaze and shook her head. "No. It was ruled an accident."

Once again, James studied her closely. Though it appeared she had every reason to be bitter, he couldn't detect it in her tone. *Perhaps she was clever at hiding it?* After all, her ex-husband, the man who'd caused her serious permanent injury, had just been found murdered. It wouldn't do to alert the police to a possible motive.

James had been a detective long enough to know that it took all types to be a criminal. The most innocent-looking person could turn out to have a heart as black as the night. He'd learned never to take anything or anyone at face value. Besides, she'd already made contact with her lawyer and then there was that flash of fear... What it all meant, he had yet to learn, but he was far from through with Aimee Li.

"Did your ex-mother-in-law tell you how her son was killed?" he asked.

The woman shook her head. "No. We didn't speak for long."

James kept his gaze trained on her. "He was shot. In the middle of the forehead. Do you know how to shoot, Miss Li?"

"No."

"Because this person knew what they were doing. The gun was fired from a reasonable distance away and yet the bullet landed dead center, killing your ex instantly. We're sure it wasn't by chance."

Once again, he eyeballed her, but she remained unflustered. Either she was very good keeping calm under pressure, or she was telling the truth.

"What's your relationship like with Doug's mother?" Wang asked conversationally.

The woman turned her attention to James' colleague. "I have no problem with Maureen Hanley, though I can't say she feels the same way about me."

"You're right," James replied. "In fact, she was the one who sent us to your door. She's convinced you were involved in Doug's murder."

Anger flickered in the dark depths of Aimee's eyes. "Then I guess I ought to be thankful she's not in charge of this investigation," she replied. Her tone was laced with sarcasm.

"You and your ex-mother-in-law didn't get on," James guessed.

The woman let out a bark of laughter. Her mouth tightened. "Oh, we got on just fine. As long as I stayed well out of her way. She was ashamed and upset her son had the audacity to marry to an Asian woman. Maureen Hanley, fine upstanding Christian lady who volunteers twice a week at a church-run soup kitchen can't stand the thought of her precious son being tangled up with a woman born in China."

And there it was. The bitterness he'd expected earlier. It was strange how it hadn't manifested itself during discussions about her ex-husband. No, it was the ex-mother-in-law who'd triggered it. *Interesting.* Just as interesting as Maureen Hanley's certainty her ex-daughter-in-law was responsible for her son's death.

As if belatedly realizing she'd let her tongue run away with her, the woman in the wheelchair collected herself and then reversing the wheels of her chair, turned and headed down a wide hall. Taking her up on her unspoken invitation, James and Wang followed behind her.

The hall ended in a bright and airy open concept kitchen and living room. James noticed the kitchen countertops had been lowered to accommodate the height of the wheelchair.

The overall color scheme was white and buttercup yellow. Furniture was sparse, but what there was had been selected with care. The room was decorated with style and flair and could have been taken from the pictures of one of those glossy home design magazines his sister sometimes flipped through.

Aimee Li sat in her chair on the far side of the room. Her back was to the window. Morning sunlight spilled over her shoulder, throwing her face in shadows. She appeared to have regained her calm façade and gone was any indication that she'd been upset by their line of questioning. A knock sounded at the door. Her expression reflected her relief.

"That will be my sister," she said.

James frowned. "I thought you were waiting for your lawyer?"

"My sister *is* my lawyer. Please, will you show her in?"

James concealed his surprise and headed back down the hall. Reaching for the knob, he opened the door and was immediately taken aback. The young female who stood in the entryway was the most beautiful woman he'd ever seen and she was spitting fire. She barely came up to his shoulder, but she stared at him with all the attitude of a mother lion who was hell bent on protecting her cub.

"I'm Sally-Ann Li."

James shook her proffered hand. It was small and slim, but her handshake was strong and firm.

"Detective James Shepherd," he said in reply.

She narrowed her eyes at him. "I'm representing Aimee Li and you want to hope like hell you haven't elicited any information from her without me being present."

James' head spun. He'd thought Aimee was attractive; this woman was stunning. Dark, almond-shaped eyes flashed with anger. Coal-black hair that shone like a satiny curtain hung loose around her shoulders and fell to halfway down her back. A generous bust line and a luscious mouth painted in bright red lipstick drew his gaze over and over again.

She wore a tailored, charcoal-gray suit and pale gray blouse. The outfit looked like it cost more than a month's wages. Belatedly, he noticed her four-inch silver heels. Though they elevated her somewhat, she was still tiny, but with her shoulders thrust back and the light of challenge gleaming in her eyes, it was obvious what she lacked in stature she made up for in attitude.

He stepped back and allowed her to enter. A wave of expensive perfume wafted toward his nose. Her sandals clacked at a brisk pace along the wooden floorboards. He followed at a more leisurely pace, enjoying the view from the rear. It was every bit as pleasing as the front. He was suddenly very interested to learn more about Sally-Ann Li.

CHAPTER 3

Sally-Ann leaned down to peck her sister on the cheek and used the time to slow down her heartbeat. The sight of the sexy detective on the other side of the door had sent her pulse into a flurry of activity. It was like a frisson of electricity had passed between them. It was so real, she'd almost gasped at the impact. She was sure he'd felt it, too. Still, this wasn't the time or place to get distracted by a handsome face and pair of startling green eyes.

"How are you doing?" she whispered to Aimee.

"I'm fine," her sister replied.

"Have you told them anything?"

Aimee blushed guiltily. Sally-Ann frowned, but kept her voice pitched low. "I thought I told you not to speak to them until I got here?"

"You did and I didn't tell them very much. They just started asking questions and I... I answered them."

Sally-Ann shot another narrow-eyed look in the direction of the good-looking detective and then focused back on her sister. "I guess it doesn't matter. It's not like you have anything to hide, right?"

Aimee nodded. "Right."

Sally-Ann cleared her throat and returned her attention to the detectives who stood a short distance away. She'd barely noticed the Chinese detective on her way in. The man was older than his colleague. Sally-Ann guessed him to be in his mid to late forties. His short black hair was graying at the temples and crows' feet lined the skin around his eyes. He stared at her with eyes that were as black as midnight. She shivered. To her relief, the younger detective stepped forward and the moment passed.

"Ms Li, this is my partner, Detective Hung Wang. We're here to talk to your sister about the murder of her ex-husband."

Sally-Ann nodded. "Yes, Aimee called me a short while ago and told me about Doug's death."

James moved closer to her sister. "We have some more questions, Miss Li."

Aimee shot a look at Sally-Ann, who nodded. "Ask away," Aimee said.

"How long were you married to Douglas Hanley?" James asked.

"Seven years," Aimee replied. "We got married right after my twenty-second birthday."

"And you've been divorced for five, right?" Shepherd asked.

"Yes. I'm thirty-four, Detective, in case you need help with the math."

The detective allowed himself a small smile. Sally-Ann caught a glimpse of even, white teeth that were in stark contrast to the tanned skin around his mouth.

"When did you last see your ex-husband?" Wang asked.

Once again, Aimee looked toward her sister and once again, Sally-Ann nodded in encouragement. As much as they'd been raised to be suspicious of the police, for the most part, they were just trying to do their job. Things often went smoother if you cooperated and with nothing to hide, there was no reason not to answer their questions.

"Doug called me a few days ago and wanted to see me. We met for coffee at the Westfield mall," Aimee replied.

"Which mall?" James asked.

"The one in Parramatta."

"You've been divorced for five years. How often did you speak with your ex?" James asked.

"We didn't speak," Aimee replied quietly. "At least, not until a few days ago. Doug's call came from out of nowhere. Until the other day, I hadn't seen him since the divorce was finalized."

Shepherd frowned. "So you hadn't seen or heard from him in all that time and suddenly, he calls you and asks you to meet. Is that right?"

"Yes."

"What for?"

Aimee's brow furrowed in confusion. "Excuse me?"

"Why did he ask you to meet with him?" Wang clarified.

Color spread across Aimee's cheeks. She stared down at her hands where they were folded in her lap. "He wanted to talk to me. He wanted to apologize for...the accident. He told me he still loved me and that he should never have walked out. He wanted us to get back together."

"And what was your response?" Shepherd asked.

"I was flattered and a few years earlier, I might have taken him up on his offer. I was heartbroken when he walked out on our marriage. It took me a long time to heal, not only from the accident, but the emotional pain took a long time to get over. But I'm finally in a place where I'm happy with who I am and where I am in life. I have a good job, a nice apartment, a small group of close friends. And I did it all without Doug. I've moved on; I don't need him in my life. I told him as much."

"And how did he take it?" Wang asked.

Aimee sighed. "Not very well. He tried to convince me to give him another go. He promised he'd try harder this time."

"And what did you say?" Wang asked.

"I told me no."

"Where were you last night?" Shepherd asked.

Sally-Ann tensed. She was certain her sister was innocent of any wrongdoing, but she'd forgotten to ask her if she had an alibi.

"I was here, at home," Aimee replied.

"Alone?" Shepherd asked.

"Yes."

"Can anyone verify that?"

Aimee shrugged. "I spoke to my mother a little

after eight. I was watching Seinfeld reruns. Mom loves that show. We talked about it. I went to bed around ten and didn't wake until Doug's mom telephoned me early this morning."

"Is there anyone who can verify that you were here last night?" Shepherd insisted.

Aimee fell silent a moment and then shook her head. "I guess not."

Shepherd and Wang shared a look. Sally-Ann had seen that look before. It immediately set her on edge. She moved so that she stood between Aimee and the detectives and crossed her arms over her chest. She eyed the men defiantly.

"My sister lives alone. She was at home last night watching television and then went to bed, like she does most nights. It's not her fault there isn't anyone who can verify her movements. It's not like she was given any warning that she'd need an alibi." She thrust her jaw out at a stubborn angle her family were well familiar with and glared at the good-looking detective. "Where were *you* last night, Detective? Is there anyone who can verify *your* whereabouts?"

The detective in question shot her a lazy look. Sally-Ann could have sworn she saw a glint of amusement in his mesmerizing eyes. "As a matter of fact, Ms Li, there *is* someone who can verify my whereabouts. I was doing the graveyard shift from six to six, alongside Detective Wang. That's how we caught your ex-brother-in-law's case. I guess we got lucky."

His tone was liberally laced with sarcasm. Heat spread up Sally-Ann's neck and crept across her cheeks. *What was she doing?* It was madness challenging the detective. He was in charge of a murder investigation, an investigation that put her sister in their sights. Sally-Ann knew they were wasting their time, but right now the detectives were pursuing every line of enquiry and unfortunately, that included Aimee. The sooner she gave them the answers they sought, the sooner they'd realize she couldn't have committed the murder and then they'd be on their way.

"How did Doug die?" she asked, modifying her tone.

Detective Shepherd's gaze remained steady on hers. "He was shot in the head in an alleyway."

Sally-Ann shook her head slowly back and forth. "Detective, does my sister look like someone capable of that? She doesn't even know how to shoot, let alone get herself into an alleyway in the middle of the night and murder her ex-husband."

The detective looked unperturbed. "It doesn't mean she didn't get someone else to do it."

Sally-Ann's lip curled derisively. "You watch too much TV, Detective. My sister wouldn't hurt a fly. She abhors violence."

The detective's expression remained unchanged. "Your ex-brother-in-law ruined your sister's life. What's worse, the law didn't see fit to punish him for it. That's fairly strong motive, Counselor."

Sally-Ann held onto her temper. There was nothing to be gained by letting the detective know how much his words rankled.

"My sister has been in a wheelchair for five

years. That's a long time to wait for revenge."

"Perhaps an opportunity didn't present itself earlier?" the detective continued in a mild tone. "Your sister told us she recently met up with her ex-husband. Perhaps the meeting dredged up old memories and renewed long-dormant anger and pain... Who's to say?"

"What about Janice Carter?"

The quietly voiced question broke through the silence. As one, Sally-Ann and James turned to face Aimee.

"Who's Janice Carter?" James asked.

Aimee grimaced. "I see Maureen Hanley didn't fill you in on *everything*," she said dryly.

James looked at Wang and then returned his attention to Sally-Ann's sister. "I don't believe she mentioned that name."

"She's Doug's ex-wife," Sally stated and felt a shard of satisfaction at the surprise that flooded the faces of both detectives.

"Hang on a minute," Shepherd said. He turned to Aimee. "I'm confused. I thought *you* were the ex-wife?"

"I'm Doug's first wife. He left me for Janice."

Detective Shepherd nodded in comprehension. He made his way over to the two-seater and lowered himself onto it. The action brought him down to Aimee's level. Sally-Ann caught a whiff of his spicy cologne. It tickled her nostrils. Annoyed that she'd noticed how good it smelled, she hovered protectively nearby.

"Tell me about Janice," Shepherd said quietly.

Aimee drew in a deep breath and eased it out

on a sigh. "Janice Carter was a nurse at the Sydney Harbour Hospital. That's where I was hospitalized after the accident. I spent months there—between the days in the Intensive Care Unit to the weeks in rehab, the hospital became my second home. Doug visited me often, right up until the day he told me he'd fallen in love with one of the nurses who'd helped look after me. He was leaving me for Janice. Life as I'd known it was over and now, apparently so was my marriage."

"It must have come as a shock," Shepherd said sympathetically.

Sally-Ann was grateful for his sensitivity. Aimee had been desperately hurt by her husband's betrayal and even more so when it came at a time when she needed him the most.

"Yes, it did," Aimee admitted quietly. "Apart from the accident, it was the worst thing that had ever happened to me. Coming right on the heels of being told I'd be confined to a wheelchair for the rest of my life, it was a little tough to take."

She said the words lightly and even managed a small smile, but Sally-Ann wasn't fooled. The whole sad episode had sent Aimee spiraling into a depression so deep, her family had despaired that she'd ever find herself out of it. But, to her credit, she'd found the strength to pull herself together and over the years, she'd learned to live with her disability. She'd even returned to work and now ran a successful counseling business in a medical center attached to the Sydney Harbour Hospital.

"When did Doug marry Janice?" Shepherd asked, his tone still low and respectful.

Aimee sighed. "I'm not sure of the exact date. They were together from the time Doug left me. He filed for divorce a few months later and a year down the track, the final papers were issued. When I spoke to him the other day, he said he and Janice were over. From what he said, I gathered the break-up was recent."

Shepherd frowned. "What made you think that?"

Aimee shrugged. "Just that he said Janice had taken the break-up hard and was hopeful they'd reconcile. He wanted no part of that. In fact, he wanted to get back together with me."

"Did you and Doug have any children?" Shepherd asked.

Aimee shook her head sadly. "No. Doug caught the mumps when he was fifteen. The illness left him infertile. Unfortunately, neither of us knew about the infertility until we started doing some investigations. We tried for a family for a couple of years before we decided to go to a doctor."

"That must have been tough," Shepherd said.

Aimee looked across at him. "Yes, it was."

"Do you think that contributed to the breakdown of your marriage?" Shepherd asked.

"Maybe. It certainly put a strain on things, though I would never have left Doug over it. I hadn't married him for his ability to provide me with children. I didn't think it was something we couldn't get past. Then I got hurt..."

Sally-Ann cleared her throat. She couldn't see how this line of questioning was relevant. All it was doing was dragging up painful memories for her sister and Aimee had already been through enough.

"Detective Shepherd, are we nearly done here?" she asked.

He shot her look that was loaded with challenge. "What do *you* think about the boating accident that left your sister a paraplegic?"

Sally-Ann bit her lip against an instinctive protest. She hated that people referred to it as an accident. Okay, the police hadn't seen fit to lay charges against her ex-brother-in-law, but even all these years later, Sally-Ann fumed against the injustice that had seen him walk away without being punished. As far as she was concerned, his reckless behavior had caused the injury to her sister. He should have been made to pay. Still, it wouldn't do to alert the police to the anger and resentment she still felt toward Doug. Not when he'd just been murdered.

"Naturally, my family and I were incredibly upset when it happened," she said, choosing her words with care. "Despite the police findings, I think he acted irresponsibly and should have been held accountable. Our parents feel the same way. It doesn't mean we wanted him dead."

Wang straightened from his slouched position up against the wall and stepped forward. "Who are your parents?"

"Chao and Fen Li. They live in Parramatta," she replied.

"We'll need to interview them," Wang stated and took down their address details.

Sally-Ann swallowed a sigh. *Great.* The last thing her parents needed was a visit from the police. Her dad would freak. She needed to call him and warn him.

"We'll also need to speak with Janice Carter," Shepherd said. "How certain are you that she still works at the Sydney Harbour Hospital?"

He directed his question to Aimee. She shrugged. "I'm not at all sure. When Doug and I spoke the other day, he didn't mention where she worked. He only talked about the fact they were over."

Shepherd acknowledged her comment with a nod and then reached inside his jacket. He pulled out two business cards and handed one to Aimee and gave the other to Sally-Ann. Their fingers brushed and tingles ran down her arm from the contact. She averted her gaze and murmured her thanks.

"Please call me if you think of anything that might help with the investigation. At this stage, it appears your sister was the last person to speak with the victim. Or at least, she was the last person he called." The detective turned back to Aimee. "Did you speak with Doug last night?"

"No. Maureen told me he'd called me, but I didn't get the call. It didn't even show up as a missed call. You can check my phone if you like."

Shepherd nodded and Aimee wheeled away toward the counter. Her phone was lying on the low bench. She picked it up and gave it to the detective. Shepherd checked the screen and then handed the phone back to her.

"You need to put your password in."

Aimee did as he asked and then handed the phone back to him. In silence, he flicked through the screens and then handed the phone to his colleague. Wang repeated the action and a moment later, shook his head.

"There doesn't seem to be any call logged to the victim last night. In fact, the only calls I can find are the ones made and received three days ago."

"That's when Doug and I agreed to meet. I already told you about that."

Shepherd nodded, appearing to be satisfied. "Yes, you did, Ms Li and we appreciate your cooperation and like I told your sister, if you think of anything, please call me."

With a final glance in Sally-Ann's direction, Shepherd headed toward the front door. Wang followed him. The door clicked on their departure and Sally-Ann's shoulders slumped on a sigh. She looked at Aimee. "We need to call Dad."

A Woman Scorned will be released on
27 August, 2017 and is available for pre-order
from favorite digital retailer.

About the Author

Chris Taylor grew up on a farm in north-west New South Wales, Australia. She always had a thirst for stories and recalls writing her first book at the ripe old age of eight. Always a lover of romance and happily-ever-afters, a career in criminal law sparked her interest in intrigue and suspense. For Chris to be able to combine romance with suspense in her books is a dream come true.

Chris is married to Linden and is the mother of five children. If not behind her computer, you can find her doing the school run, taxiing children to swimming lessons, football, ballet and cricket. In her spare time, Chris loves to read her favorite authors who include Richard North Patterson, Sandra Brown, Kathleen E Woodiwiss and Jude Devereaux.

You can find out more about Chris and sign up for her newsletter at her website:

http://www.christaylorauthor.com.au